Deadly Risk

Jane Blythe

Bear Spots Publications
Melbourne Australia

Paperback
ISBN-13: 978-0-6456432-0-6

Cover designed by RBA Designs

SOME QUESTIONS HAVE NO ANSWERS
SOME TRUTH CAN BE DISTORTED
SOME TRUST CAN BE REBUILT
SOME MISTAKES ARE UNFORGIVABLE

Candella Sisters' Heroes Series

LITTLE DOLLS
LITTLE HEARTS
LITTLE BALLERINA

Storybook Murders Series

NURSERY RHYME KILLER
FAIRYTALE KILLER
FABLE KILLER

Saving SEALs Series

SAVING RYDER
SAVING ERIC
SAVING OWEN
SAVING LOGAN
SAVING GRAYSON
SAVING CHARLIE

Prey Security Series

PROTECTING EAGLE
PROTECTING RAVEN
PROTECTING FALCON
PROTECTING SPARROW
PROTECTING HAWK
PROTECTING DOVE

Prey Security: Alpha Team

DEADLY RISK

Christmas Romantic Suspense Series

CHRISTMAS HOSTAGE
CHRISTMAS CAPTIVE
CHRISTMAS VICTIM
YULETIDE PROTECTOR
YULETIDE GUARD
YULETIDE HERO

I'd like to thank everyone who played a part in bringing this story to life. Particularly my mom who is always there to share her thoughts and opinions with me. My awesome cover designer, Amy, who whips up covers for me so quickly and who patiently makes every change I ask for, and there are usually lots of them! And my lovely editor Lisa Edwards, for all their encouragement and for all the hard work they put into polishing my work.

CHAPTER ONE

The hairs on the back of his neck stood up.

Something wasn't right.

Luca "Bear" Jackson halted his team. The island was too quiet; he'd expected to meet some sort of resistance before now, but so far, they hadn't encountered anything.

A crash of thunder rumbled through the dark night, quickly followed by a bright flash of lightning arcing across the sky. Raiding a compound belonging to a domestic terrorist who had fled the country after almost being caught in the middle of a thunderstorm wasn't ideal, but unfortunately, they didn't have much choice.

When Storm Gallagher had disappeared, he'd gone to Uganda—to Lake Victoria—the place in the world that had the most thunderstorms. Bear was pretty sure that wasn't a coincidence.

What they knew about the man was that he was delusional; he hated the government and the military, although nobody seemed to know where this hatred had begun; and he had plans to use veterans to try to bankrupt the government, as well as plans to set off multiple explosions.

Storm Gallagher was a dangerous man, but he wasn't stupid. After his plans to use a former Ranger turned K9 trainer to kick off his campaign of terror were foiled, the man had disappeared— moved here—but Bear doubted he was playing things foolishly.

Storm had hidden out with a bunch of survivalists: vulnerable

1

men and women he had managed to convince to join his cause. Most of them had been either caught or killed when the compound was attacked, but Storm had enough men left to start over.

Here.

On this small island.

Which appeared to have been abandoned.

Only Bear would have bet his one remaining leg that there was no way Storm would just abandon this place. The man had an obsession with storms that he'd taken as far as having a lightning bolt tattooed around one of his eyes and a tornado around the other.

This place meant something to the man, and there was no way he'd give it up without a fight.

And if a fight was what Storm wanted, then it was a fight he was getting, because this was personal to Bear and his team. The K9 trainer he'd targeted was now engaged to Dove Oswald, who was one of six owners of Prey Security, the company Bear and his team worked for. They were more than just boss and employees; they were a *family*.

The only family Bear had left after his own had disowned him.

There was no way Prey was backing away from this; they would hunt the terrorist to the ends of the earth—as they had—because nobody messed with the Prey family and got away with it.

Storm Gallagher was going down, the easy way or the hard way. All they could hope for now was that he wouldn't bring anyone else with him.

Another bolt of lightning lit the night, and once it was dark again, Bear gestured for his team to move.

As they crept between the trees, the team split up. Images from the drones they'd used to do recon over the last couple of days showed that the compound was basically one large building in the middle of the island. The building was surrounded by the trees, and those and the water provided the first layer of protection, but Bear expected there to be men hidden in the trees ready to pick them off as they approached.

Attempt to pick them off, because Bear and his team were the best.

All of them might have sustained injuries that ended their military careers, but they were in top physical condition. They trained relentlessly when they weren't on missions and were as physically fit as when they'd served. They were also highly trained, and thanks to Prey being the most successful private security company in the world, they had the very best equipment to back it up.

But things could still go deathly wrong.

Had gone deathly wrong before.

This time will be different, Bear swore to himself.

According to his night vision goggles, there was no one in the trees as he and his team split up and made their way toward the building in the center of the island. No shots were fired. Nothing moved. The only sound was the rumble of thunder, and while that could mask any other sounds, Bear didn't get the feeling he was being watched.

Despite that, the hairs on the back of his neck stood at attention.

He continued creeping soundlessly forward, no one would see him unless he wanted to be seen; of that, he was confident. You didn't spend almost half your life in the military and not know how to make yourself invisible. Not when you worked for the elite Delta Force.

When he reached the building, he found a huge concrete monstrosity: five stories high, with possibly more levels underground. He counted at least six windows on the first story, meaning the building had a minimum of thirty rooms that would all have to be cleared.

Bear hovered under the cover of the trees, wondering if

perhaps Storm had decided to rally his men here and hold down the fort. But there were no gunshots fired, and the compound looked quiet and abandoned.

Why would Storm run?

And how did he know he needed to?

Bear was contemplating that as he moved, intending to enter the building, when he felt his foot land on something that felt different than the ground.

Something that shouldn't be there.

Something metal.

He scanned the area, sensing suddenly that he wasn't alone. When he looked beneath his feet, he registered a heat signature.

Someone was down there.

Is that where Storm and his men were hiding? In underground tunnels and rooms?

Carefully, he dropped to his knees and felt around until his fingers curled around a handle. He tried pulling on the trapdoor, but it didn't budge, and he found a padlock. If Storm was using a hideout down there, then this wasn't the entry point, because it was locked from the outside.

After sliding his pack off his back, Bear rifled through it, found what he needed, and cut the padlock off. He put his pack back on, then held his weapon in his hands and carefully eased open the trapdoor.

No one came out. There were no gunshots, no shouts, and nobody moved toward him. In fact, if he couldn't still see the single heat signature, then he would be positive there was nobody down there.

Keeping his weapon trained at the heat signature that hadn't moved, he jumped down, finding himself in a small—perhaps six-by-six-foot—hole in the ground.

The smell down here was awful: human waste, sweat, fear.

It was the fear that hit him the hardest.

But he wasn't going to let his guard down. If there was one

thing Bear knew, it was that nobody, no matter who they were, no matter what they said, no matter what they claimed, was trustworthy. People lied, they were selfish, and they cared only about themselves and what they wanted.

"Who are you?" he demanded as he stepped toward the huddled figure. The person was dressed in white, wild dark curls stuck up in all directions, and didn't respond to his question.

A trap?

Had someone been left down here to provide a distraction? Allow him to be ambushed?

Other than the occasional crash of thunder, Bear couldn't hear anything else, and he took another step toward the figure.

"Hey, get up, now," he ordered. "Hands on your head."

Very slowly, the other person's head lifted, and a moment later, he was looking into the terrified face of a young woman.

She appeared to be in her mid-twenties and had chocolate-brown hair and huge dark eyes that seemed too big for her thin face. When her gaze met his, she let out a startled squawk, and he quickly lifted the weapon, aiming it at her head in case she was one of Storm's brainwashed minions.

At the sight of his weapon, she shrank further in on herself, her scared eyes locked on him as though she suspected he was seconds away from hurting her.

She was right.

If she was a threat, he wouldn't hesitate to eliminate her. The safety of his team came first. Always.

"Who are you?" he demanded, allowing the growl he was well known for to edge into his voice. The nickname Bear had come because of his large physique and the way he tended to growl at people.

"I'm M-Ma-Mackenzie," she stammered, wrapping her arms around herself in a gesture of self-comfort.

Given that the woman hadn't made any move to be aggressive, had been locked away in here for a while if the strength of the smell was anything to go by, and was clearly afraid out of her mind, he had to wonder if she was here by choice.

Had she gotten in over her head when she agreed to join Storm and wound up locked away down here when she said she wanted to leave or did something Storm hadn't approved of? Or had she been brought to the island against her will?

"What are you doing here?" he demanded.

"M-my brother k-kidnapped me."

"Your brother?"

"Y-yes," she said. "My brother. Storm Gallagher."

* * * * *

September 27th
2:36 A.M.

Mackenzie was terrified of the huge man pointing the gun at her.

It was dark down in the hole where she'd been thrown when her brother kidnapped her and brought her here. He hadn't taken her out, and as much as she hated it down here, anything was preferable than being in Storm's company.

Her brother scared her.

No, he flat-out terrified her.

More than the man with the gun.

Ever since she could remember, Storm had taken great pleasure in tormenting her, from sneaking into her room to watch her while she slept, to breaking her toys, to whispered threats and physical violence. She had no idea why it was exactly that he hated her, but she knew he did, and the fact that he'd abducted her and brought her here proved just how much.

For weeks, she'd been praying for rescue, for someone to find her, but in all her daydreams of that happening, none of them had gone anything like this.

Despite the darkness, she could see the hard lines of his face beneath the black paint, feel the distrust oozing off him, although she had no idea what possible reason he could have for distrusting her. Did he think she'd locked herself down here for fun?

"You're Storm Gallagher's sister?" the man growled at her, his weapon never wavering, remaining steadily pointed at her head. She was afraid to move in case he shot her.

"Y-yes."

"Storm kidnapped you, brought you with him when he fled the country, and then locked you away down here?" The disbelief was evident in his tone, but she didn't know what she could possibly say to convince him.

Yes, her brother had broken into her house and kidnapped her.

Not before beating her unconscious.

When she'd awakened, they'd been on a plane. Then there had been a car ride, a boat ride, and a hike across the island until they got to the house. There, she'd been viciously beaten again and thrown down here. She hadn't been let out since, and it had to have been five, maybe six weeks.

"Yes," she said softly. Whether the scary man believed her or not it didn't change the facts.

"Why?"

"Because Storm h-hates me." Maybe it was because his mother had remarried after his father's death, that she'd had both her parents while his father had almost gotten him killed. She didn't know, and right now she didn't care. She just wanted to go home.

"Stand up," he ordered.

Even though it had been weeks since she'd received the two beatings so close together, her body was still achy and weak, no doubt because she hadn't been given any medical treatment and had been kept in this hole in the ground, fed nothing but scraps of food.

Still, there was no way she was going to disobey a clear order from the man with the gun, so she braced her hands on the wall and used it to help her get to her feet.

As soon as she was standing, her weak body swayed, and the familiar twinge in her ribs had her muffling a moan. The last thing she wanted was to do anything to make the man shoot her, and she had a feeling it wouldn't take much.

"Turn around." The next order was delivered with the same authority. An authority that clearly communicated he was used to being obeyed and if she even thought about refusing, she wouldn't like the consequences.

"W-why?" she asked. What was he going to do with her? Was he one of Storm's men? Things had gotten quiet a couple of hours ago; she had no idea why or what was going on. It wasn't like anybody bothered to keep the prisoner informed. Had some of his men come back to collect her?

"I'm going to cuff you until we get out of here, you've been interviewed, and it's ascertained that you aren't working with your brother."

Working with Storm?

With the brother who had tormented her her entire life?

Who scared her even more than this man did?

Who had kidnapped her, beaten her, and kept her locked away with plans to do who knew what with her?

Yeah, right.

The man was insane.

Working with Storm wasn't something she'd do in a million years, not even if there was a gun pointed at her head. Which reminded her that at this moment, there was indeed a gun pointed at her head.

"D-do you w-work for Storm?" she asked. She had to know. If he did, she'd rather he just shot her now and got it over and done with, because she knew whatever her brother had planned for her would be worse.

"Work for Storm?" He sounded offended at the idea. Well

good, he'd said the same thing about her, and she'd taken it as an insult too.

"How did you find this place? Why did you come? Are you going to arrest Storm? I think he has plans to do something awful." Hysteria was starting to bubble inside her. So far, she'd managed to hold it together fairly well, although she had no idea how, but now she felt dangerously close to falling apart.

"Turn around, Mackenzie. Now." His tone brokered no argument and allowed no room for disobedience, and she decided she may as well comply. At least he would be getting her out of here, away from her brother, and she was sure she could clear everything up once they were someplace safe.

"You're sure we're leaving here?" she asked.

"Positive."

"And y-you won't let Storm hurt m-me?"

"No. I won't let him hurt you." His voice softened somehow as he said that. It was still growly, still intimidating, but she got the feeling he was starting to believe she was, in fact, terrified of her brother and not part of whatever Storm had planned.

"Okay." All out of fight and convinced that this man would get her back home even if it was only so she could be interrogated about Storm, she turned and moved her hands behind her back. The position tugged on her ribs; she was sure several of them had been broken when Storm had had her beaten.

Large hands circled her wrists, and she realized in that moment what a terrible tactical error she might have made. This man was so much bigger than she was, he could crush her in a second if he wanted to. He tightened his hold, pushing both her wrists together, and she couldn't quite hide her wince of pain.

He loosened his grip immediately. "What's wrong? Are you injured?"

"Storm had me beaten the night he kidnapped me and again when we got here. He's not big on offering medical attention to his prisoners. I'm mostly healed, but my ribs are still bothering me a little. When you pulled my arms like that, it just twinged them." Mackenzie straightened her spine. She'd done nothing wrong and saw no reason why she should cower at this man's feet. "Don't worry, I can take it."

He grunted. She had no idea what that meant, but then he released her and turned her around, bringing her hands together in front of her instead. He still bound them with a plastic zip tie, but his apparent concern over her being in pain calmed her a little.

The man had to be military, which meant he was here to capture Storm and stop him from putting his plans into action. Of course he had to doubt her—he didn't even know her—but she was sure at heart he wasn't a bad guy.

"I'm going to have to put you over my shoulder to get out," he warned her, and if she wasn't mistaken, there was a hint of regret in his tone.

Because she didn't want him to feel bad for doing his job, she rested her bound hands on his forearm. It was thick with muscle, and she felt power ripple through it. If anyone could protect her against her brother, it would be him. But as soon as he dropped her off with whoever was going to interrogate her, she had no doubt he would disappear and she'd never see him again.

Too bad.

The thought caught her by surprise. Mackenzie was wary about who she let get close to her because of what her brother had put her through, but this man provided a sense of security not much else ever had.

"It's okay. I can take it," she assured him. It was true too; she was no stranger to injuries inflicted by her brother, even if these were the worst he'd ever given her.

The man merely nodded, but she felt rather than saw the glimmer of respect in his dark eyes, and another layer of distrust melted away. His large hands circled her hips, and he lifted her, resting her across his shoulder. There was a stab of pain in her chest at the awkward position, but it wasn't so bad.

Like some sort of monkey, he managed to climb out of her prison with her on his shoulder, his pack on his back, and his weapon in his hands.

No sooner had he set her on her feet than bullets began to fly.

CHAPTER TWO

September 27th
2:49 A.M.

Bear muttered a curse as he lunged at Mackenzie, wrapped an arm around her waist, and tackled her to the ground.

His distrust for her was back.

Coincidence that someone was shooting at them as soon as she was out of the hole in the ground?

There was no way to know, but he didn't believe in coincidences.

It could have been a trap. She could have somehow signaled her brother and his men, let them know it was time to strike.

The bullets were coming from the outer parts of the island, not from the house, which meant Storm had taken his men and left on boats before Bear and his team arrived on the island. They'd then come back to defend their home once they knew the team sent in to raid the compound would be trapped in the house.

It was a good plan, and he respected it, but it also meant that Storm had been tipped off.

He'd known a raid was coming.

Despite his misgivings about the pretty brunette, Bear cupped the back of her head with his hand and rolled so he took the brunt of the fall, then tucked her beneath him, covering her small body with his as he maneuvered them both under the cover of a fallen tree.

Her slight moan didn't go unnoticed, even though he got the feeling she was trying to hide her pain from him, and he hated—*hated*—that it got to him.

This woman was nobody. She was potentially involved in a detailed plot to blow up several buildings as well as abduct and hold former military men like himself for ransom.

Nothing about her should get to him, certainly not her pain. If she was working with her brother and had been beaten because she'd gotten herself on Storm's bad side, then she deserved whatever she'd been given.

But what if she really had been kidnapped and brought here against her will?

There was no time to worry about it right now.

"Report," he said into his comms. The most important thing to him was that his men made it out of here alive. Trust had to be earned. He'd learned that lesson the hard way, throwing his trust at people who hadn't deserved it. But his team had earned it. He respected every one of them, liked them, and wouldn't allow them to be hurt or killed.

"Under fire," Asher "Mouse" Whitman replied. Mouse was his oldest friend. They'd served in Delta together, and Mouse had followed him to Prey and was his second-in-command. He was also the father of an adorable six-year-old little girl who had all the big, tough warriors on her father's team wrapped around her cute little finger. Himself included.

"Brick was hit," their team medic Antonio "Arrow" Eden announced.

"Bad?" Bear asked, fighting against the tightening in his chest.

"He'll live," Arrow replied.

"They're coming from the edge of the island," Dominick "Domino" Tanner added.

"They knew we were coming, evacuated, then waited till they knew we'd be trapped before coming in to take us out," Christian "Surf" Bailey said, his tone lethal, belying his good looks and easy-going attitude. Despite his love of fun, his ability to get along with anyone, and his laidback ways, Surf was still a warrior, one who never hesitated to do what needed to be done.

"I know. I'm not alone," he told his team. He was still wary of Mackenzie, even if her small hands were currently twisted in the front of his fatigues and her face was pressed against his chest in a way that made him feel … something he didn't want to.

"Friend or enemy?" Mouse asked.

"Uncertain yet. I'll explain later. We're evaccing, Storm won't be here. He'll have used his men as a distraction like he did last time." Last time, when Dove and Isaac had almost been killed, Storm had been a coward, sacrificing his people so he could make his escape. It had worked then, and it would work now, but this time, they had something Storm wanted. Innocent bystander or co-conspirator, Mackenzie was Storm's sister, and he had a feeling the man wouldn't let her go so easily.

"I-I'm not working with S-Storm." Mackenzie's imploring brown eyes stared up at him. "I'm t-terrified of h-him."

Why did her softly spoken words affect him?

Because she was in obvious pain and yet had taken the time to try to make sure he didn't feel bad about causing her more pain?

Because even though she was clearly scared out of her mind, she still hadn't fought him on his need to cuff her?

Whatever it was, he didn't like it, and it had to stop.

The last thing he wanted was to be feeling anything for a woman.

"We'll get it sorted out," he said briskly, although as much as he hated it, he believed her. No one could fake the raw fear he could feel wracking through her body.

Her mouth opened to say something, but he could hear the distinct sound of footsteps, so he clamped a hand over it. Storm's men might be trained, but they had nothing on him and his team, and he moved himself and Mackenzie further under the cover of the fallen tree trunk as he caught sight of shadows moving through the trees.

Knowing his team could take care of themselves and would watch each other's backs, it was his job to get himself and

Mackenzie to the boat.

The thunder and lightning had thankfully died down, and the darkness was working in his favor. Storm's men no doubt thought he had run and would be attempting to track him, but he was going to wait right here until they passed him and then grab Mackenzie and run.

Whether or not she was working with Storm, she likely knew something of his plans. She was a valuable commodity in bringing down the terrorist, so it was imperative that he get her back to Stateside in one piece.

That was definitely the only reason he didn't want her falling back into Storm's hands. It was absolutely not because he was worried about what her brother would do to her.

Definitely not.

Slowly, he let his hand drop from her mouth and grabbed hold of her, ready to run as soon as the last of Storm's men went past.

A rumble of thunder crashed through the night just as he was about to move, a bolt of lightning followed quickly after.

The timing sucked.

Mackenzie's eyes grew wide, and her bound hands shoved at him to try to push him out of the way.

Damn woman. It wasn't her job to try to protect him, and he had been well aware of the figure creeping up behind him.

Pulling out his knife, he spun and buried it in the man's neck in one smooth move, then tossed the knife to Mackenzie, who was staring up at him in shock. "Cut your hands free and run. Boat is straight ahead that way," he told her gesturing due east. "Wait for us there."

He'd take out as many men as he could, make sure she got away safely, then follow her. If she didn't go to the boat, then he'd know for sure that she was in on whatever her brother was planning.

"You're not coming with me?" Mackenzie asked, managing to pick up the knife and slice through the plastic zip tie at her wrists.

There was fear in her voice at the prospect of being left alone, and he was forced to acknowledge this woman was the real deal. That, or she was the best actress ever and should be finding herself a job and winning an Oscar.

"I'll catch up."

"Please come with me," she begged. There was such trust in her gaze, and it burned like acid in his stomach. Bitter betrayal upon bitter betrayal had all but decimated his ability to trust, and yet there was something about that open honesty in her eyes that soothed something inside him.

He was losing it.

The woman had him not knowing which way was up, and he'd only spent ten minutes in her company.

"Look out!" she screamed a second before he felt a bullet rip through his leg.

That's what happened when you let yourself get distracted. Someone always got hurt.

"Run," he ordered Mackenzie. The best he could do now was stay here, prop himself up against a tree, and lay down covering fire so she could get away.

"I'm not going without you." The stubborn thing slipped up beside him and under his arm, wrapping hers around his waist and attempting to take his weight.

"Mackenzie, run," he growled, firing a spray of bullets at the approaching soldiers.

"No."

"Get out of here," he ground out.

"Not without you." She tugged on him like she actually stood a chance at moving him, and he sighed. He was hurt, and she clearly wasn't going anywhere on her own. He may as well get her to the boat, then wait for the rest of his team there.

Shoving her ahead of him, he lay down more covering fire, then took off after her. The bullet had gone through his thigh on the side he was missing the bottom half of his leg. For now, adrenalin masked the pain, but unless he got himself and Mackenzie to the boat quickly, he'd lose the strength in the muscles he needed to keep his balance with the prosthetic.

He hadn't gone more than a couple of dozen yards when he found Mackenzie bouncing anxiously from foot to foot.

Waiting for him.

When she spotted him, she hurried over and resumed her position at his side, her intentions to help him more than clear.

This was not good.

Her refusal to save herself and wait for him left him confused and poked at something inside him best left alone. This grudging respect he felt for her was unwelcome, and he didn't like it in the least. He wanted away from Mackenzie the sooner the better.

* * * * *

September 27th
3:03 A.M.

The man was huge.

Mackenzie knew he was taking most of his own weight despite the fact she knew he'd been shot in the leg, and she was still struggling to help keep him on his feet.

Or maybe she was making things worse and getting in the way. She wasn't sure, but what she did know was she wasn't letting go of him for anything. He was her only hope of getting out of here, away from her brother.

Even though she was still intimidated by him, he was big and growly and, okay, pretty terrifying, but he also made her feel safe, and after spending weeks trapped in an underground prison, she was latching on to anything even resembling security and never letting go.

"Get down." His words were accompanied with a hard shove that sent her sprawling to the ground. She managed to keep in a cry of pain. Mackenzie knew it wasn't a good thing that she was still in pain after so many weeks, but two beatings hours apart and zero medical treatment meant she had no idea of the kind of damage Storm's men had inflicted on her.

A moment later, the man, whose name she still didn't know, fired off a round of shots.

It was so loud.

She'd learned to shoot as a child; her dad had insisted. Her father had served as a Navy SEAL until an injury ended his career. He'd gone into politics after that. Storm's father had also served—he'd been a Marine—but after acquiring a traumatic brain injury, he'd gone off the deep end, become obsessed with storms, and ended up killing himself and very nearly four-year-old Storm when he'd gotten himself and his son caught in the path of a tornado.

Although she knew how to shoot and was even a fairly decent shot, she'd only ever gone to a range. She'd never known until this moment what gunfire in a battle sounded like, and it was terrifying.

"Let's go."

A hand clamped around her arm, dragging her to her feet, and then she was flung over the man's shoulder, and he took off running. His pace was faster than she could have gone on her own, and he had been shot and was carrying her and some huge backpack. The guy was like some sort of superhero.

"Do you know a way off this island?" he asked as he ran.

"No," she managed to force out past the pain in her chest.

Her broken ribs were healing, but being crushed like this against a hard shoulder and bounced about brought back the same pain she'd suffered in the early days, back when every breath had been torture.

"Storm's men beat me unconscious when they broke into my house. I remember being on a boat and walking to the house, but it's hazy. I was in and out of consciousness. My only clear memory is being beaten again before they threw me in the hole. They didn't let me out, just threw food down to me once a day. If you hadn't rescued me, I'd still be trapped there."

A scary thought.

She had no idea what Storm had planned for her, but she knew it wasn't good.

The stuff of nightmares.

She was well-versed in those. Her entire childhood had been one until her mom finally kicked Storm out of the house.

"How long were you in there?"

"Five, maybe six weeks."

"So he took you right when he fled," the man said thoughtfully. "Right after the compound was raided."

Mackenzie had no idea what he was talking about. "I hadn't seen him in almost two years. I thought he finally got the message. I was even thinking of letting the restraining order lapse."

"You had a restraining order?"

"Since Mom kicked him out when he was sixteen." The relief she'd felt when she realized her home was finally going to become a safe place had been quickly squashed when it became clear Storm had no intention of ending his torment of her whether he lived in the same house or not.

"So you really don't know anything about your brother's plans." There was an odd mixture of disappointment and relief in his voice, but she didn't have time to analyze it.

Shouts sounded, and the man stopped, set her on her feet, and pushed her toward the shore, which was visible through the thinning trees.

"They're going to get us," she said, hating that her words came out as a whimper, but she was scared out of her mind about her brother getting his hands on her again. There would be another beating, she knew that, but it was what was coming next that just about choked her.

"Hey." The man gripped her shoulders and leaned down so

they were eye to eye. "They are not going to get us. Go to the shore. See if you can find us a boat. We're on the opposite side of the island that my team and I came in, but your brother and his men had to get here somehow."

"You're coming, though, right?" Was he planning on leaving her? She had no idea where they were or how to get someplace safe. Mackenzie didn't think he still thought she was working with her brother, but that didn't mean he wouldn't dump her. Especially if she didn't have the intel he'd been hoping she might.

His grip on her shoulders tightened. "Kenzie, go. I'm coming."

Then he turned his back on her and began firing his weapon.

Knowing she had no choice but to trust that he was a man of his word, she ran toward the water. There were a few wooden boats on the sandy shoreline, their oars sitting inside. They wouldn't be the best way of escaping, but it was probably all they had.

There were three boats. If she didn't get rid of the other two, then Storm's men could follow them. Running for the first boat, she shoved against it. It was much heavier than she thought it was going to be, and even putting all her effort into it the thing didn't move it very quickly.

Once she'd managed to get it into the water, she waded in after it and gave it a shove, sending it away from the shore. Then she ran to the next boat. She had it only part way into the water when she heard someone running toward her.

Mackenzie spun around on a strangled scream and almost sagged in relief when she saw it was just her rescuer.

"What are you doing?" he demanded.

"Getting rid of the other boats so they can't follow us."

He gave her a funny look but then nodded approvingly. "Go get in the other boat. I'll push this one out."

Because she knew he was stronger, she did as he said, going to the third boat and climbing inside.

It didn't take long for him to push the other boat out into the water, and then he was pushing hers off the sand.

Panic hit hard.

Was he just going to get rid of her? Send her off and let fate do with her whatever it wanted?

He'd said he was coming after her, and he had, but he hadn't said he was coming *with* her.

Her breathing grew choppy, and she huddled in the bottom of the boat, suddenly freezing. She was sitting in a couple of inches of water, the bottom of her nightgown soaked up to the knees. The cotton was thin, and it had no sleeves, and she was probably going into shock. There was no way on earth she could still the tremors wracking her body or stop her teeth from chattering.

And then her savior was rising out of the water like some sort of mystical hero and clambering into the boat.

"What's wrong?" he demanded as he grabbed the oars and started rowing.

"I-I thought you l-left me," she said through her chattering teeth.

"I said I was coming."

"And you came. You just never said you were going to save me."

"I thought it was implied."

"I wasn't sure," she said softly, the shakes slowly easing. "Sometimes I find it hard to trust people."

Mackenzie could have sworn she saw him wince at that, but she was no doubt projecting all her issues onto him. This man was big and strong. What did he know about being betrayed?

"Kenzie." He waited till she lifted her gaze to look at him. "I'll get you home safely. That, you can believe."

She wanted to trust him, she really did, so very badly. But when your own mother wouldn't do what was necessary to keep you safe, it made it hard to believe in anyone.

Especially a man she didn't even know.

"I don't even know your name."

"Bear."

"Your name is Bear?"

"It's what everyone calls me. My name is Luca."

"Luca. I like it. Although I can see why people call you Bear. You're so big, and with the scruffy beard and the growly voice, the name suits you."

He merely grunted in response. "Why don't you get some rest."

She watched as his strong arms moved the oars through the water with ease, his muscles bulging against the fabric of his fatigues. He was strong, but he was also hurt. Even exhausted as she was, she was she couldn't let him do all the work. "I'd rather help."

Mackenzie moved to sit beside him and took one of the oars. Then side by side, they rowed away from the island where she had been convinced she was going to die.

Now her only hope was that they weren't rowing toward a fate worse than death.

CHAPTER THREE

September 27th
5:14 A.M.

Patience was not his strong suit.

Actually having to wait made him feel like ripping out his own hair.

"Well?" Storm Gallagher demanded as his second-in-command entered his room. He'd been waiting for word for hours now, but nobody seemed to know anything.

It was the one thing he hated about living out here on Lake Victoria in Uganda. The island he had made his home was gorgeous, and the fact that it stormed here more days than not was exactly why he had come here, but the place was remote, technology rarely worked, there was no electricity, and the power from the generators didn't allow them to do much of anything.

They had satellite phones, but with the interference of the electrical storms, sometimes reception could be choppy and unpredictable.

"I'm sorry," Ezra announced.

The man had served in the Army but had been dishonorably discharged after serving less than a year. Ezra had a mean streak and anger management issues, but he also had plenty of hatred toward the military and the government, which made him the perfect choice to be Storm's second-in-charge. Right now, the man looked anything but sorry; in fact, he looked furious.

"You're sorry why exactly?" he demanded. It paid to have friends all over the lake; as soon as word got back to him that a team of military men had shown up, he knew they were there for him. He'd evacuated his people to one of a few backup locations he had set up. Then when he was sure whoever was after him would be trapped in the middle of the island, he'd sent some of his best men in after them.

The plan had been to capture them alive so they could be interrogated. He needed to know who was out to get him and how likely they were to keep trying. And his half sister had been left alone on the island. He needed word that she was being brought to him. Mackenzie played a large role in his plans, not that she was aware of that, and he wanted her here with him now.

"Whoever came after us was good. Really good. Probably former special forces, but maybe a team of SEALs or even Delta. We had them at the manor; they were trapped but somehow got away. Took out almost a dozen of our best men. We hit at least two of theirs, though," Ezra said smugly.

If they were that good, then he knew exactly who they were.

He was up against a formidable opponent, but nothing was going to stop him.

Not now.

Not when he was right on the precipice of bringing in a new age.

The age of the regular people.

No longer was the world going to be ruled by the wealthy. Those who bought and sold politicians, who fought wars that weren't their business because it made them more money, their time was over. Once he bankrupted the government and destroyed their armed forces, then it was time for a brand-new day.

"I know who they were," he said.

"Who?"

"Prey Security."

Ezra's eyes widened and then narrowed, and from the fury bubbling in the man's black eyes, Storm assumed Ezra had been turned down by the elite security company. Prey did everything from personal security for the wealthy to black ops for the government and were expanding to include K9 units, search and rescue, and a dedicated serial killer hunter team.

"How do you know it was them?" Ezra asked.

"Because it's personal for them."

Before he'd been forced to flee the country, he'd almost abducted the youngest of the six Oswald siblings who owned and ran Prey. She'd become involved with a former Ranger turned K9 trainer who'd happened to live next door to the survivalist compound he had built and was grooming to turn into domestic terrorists.

Inspired by the prospect of being able to use the woman to control her money and her company, he'd had her and the boyfriend kidnapped. It had almost worked out, but Prey had sent in men to rescue them, and he'd lost almost all his own men in the process.

"They going to be a problem for us?" Ezra asked.

"Yes." Storm didn't hesitate to reply. Prey were absolutely going to be a problem. If he had to guess, they were going to pursue him relentlessly, but they had underestimated him. There was no one more zealous for their cause than he was. "Are our men bringing Mackenzie back with them? We won't be able to go back there, as that location is compromised, but they obviously don't know about this island. If they did, they would have hit all our islands at the same time."

Thankfully, Prey didn't seem to realize just how well he was being financed. He wasn't the only one who wanted to bring in a new era, and there were certain people who were more than happy to finance his mission, which meant he had several island hideouts at his disposal.

Ezra hesitated, and Storm got a bad feeling in his gut.

What had happened that his second-in-command, who cared about no one but himself, who Storm sometimes doubted even had a soul, was worried about telling him?

Storm pushed back the chair at his desk and stood, fixing the man with his very best glower. "What is it? Where's Mackenzie? What's her ETA?" He had plans for his baby sister, plans he was ready to start enacting.

"She was gone," Ezra announced.

For a moment, it felt like the world stopped spinning.

Mackenzie gone?

She couldn't be gone.

He needed her.

"What do you mean gone?" he demanded. There was no way he could have lost her. She was a vital piece of the puzzle. Without her, there was no way to achieve what he wanted. He might be bringing in the new era, but he wasn't going to be the one to rebuild the new world. That job would belong to another.

To his son.

The son he and Mackenzie would create together.

Without her, everything he was working toward would all be for naught.

"When the men went to get her, the door to her prison was open and she was gone. One of the men from Prey must have found her and taken her with them. A few of the boats were pushed out into the water, and one was missing. At least one of the Prey men must have been separated, taken it, and fled."

Storm had stopped listening after he'd heard that Mackenzie had been taken.

Stolen from right out beneath him.

He'd waited so long to get her, and now she'd been snatched away. Anger rolled through him, crashing at his insides like a bolt of lightning.

This wasn't acceptable.

He was sick of people trying to keep him away from his sister. His hatred for her was equal to his need for her. She was the good child, the wanted child, and could do wrong. She had friends, got good grades in school, played sports. She was sweet and good and everything he wasn't.

She was the golden girl, and he despised her for it.

But that was also why he needed her. A child with her skills, intellect, and generosity and his determination, drive, and desire for change could change the world. *Would* change the world.

Which meant he needed her.

"We need to find her," he said, crossing to his window and looking out into the early morning light. A jagged cut of lightning split the sky in two, and he watched in awe as it was followed by another bolt and another. The jagged lines matched the scars inside him and the scars on the outside.

The power of the storm had entered him when he was a small boy, and it lived there to this day. It was why he had come here. He needed to be close to his roots, and his roots laid in the rumble of thunder and the spark of lightning. He was part of the storm, and now that he was here, he could harness its power and do what he had to do.

"We don't need the girl," Ezra snapped. "I keep telling you that. She's not important. She's nothing. She's—"

Storm didn't remember moving. The next thing he knew, he had the man on the floor, his knee pressed against Ezra's neck. "She is important. She is part of this. She is everything. We will find her, and we will get her back. I need her for this. Ezra, if you ever defy me again, I'll kill you. I know what I'm doing, and I won't allow doubters to ruin my plans."

Slowly, he forced himself to stand. It had been a long time since he had lost control of himself like that. After being kicked out of the family home, he'd learned to harness the storm inside him; he'd learned that you caught more flies with honey than with vinegar. But when the entire fate of the world rested in his hands, it was no wonder his nerves were so strung out.

If he failed, the entire world would fall with him.

CHAPTER FOUR

September 27th
5:52 A.M.

If they stayed out on the water much longer, they were going to be spotted.

Spotted and shot at.

Bear scanned the lake. There were no signs of anyone approaching, but he was way off course for where he wanted to be. His plan when he'd pushed the boat off into the water was to circle around the long way to their extraction point, but when he'd been making his way there, he'd encountered boats he was sure contained more of Storm's men.

His NVGs had alerted him to their presence before they'd been spotted, and he'd adjusted his course, but now they were miles from where he wanted to be, they'd missed the evac time, and while he knew Prey would send a helo back for him, he had that feeling in his gut that warned of something happening.

They hadn't planned on finding a prisoner, and he certainly hadn't planned on getting shot and being stuck in a small wooden boat with said prisoner in the middle of Lake Victoria.

With the sun rising soon, they'd be too easily spotted out here, and Storm was going to be looking for them. If he'd gone to all the trouble of kidnapping his sister and bringing her with him when he fled the country, then she was an important part of his plan, whether she knew it or not.

Bear's gaze dropped to the woman curled up at his feet.

Mackenzie had helped him row the boat for over an hour before exhaustion claimed her. Her strokes had gotten slower, her head had started drooping, and when her forehead touched his shoulder it nestled there, stabbing something unfamiliar and unwanted into his heart, he'd ordered her to lie down and get some rest.

Although she'd argued that it wasn't fair that he did all the work, especially since he'd been shot, he'd insisted. The last thing he needed was to be sitting beside her, their thighs pressed against one another as they sat on the narrow wooden bench. The damn woman was making him feel things, and it was completely unprofessional … and completely unlike him.

He didn't allow people to make him feel.

No stranger to betrayal, he kept his emotions locked down along with his heart. His team and the Oswald family had his undivided loyalties, and he'd lay down his life for any of his men, the six Oswald siblings, and their partners and children. Bear didn't like the feeling that he could quite too easily offer that same loyalty to the woman who had snuggled as close to his feet as she could get.

She trusted him.

He'd seen it in her eyes, in the stubborn way she had tried to help him after he'd been shot, the way she'd panicked when she'd thought he was leaving her. Mackenzie trusted him, and he wished she wouldn't. The last thing he needed was any sort of entanglement, even one as pretty as Mackenzie.

Deliberately moving his gaze away from her, he scanned the lake again. All was quiet, but that wouldn't last. He'd put a fair bit of distance between them and the small islands dotting the lake. The local fisherman would already be out starting their days, and he knew there was no way he could hide who and what he was. He had warrior practically tattooed on his forehead, and he wasn't going to leave his weapons behind; they'd need them until he could get Mackenzie back to the others.

They were out of range, so his comms were useless, but once he got them someplace safe, he'd use his sat phone to call in and ask for an exfil. The helo would have picked up the others—Brick needed medical treatment—but Prey wouldn't hesitate to send someone in for him as soon as they had a location locked down. Then Mackenzie would be taken back to Prey, where she would be questioned until it was clear she wasn't in cahoots with her brother and until any knowledge she might have, consciously or subconsciously, had been discovered.

Looking down at her, Bear almost felt sorry for the poor thing. The questioning wouldn't be done gently; although she wouldn't be physically harmed, she'd be put through the wringer, asked the same questions over and over again, and would be treated like she was guilty until she proved her own innocence.

Maybe he'd ask Eagle to make sure he went easy on the woman. It didn't seem fair that Mackenzie would have to pay for her brother's crimes.

That he thought that only went to prove just how much she was messing with his head.

It wasn't like him at all to be infatuated with a gorgeous woman. When he had needs that had to be attended to, he found a woman who knew the score—quick and dirty sex, no intimacy, no emotion, no expectations. Most of the time, he dealt with his needs with his own hand, but there were times when he needed a connection, however brief and devoid of anything real. When that was the case, he always picked women like him, hard and disillusioned, cold inside, ruined by the world.

Mackenzie wasn't like that.

Although she had admitted to having trust issues, there was a softness about her that called out to the hardness inside him.

For a moment, he ached to let that softness soothe him, but he shoved away the feelings with a ruthlessness born of self-preservation. She might not be involved with her brother's schemes—and he suspected she wasn't—but that didn't mean she wouldn't wind up betraying him like everybody else.

There was safety in guarding his heart and his emotions, a

safety he wasn't prepared to abandon for a woman he didn't know.

Bear registered the approaching boat a moment before they noticed him.

Any hope that it was just a fisherman heading out for the day was quickly dashed when he heard shouts. Seemed whoever was in the boat had recognized him as well. He had no idea how many of Storm's men had survived or what they had seen and reported back, but he had to assume it was worst-case scenario, which was that they knew he and Mackenzie were out here alone.

"Kenzie, wake up," he ordered as he shifted his weapon, ready to take aim. He'd prefer not to have to shoot, not because he cared about these men and their lives—they were the enemy and out to kill thousands of innocent people—but because it would alert others—human and animal—to their location. He wasn't kidding himself. He was skilled, but he was outnumbered and had an untrained woman with him; plus the waters of Lake Victoria were teeming with hippos and crocodiles, neither of which he wished to encounter.

"Luca?" she mumbled, sitting up and brushing sleepily at her eyes. It would have been adorable if they weren't about to fight for their lives.

"Can you swim?"

"Swim?" She cast a concerned glance at the dark lake. "Yeah. Why?"

"Because we've been spotted." He'd barely gotten the words out when the first shots came. Whoever was shooting at them was proficient. While the bullets missed them, they peppered the sides of the boat, causing water to immediately begin to flow in.

At least Mackenzie could swim. The last thing he needed was to be dragging his pack, his weapon, and her through the water, avoiding the men shooting at them and whatever was lurking beneath the surface.

"Go," he ordered, firing back at the boat and managing to take out two of the men on board.

She hesitated for only a moment before fixing him with a determined stare. "Which way is the shore?"

"That way," he replied, impressed with her attitude.

When he heard the splash telling him she'd jumped out of the boat, he fired off another round of shots at the approaching boat, managing to hit the third man on board.

They were safe for the moment, but more men would come, and they'd just lost their mode of transport.

His leg had stiffened during the hours of inactivity, and it protested vigorously when he dived into the water and started to kick. It didn't take him long to catch up to Mackenzie. She was swimming in the direction he'd pointed her in with smooth, determined strokes, and he realized she knew more than just how to swim.

"Are you okay?" she asked when he drew up alongside her. "How's your leg?"

That the first words out of her mouth were concern for him made the wall around his heart want to crack, but he firmed it up. She was asking because she needed him to stay alive, not because she cared.

"Fine."

His answer had been curt, but she didn't comment, just continued swimming, and her nonresponse made him feel bad. She didn't deserve to be on the receiving end of his anger and distrust. She hadn't done anything to betray him; she'd just had the misfortune for having a lunatic out for blood as her brother.

Still, although he felt bad, he didn't make any attempts to smooth things over, and they swam side by side in silence as the sky began to brighten and the sun slowly began to rise. For the first time in years, since the mission that destroyed his team and cost him his leg, his wife, and his family, he actually wished he wasn't hardened by betrayal and determined to keep everyone at a distance.

He'd hurt Mackenzie by being rude, and it left him as unsettled as the splintering cracks the pretty brunette was creating in his walls.

* * * * *

September 27th
3:44 P.M.

Mackenzie's legs felt like they were about to fall off.

How many hours had they been walking?

It had to have been most of the day, although she didn't really know because she wasn't wearing her watch. That was one of the things she'd hated most about being trapped in that hole her brother had locked her in. There was no way to tell time down there. Her days were divided simply between day and night. Nothing to do but sit there, try to stretch her muscles as much as she could, eat whatever scraps she was thrown, and try not to lose her mind.

Yoga had been her saving grace, but there was no time to do yoga now.

She chuckled to herself as she pictured the look on Luca's face if she told him she needed to stop for a break so she could work through her yoga routine. He'd think she was insane.

"What?" he asked, stopping and turning to look back at her. He seemed to know where they were going, which was a good thing because she only knew what country they were in thanks to him telling her they were at Lake Victoria in Uganda.

"Nothing," she said, the smile falling from her lips. Darn, the man was intimidating. She didn't even think he tried to look scary. It just seemed to come natural to him.

The look he shot her clearly communicated he was annoyed with her again, and she had to wonder what she'd done to make him hate her so much. It seemed like he'd hated her on sight, and okay, she got it when he thought she might be working with her brother, but surely he knew by now that she wasn't.

Mackenzie was doing her best not to be too big a burden. Because she knew she was woefully inadequate to be helping Luca defend them or find their way to wherever he was heading, she was trying to do what she could. Which mainly consisted of not complaining, walking where he told her to, matching his pace as best as she could, and following his orders without questioning them.

It didn't feel like enough, and maybe that was why Luca was so mad at her. Did he wish that he'd left her behind so he wasn't stuck out here with her?

If it wasn't for her, he would have been able to meet up with his team and would have left with them; instead, he was here with her, and he obviously didn't like that very much at all.

"Water," he grunted, thrusting the canteen at her.

"Thanks," she mumbled as she took it and drank a few mouthfuls.

It wasn't too muggy today at least, and the temperature was bearable, but they'd been walking for hours, on top of swimming for at least an hour, and she was trembling with exhaustion. The short nap in the boat hadn't even come close to making in a dint in the exhaustion that came from weeks of being in pain and scared for her life.

"Food." This time, he thrust one of those protein bars he seemed to have a whole stack of in that pack of his into her hand.

It didn't taste all that good, at least the one he'd given her when they'd first made it to shore hadn't, and neither had the one he'd given her when they'd taken their first break. This one had a different wrapper, so she assumed it was a different flavor, but her hopes she'd enjoy it more than the last ones weren't high.

He took a protein bar for himself, and they stood side by side in silence while they ate. Mackenzie wanted to try to reach out to him, make small talk, get to know him. She hated awkward silences like this, but she didn't know what to say, and since Luca seemed to dislike her so intently, she kept her mouth shut.

When he was ready to go, he didn't even say anything to her, just hefted his pack back onto his back and started walking.

With a small sigh, she followed.

Not only were her legs aching with fatigue, but her feet were a throbbing mess. It had been the middle of the night when Storm and his men broke into her house, so she'd been in bed in her nightgown, which meant she didn't have any shoes. It hadn't been a big deal while she was trapped in that hole, and back at the other island, she'd barely noticed because Luca had carried her most of the time, but now that they'd been walking for hours, she couldn't ignore it any longer.

Luca had given her a pair of his socks to wear when they'd first come out of the lake, but that was hours ago, and traipsing across so many miles of wild forests had pretty much torn them to shreds.

Still, Mackenzie wasn't going to complain. After all, Luca was walking with a bullet hole in his leg and didn't seem to be having any trouble. She wished she was a superhero like he apparently was, but she wasn't. She was just a plain old regular woman who didn't work out quite as often as she should because she was always too busy and therefore wasn't as fit as she could have been.

She could deal with pain, though.

That was one thing she'd mastered long ago.

There really hadn't been a choice, because Storm took advantage of every opportunity he could to inflict it on her.

So, despite the exhaustion and the pain, she would keep walking for as long as it took.

Besides, when she thought about it logically, the trade-off of getting back home where she would be safe and away from her brother was more than worth her current discomfort.

Ahead of her, Luca stumbled, and she hurried forward.

"Are you okay?" she asked, laying a hand on his forearm. He

flinched, and she quickly snatched her hand back.

"Fine," he snapped like it was her fault he'd stumbled, and she took a step back but still met his eye squarely.

"It's your leg. We need to take a look at it," she said softly but firmly.

She'd wanted to look at it when they'd finally made it to shore. They'd both been exhausted, both laid on the grassy shore for several minutes, then Luca had jumped to his feet and told her they had to start walking. When she'd insisted it wouldn't take long to clean and bandage his wound, he'd told her it could wait.

She'd disagreed but had quickly learned he wasn't really one for discussion. Obviously, in his world, he was used to his word being law. Any argument she would have offered would have been futile, so she'd accepted the pair of socks, eaten the protein bar, and then followed after him.

"It's fine," he gritted out, but there was a flush to his cheeks that hadn't been there before, and his dark eyes glittered and certainly not with lust.

Without thinking, she reached out and touched the back of her hand to his forehead.

Hot.

Feverish.

He was running a fever, which meant his wound was infected. If they didn't stop to take care of it now, then he'd be in real trouble later.

"What are you doing?" he demanded, stepping back so her hand fell away. When he almost stumbled in his haste to get away from her, she stupidly reached out to help steady him, only to have him aim a piercing glare her way.

It shouldn't hurt that he was acting like they were five and he thought she had cooties, but it did. Just like it had hurt in the lake when he'd been rude when she'd asked about his leg. He'd been shot. It was only natural for her to be worried about it. Why did he keep acting like that was such an awful thing?

"We need to keep walking," he said, sidestepping around her and trudging off through the jungle. His limp was more pronounced, and he was running a temperature. This wasn't something he could just brush off and ignore.

"Your wound is infected," she said as she hurried after him.

"It's fine."

"No, it's not. We need to tend to it now before it gets worse."

"It's fine," he growled.

"No, it's not," she said again, more firmly this time. "Why are you being so ridiculous about it? If we don't take care of it, you could wind up losing your leg."

"I said it's fine," he yelled, whirling around so fast she squealed and stumbled backward, landing hard on her backside.

There was something dangerous in his eyes, something that told her she had inadvertently struck a nerve. Mackenzie had been sure that while the man was growly and intimidating, every bit the bear he was named after, he wouldn't actually hurt her.

Now she wasn't so sure.

Like she always did when she was threatened by someone bigger and stronger than her, she curled in on herself, trying to become as small a target as possible.

Regret flashed across Luca's features, and he raked his fingers through his brown locks. "I'm sorry, I didn't mean to yell at you. My leg will be fine, and we need to put as much distance between ourselves and the lake, so let's just keep walking."

Mackenzie gave a weak nod but ignored his hand when he held it out to help her up and got back on her feet herself.

The regret deepened, but then Luca shoved it away, and his expression blanked again. Without another word, he turned and started walking.

With no other choices, Mackenzie followed him.

CHAPTER FIVE

September 28th
1:56 A.M.

Why did he have to be such a jerk?

Bear was still beating himself up over the way he'd treated Mackenzie hours later.

It was clear that his little outburst had scared her. She'd been keeping her distance ever since, not getting too close, keeping her gaze fixed anywhere but directly at him when they'd taken breaks, and she hadn't offered to check his wound again.

Stupid pride had made him yell at her.

His leg was a sensitive topic. The mission that had cost him half of his leg had also cost him his entire family, but of course Mackenzie knew none of that. All she was trying to do was help. There was no possible way she could have known he had already lost most of that leg.

Pride.

How many times was he going to allow it to destroy his life?

You'd think he would learn his lesson. The more he clung to his pride, the more he pushed away the people in his life. After losing his leg, his wife had begged him to move back to take over his parents' ranch, but he hadn't been ready to face the fact that the military no longer had a use for him.

No leg; no job.

It was as simple as that in the military's mind.

He'd dedicated his entire adult life to them, defied his parents and his wife's wishes to do what he wanted rather than what was expected of him.

His family hadn't understood what would possess him to give up a comfortable lifestyle running a successful ranch to become a special forces operative, but he'd always wanted more out of life than a cushy life on a gorgeous ranch. He'd wanted to make a difference. And he had.

When Eagle Oswald had approached him when he was starting up Prey Security and asked him to head the first team, it had been a no-brainer. Bear had needed to prove to the world—and himself—that just because he was missing part of one leg didn't mean he was useless; it didn't mean he couldn't still do what he'd trained to do.

His wife had given him an ultimatum: come back with her to run the ranch, or she was leaving him. When it hit him how easy a decision it was, he realized he'd never loved Natalia. His parents had sided with her, saying they'd cut off contact if he divorced his wife and didn't come home. He hadn't spoken to them in nine years.

Said leg had cost him everything—his wife, family, his ability to trust in people, especially women—but it had also shown him what he was made of. Bear had worked hard to rebuild his strength and muscle mass, to keep his skills sharp, and he thought it was a credit to all that hard work that he was one of the deadliest men on the planet.

"Luca?"

Mackenzie's soft voice drew him out of his thoughts. She sounded sweet, like a siren luring him in, only if he allowed himself to be lured in, he'd wind up dashed against the rocks, and this time, he might not be able to rebuild himself.

"Luca?"

"What?" he growled. It wasn't fair to punish her for being nothing but sweet and thoughtful, but he had a raging headache to go along with the burning in his leg, and he was barely to clinging to control.

"Are you okay?"

"Fine," he said shortly.

They'd stopped around nightfall for a few hours. Mackenzie had promptly crashed after eating some MREs, but he'd lain there, twisting and turning, his weapon in his hands, his gaze all but glued to her soft curves. Never before had he been as turned on by a woman as he was by Mackenzie.

Natalia had been his high school girlfriend. He'd been the star quarterback, and she'd been head cheerleader. She'd been hot with large breasts and legs that seemed to go on forever, but she was rude and nasty, bullying those she saw as beneath her, and for the life of him, he didn't know what had possessed him to propose to her.

No, scratch that. He knew why he'd proposed. He'd already upset his parents by signing up to join the Army. He'd thought he should at least give them the daughter-in-law they wanted. A trade-off of sorts. He was away more than he was home anyway, so it wasn't like he'd had to spend too much time with Natalia.

But Mackenzie was the kind of woman it would be hard to leave behind when he went on a mission.

She was the kind of woman you cherished, who deserved every part of you, who it was no sacrifice to worship her body and her soul.

"Luca?"

"What?" he snapped.

"You zoned out. I'm worried about you." Her brows were scrunched together, forming a small v, and even in the dark, he could see the concern in her pretty brown eyes.

Pretty eyes?

He didn't notice woman's eyes.

Well, not unless he was in a bar and he could see they were mentally undressing him.

Maybe Mackenzie was right to worry.

Still, he felt an almost irrational need to push her away lest he do something completely stupid like kiss those full lips. "I didn't ask you to worry."

"I know you didn't, but that doesn't mean I can't."

Turning his back, he threw over his shoulder, "There's no need to."

"Luca." She sounded exasperated and hurried around him to block his path. "We're walking in circles."

He froze.

Impossible.

He'd joined the Army at eighteen, joined Delta a few years later, served for a couple of years before his injury sidelined him. He didn't get lost.

"Not possible," he gritted out, throwing everything into the dark glower he sent Mackenzie's way.

Her throat moved as she gulped, but there was an air of determination in her eyes that said that while she might be intimidated by him, she wasn't backing down. "I wasn't sure at first because even though I've been camping a few times, I'm not an expert, but then I made this mark. See?" She pointed to two branches she'd twisted together to make a vague heart shape.

Why did she have to pick a heart?

Why did he immediately think of the woman lodging in his heart?

Rubbing a hand wearily over his eyes, he wondered if it was true. Was he really leading them in circles?

Tentatively, Mackenzie reached out and rested a hand on his forearm. The touch was like an electric shock, only instead of giving out pain, it brought pleasure. Warmth, softness, gentleness, care … She offered whispered promises of peace and happiness, and she didn't even realize it.

"Luca, you've been weaving all over the place. You can't walk in a straight line. More than once, I thought you were going to fall. You need to stop being stubborn and get some rest, and you need to let me look at your leg." There was her own brand of stubbornness in her voice, and her chin was jutted out, daring him to disagree. Beneath the gentleness, there was a strength he hadn't noticed before, and it was hot as hell.

"We'll walk a little longer, then I'll rest," he said, but he could feel his body beginning to give out on him. She was right. His wound had to be infected. The only reason he was still on his feet was pure stubborn determination. He didn't give up. Ever. He wouldn't. Not for anything. Especially not while this sweet woman's life was on his shoulders.

"You're impossible, you know that, right?" she called out to his back as he turned away and started walking again.

All right, so he was staggering more than walking, but he was still standing.

Better than nothing.

"You know it, sweetheart."

Did his voice just slur?

The ground seemed to wobble beneath him.

The trees looked like they were swaying.

No wait.

That was him who was swaying.

His skin suddenly felt too tight. Too hot.

Constricting.

His leg felt like it was fire.

Don't give in. Don't give up.

That had been his mantra when he'd been battling his way through physical therapy, learning to walk again and rebuilding the muscle mass he'd lost being stuck in bed for weeks.

Don't give in.

Don't give up.

Mackenzie needs you.

Bear didn't even realize he'd gone down until he heard Mackenzie's panicked voice call his name.

Then there were small hands smoothing across his forehead. Her cool fingers felt like heaven against his burning skin.

Mackenzie was worried.

Scared.

He had to get back on his feet.

Had to get her home.

She was counting on him.

This was why he didn't let anyone get close. He couldn't stand the thought of someone relying on him and failing them.

Failure.

He'd been a failure as a son.

A failure as a husband.

He'd failed his team that day too.

No way could he fail Mackenzie.

Not the sweet woman who'd been beaten nearly to death by her brother and then faced his suspicions with grace and understanding. No complaints while they trudged through the forest. She'd sat by his side and helped row the boat until exhaustion had claimed her.

He couldn't fail her.

"Shh," she soothed, her fingertips stroking his cheek. "Don't worry, I have you."

Those were the last words he heard before the world faded away into nothing.

* * * * *

September 28th
4:02 A.M.

Why did he have to be so big?

Mackenzie let go of Luca's shoulders and slumped back to rest against the nearest tree trunk.

She was exhausted.

After Luca had passed out, she'd torn at his pants where the bullet had already ripped a hole and examined his wound. It looked bad. Bad enough that she was concerned that if they didn't get wherever he was going soon, he might die.

Not for the first time, she wished she'd asked where they were going. Just because he was the expert here and she had zero training in evading armed terrorists didn't mean she should have just completely surrendered all control of herself and her life to someone else. Particularly a stranger who didn't even like her.

No way would she be making that mistake again.

Taking care of herself was something she'd always done. Her parents loved her the best way they knew how, but her father was always busy—politics was his first love—and her mom was always torn between her and Storm, which meant home hadn't been a safe place for her. So, she'd always taken on responsibility for her own safety.

Until Luca.

When he'd sprung her from that hole, she'd just been so glad she wasn't alone anymore, that there was someone bigger and stronger who was willing to stand between her and danger. She had allowed herself to be weak, and because of that, both she and Luca were now in even more danger.

"No, stay ... over ... gone ..." Luca mumbled incoherently, and she dropped to her knees beside him, smoothing a hand over his forehead. He was still burning up. She'd cleaned out his wound as best as she could, used the antibiotic cream in his first aid kit, then bandaged him up. There had been a couple of vials of antibiotics in there as well, and even though she'd never given another person a shot before, she figured she couldn't make him any worse by trying it, so she had.

Her medical training was limited to a first aid class she'd taken in college, so she had no idea how long it would take for the antibiotics to start doing their thing or even if Luca was already past the stage of them being able to help him much. But there were two more shots worth of the drugs, so her plan was to get Luca someplace safe—or at least relatively safe where they could hide out—then give him another shot tonight and one again in the morning.

If after that he hadn't improved any, then she'd have to admit that she'd failed and Luca would die. Leaving her alone. Again.

"Please don't die," she whispered as she stroked her fingers through his hair.

It made her a coward, she had no choice but to acknowledge that, but the idea of being alone out here, no idea where she was or where she should be heading, knowing her brother would be sending more men after her, left her utterly terrified.

Why couldn't Storm just leave her alone?

What had she ever done to him other than be born?

"Don't die, Luca, okay? I need you, and I don't like needing people, because when you need people, they can let you down. I know you don't like me, but please, pretty please with sprinkles on top," she added with a half laugh half sob, "don't die on me."

His dark flashes fluttered on cheeks that seemed to be losing color, making his scruffy beard appear even darker. He opened his eyes, but they seemed to look right through her, and in the dark, he probably couldn't see much of her anyway. When he'd passed out, she had commandeered the night vision goggles since he had no use for them, and they'd definitely made navigating the forest a whole lot easier.

"Luca? Are you feeling any better?"

There was no answer, and though his lips moved, no sound came out.

He wasn't really with her, awake but not really, stuck in some fever-induced haze where he didn't know where he was, who she was, or what he was doing.

"You hold on, okay? I'm going to do my best to get you out of here. I know I'm not trained like you are, but I'm stubborn and promise you I'll do everything I can. I won't give up on you, but that means you can't give up on me either. You have to keep fighting, okay? No dying."

She went to move, stand back up, and start dragging him along with her, but his hand snapped out and circled her wrist.

Mackenzie gasped, but there was no fear this time.

Now she understood his earlier outburst. She'd made a faux pas when she'd made the comment about him losing his leg if they didn't stop and tend to his wound. There was no possible way she could have known part of his leg was gone, that he used a prosthetic, because she'd seen him run, carrying her weight as well as his heavy pack. Still, intended or not, she had struck a nerve and couldn't blame him for lashing out.

No wonder he hated her. He thought she was working with her brother, who was apparently some sort of terrorist, she'd gotten him shot, he was stuck out here with her instead of safe with his team, and she said stupid things that upset him.

If she was him, she'd probably hate her too.

His hand was huge in comparison to hers. She liked guys with big hands, and it had nothing to do with sexy times. She liked the way they made her feel safe. Security hadn't been a part of her childhood, and she craved it now as an adult. When she dated, she always chose the safest men she could find, big with jobs where they protected for a living—cops, doctors, firefighters. She'd never dated a military man before, though.

"It's okay, Luca," she soothed, ready to get moving again.

Instead of releasing her, he brushed his thumb softly across the inside of her wrist, making her shiver. Hands could cause so much pain, she knew firsthand, but they could also be healing; she knew that too.

When she was small, it always seemed such an odd dichotomy to her that her brother's hands could hurt her so badly, then her mother's would patch her back up. Even as a child, the irony of the fact that her mom played healer while simultaneously allowing her brother to keep hurting her never eluded her.

"Kiss me," Luca murmured.

That wasn't good.

Luca hated her, so if he wanted to kiss her, then he really had no idea where he was. And if he had no idea where he was, then he was really sick.

There was no ring on his finger, but that didn't mean he wasn't married. Maybe he was just worried about losing his wedding ring while on a mission and left it at home.

Why did the idea of him being married make her eyes go all misty?

That was stupid. The man hated her, and he wasn't the kind of man she would ever choose to date, and yet ...

Mackenzie couldn't deny that there was some invisible rope pulling her toward Luca. He hadn't hesitated to put himself in the line of fire to protect her, and when he'd told her to run and leave him, she'd felt ... something in her chest.

Fear.

But not just for herself.

Fear for him.

Which was utterly insane because she knew he had doubts about where her loyalties lay, and she had no doubt that her brother kidnapping her had put her in a position where she was going to have to fight to prove her innocence even though she had no idea what she'd supposedly done.

Feeling anything for Luca was a recipe for disaster.

Still, she couldn't deny a pleasant flush had come over her when he said he wanted to kiss her.

Attraction.

That was all it could be, all it would ever be, but maybe Luca would be starring in a few of her fantasies when she got back home.

If she got back home.

"I'm not who you think I am, Luca," she said, gently tugging her hand free from his grasp and instantly missing his touch. It would be so easy to accept the kiss—her lips were already tingling in anticipation—but it would be wrong. It would be taking advantage of him and would only prove to him that she was the unscrupulous traitor he thought her to be.

So, she resisted temptation and stood, reaching down to grab hold of his shoulders again to start dragging him through the forest in the direction he'd been heading before he passed out.

Before she took hold of him, she allowed her fingertips to brush across his forehead one more time.

Just to check his temperature, she assured herself.

Not because she liked the idea of touching him, liked the idea of him touching her, liked the idea of kissing him even more.

Patriotic heroes didn't take an interest in suspected traitors, and she didn't want him to take an interest in her anyway.

CHAPTER SIX

September 28th
7:22 P.M.

Angels wore white, didn't they?

Did that mean he was dead?

Bear's head was still throbbing with a vicious headache, and he was about ready to sacrifice the rest of his leg if it meant getting away from the pain, but it was the way the world seemed to have gone all dreamlike that was the worst.

At the back of his mind, he knew he was supposed to be protecting someone.

No.

Not someone.

Mackenzie.

The gorgeous woman with smooth skin that felt as soft as it looked and wild corkscrew curls that framed a face that held too much pain.

Pain that seemed to find cracks in the walls around him and somehow slip through to his heart underneath.

He didn't want to feel her pain.

Didn't want to give her the opportunity to betray him.

Why would he expect that she wouldn't?

Her brother was a wanted terrorist, and while he did believe her story that she had been abducted and was being kept prisoner, there was every chance she was lying.

Could he even tell anymore?

His parents hadn't hesitated to take his ex-wife's side when he told his family he wouldn't be coming home to run the ranch but rather going to work for a private security company. While he'd always known it wasn't love that brought him and Natalia together, he had at least believed that she cared for him.

Wrong.

He'd been so wrong.

He hadn't realized that his parents saw him only as an heir, not as a person with his own plans for his life, and Natalia saw him as an easy meal ticket. Her family's business was going bankrupt, and she'd thought she could marry him and have access to his family's money. But it was a member of his Delta team betraying them, getting the entire team killed except for Bear and the traitor, that had been his first taste of betrayal. He'd never seen it coming, had trusted his team implicitly.

There was no way he would make that mistake again.

Trust had to be earned, and even then, it should only be handed out cautiously.

Mackenzie could very well be involved in her brother's schemes. She could be plotting to kill him. She could be a traitor to her country.

The sound of humming drew his attention, and he saw his angel in white moving between him and the water.

Water?

They hadn't been near the water earlier.

He'd moved them away from it because they'd be easier to spot if they were closer to the lake. There were villages along the shores of Lake Victoria, and Storm's men would likely assume they'd move along the shore and be patrolling the area, hoping to catch sight of them.

Had she known that?

Was she trying to find her way back to her brother?

As he watched, Mackenzie sat down in the water and began to wash her feet.

Shoes.

She hadn't been wearing shoes, he remembered. He'd given

her his spare pair of socks, but they wouldn't have provided her a whole lot of protection from the sticks and rocks they'd been traipsing over.

Shame hit him, shoving away a little of the foggy dreamlike quality. He hadn't given a whole lot of thought to how unpleasant it must have been for her. She hadn't complained, and he'd been spending all his time trying to convince himself the woman was likely working with her brother.

Lies.

This time he was the liar.

Bear knew without a shadow of a doubt that Mackenzie was no terrorist, no traitor, nothing but an innocent victim dragged unwillingly into her brother's dark web of treachery.

He had to go to her.

Apologize.

That thought propelled him to his feet.

He swayed as he stood, his head vigorously protesting being upright. His leg felt numb, and a brush of his fingers over his pants confirmed the presence of a bandage she'd wrapped a bit too tightly around his wound. He wondered if she'd left his prosthetic on while helping him but shook the thought free.

The headache thundering in his mind took offense to the sudden movement, but he stayed standing and took an uneasy step. He really should have stayed sitting, but something was pulling him toward Mackenzie.

The woman who very well might have saved his life.

She hadn't left his side after he'd been shot, had been quick thinking enough to get rid of the other boats so they couldn't be followed when they fled the island, had tended to him while he'd been unconscious.

If she was going to turn him into her brother, she'd had ample opportunity to do it.

Instead, she'd taken care of him.

He staggered toward the water, drawn to Mackenzie, his siren, who was bringing him closer to the rocks that could destroy him and didn't even realize it.

Not just a siren, though; she was also an angel.

A sweet angel dressed in a white nightgown who had a quiet strength he wasn't even sure she was aware of.

As he got closer, he couldn't not notice the swell of her breasts. The thin, white material was wet and clinging to her like a second skin, giving him the perfect view of her pebbled nipples.

Blood rushed south.

The woman was gorgeous, the opposite of Natalia in every way. Natalia had been tall, with long legs, big breasts, blond hair flowing down her back, and ice-blue eyes he hadn't realized had been cold until she'd delivered her ultimatum. Mackenzie was short, her breasts much smaller, her curls just touching her shoulders but he knew would fall most of the way down her back if straightened. Her eyes were the warmest shade of brown, like the melted hot chocolate he used to drink on cold winter's nights as a child.

They were the kind of eyes you could get lost staring into.

The kind of eyes he found himself *wanting* to get lost in.

It wasn't like him, and as much as he didn't want to feel this way, he couldn't break away from the pull that kept him moving toward the pretty little siren.

When his feet splashed into the water, Mackenzie gasped and whipped to her feet, spinning around to face him. His weapon was in her hand, and she aimed it at his head. Her hands were shaking, but he didn't doubt she would have shot him if he were a threat.

Pride had his lips curling up, but then he saw her cheeks were wet, and not with water from the lake.

Tears.

She'd been crying.

Her eyes were red-rimmed and puffy, and the sight of them did weird things to his insides.

An urge to take her pain and make it his own caught him by surprise. He cared that she was hurting. No, more than that, he hated that she was hurting and wanted to do whatever it took to make it stop.

"Luca," she said, lowering the weapon and hurrying to his side. "What are you doing up? You shouldn't be standing. You're still running a temperature, but your leg is looking a little less red and enflamed. I've given you two shots of the antibiotics in your first aid kit. There's still one more. I think it's enough to get your fever down."

It wasn't her words that made him smile, but the concern behind them.

She was worried about him.

Genuinely worried.

She was sweeter than honey, this one, but that just meant he had to be even more careful. The last thing he wanted was to wind up getting stuck in all that sweetness; he had zero intentions of ever allowing another woman into his heart.

Yet when her small hand reached up to touch his forehead, he felt a need so strong it was hard to ignore.

He caught her hand and touched his lips to the sensitive skin on the inside of her wrist.

Mackenzie gasped, her eyes flying to meet his, but she didn't pull away.

Bear touched another kiss to her wrist, this time sweeping his tongue across her soft skin. They were both filthy and yet she tasted every bit as sweet as he'd been imagining.

"What are you doing?" she asked breathily. There was heat in her eyes, desire, want, even need, and she hadn't pulled away from him yet. She wanted it as much as he wanted to give it to her, so why did he feel guilty?

Because Mackenzie is a woman who deserves forever, and forever is the last thing you want, a voice whispered in his head.

This was wrong.

The fever was clouding his good judgment.

But it didn't stop him from dropping his head, catching a couple of stray tears with the pad of his thumb before capturing her chin and tilted her face up. His mouth stopped a millimeter from hers. "I'm kissing you," he whispered, giving her ample time to pull away if this wasn't what she wanted.

Part of him prayed she would. He needed her to be the smart one right now, because he'd become obsessed with this woman and his need to kiss her.

Just once.

Just one kiss. It was all he could afford himself.

But he knew it would be a kiss he'd replay many times over the years.

Mackenzie didn't move, and he finally allowed himself to taste her. Her lips were perfection, and she immediately opened for him, her body shifting closer.

Knowing he would regret it, Bear grabbed her hips, dragged her closer still so she was flush against him, and kissed her like his life depended on it.

In this moment, if felt like it did.

No, not his life, his heart. His heart seemed to depend on this kiss. He had a feeling this woman might just possess the ability to heal his cold, dark heart, but he couldn't afford the risk of falling for her only to be betrayed down the road.

This kiss was all they could ever have, so he better make the most of it.

* * * * *

September 29th
6:29 A.M.

The sun was rising. Luca's fever seemed to have broken, although he was still weak. Today he might even be strong enough to tell her where they needed to go, and yet Mackenzie felt nervous and unsettled.

She'd always had a nervous stomach. When she was stressed, it seemed to twist itself into knots, and that was exactly what it was doing right now.

What had she been thinking, allowing Luca to kiss her?

He was running a fever. He hadn't known what he was doing. He likely thought she was the wife she was beginning to suspect he had. It had been up to her to be the sane one, to push him away. She didn't touch married men, but she'd been weak.

As she washed her battered feet, the hopelessness she'd been trying to keep at bay had settled over her and the tears had come. Then Luca had been there. She'd thought he was one of Storm's men at first, but when she'd seen him, swaying on his feet, she couldn't not run to him.

And that was the problem.

Given her past, she was a sucker for a man who protected her in any way, but she knew from experience that it rarely worked out. Sooner or later, the man would wind up letting her down, and then she felt like she was dealing with her mom all over again.

It wasn't fair; she knew that. She was looking for someone who was perfect, and no such man existed.

There was no way to be in a relationship and not have both parties hurt each other eventually. It was just the way people were. And yet every time a man let her down, she ran, images playing through her mind of the number of times she'd pleaded with her mom to save her from Storm, only to have her mom promise and then back out when Storm raged that she was giving up on him and choosing her daughter over her son.

Luca could break her heart oh so easily.

So why was she giving him that opportunity?

Already, her heart was sneaking toward him, wanting to accept the protection he would so easily offer, but that felt like she was using him. He was more than a protector, and maybe that was the problem. She could sense his pain, and she wanted to make it better. She wanted to soothe it, to fix his problems for him, and that would lead to only one thing: heartache.

Because you couldn't fix other people. How many times had her mom tried to fix Storm?

And wanting to fix people meant caring about them, and caring about them meant falling for them, and she was terrified she was already starting to care and fall for the big, gruff bear of a man.

Movement behind her caught her attention, and she turned from the water, expecting to find Luca on his feet. He was definitely better, had even eaten a little late last night, but she wasn't sure he was strong enough to be doing much on his own.

But it wasn't Luca standing behind her.

It was a man dressed in black, a white lightning bolt on the right shoulder of his dark fatigues.

One of Storm's men.

The man hadn't seen her yet. He was leaning down over Luca, prodding him with his weapon.

Luca was out of it, asleep. At least that's what she thought, but all of a sudden, he rolled and came up swinging his weapon in the other man's direction.

Even feverish and weak, Luca had still known there was a threat, which was pretty impressive and only went to show how well trained he was, always aware of his surroundings, even when sick.

"Mackenzie, run," he ordered as the other man lunged, managing to knock Luca's weapon to the side.

As skilled as Luca was, he was still sick and weak and thus no match for an opponent right now. He should be resting, not fighting for his life, for both their lives.

She couldn't run and leave him. The man would kill him. Storm wanted her and didn't care about whoever had taken her. They were just a nuisance to be eliminated.

Luca swung a fist at the other man, connecting with his jaw and sending him stumbling backward. Luca wasn't going to go down without a fight, but she wasn't sure this was a fight he could win.

He'd taken back the automatic rifle after they'd kissed yesterday, but he had a backup weapon, more than one, and had given her another of his guns. She was supposed to keep it on her at all times, but she'd only walked away to go to relieve herself behind a tree. She hadn't thought she'd need it.

A mistake. One she and Luca might pay for.

Luca swung a fist at the other man again, but this time, their attacker managed to block it and deliver one of his own.

The force of the blow made Luca stagger backward and sink to his knees.

Even from a dozen yards away, she could see the fatigue on his face.

The other man delivered a kick to his chest and then one to the side of his head, and Luca went down.

He didn't get back up.

Mackenzie was frozen in place. She had no idea what she should do.

When Storm's man raised his weapon and aimed it at Luca's crumpled form, she didn't think; she just acted.

Running at him, she threw her entire bodyweight behind it and slammed her fist into the side of his head.

It did little more than draw his attention to her, but that was okay. As long as his attention was on her, he wasn't going to shoot Luca.

"Well, well, well, what do we have here?" the man said, shooting her a smile that made her insides quiver. "If it isn't the runaway sister."

He took a step toward her, and she quickly took one back. What was she going to do next?

Try to get to Luca's discarded weapons?

"You know your brother isn't pleased that you're gone. I reckon I'll get a reward for being the one to bring you back. He promised us we could play with you after he was finished with you," the man said, and from the leer on his face, she knew exactly what kind of games he wanted to play.

Her gaze darted to the weapon, and she jumped at it, but the man moved with surprising speed, grabbing her and throwing her to the ground. The next thing she knew, she was flat on her back, her wrists pinned together above her head, one of the man's knees between her legs.

She bucked and twisted, doing her best to throw him off as she tried not to hyperventilate, but all it earned her was a blow to her temple that had her head snapping painfully sideways.

"Nobody will know if I have a little ride of you now," he said, his dark eyes glittering with lust.

His free hand shoved her nightgown up around her hips. She wasn't wearing any panties; she'd discarded them when she'd been trapped in the hole and gotten her period.

"These are smaller than I like," he said gripping one of her breasts in a bruising hold, "but I bet you're tight down here, aren't you." His hand moved between her legs.

"Don't, please," she begged, knowing it would do no good. The man wanted her, he was bigger and stronger, she couldn't fight him off, and Luca was unconscious, unable to save her.

"I love it when you beg, love it even more when you scream," he said, his finger prodding at her entrance.

There was no way out of this.

No way to stop it from happening.

He released her wrists as he unbuckled himself, and she knew what he wanted. He wanted her to fight him. He wanted her to know that he was going to use his size to his advantage and take from her what she didn't want to give him. It turned him on.

If he wanted a fight, he was going to get one.

Mackenzie punched and slapped at him, scratched with her

nails, and tried to kick at him as best as she could with his knee between her legs.

As he shoved his pants down enough to free his length, she caught sight of a knife strapped to his thigh.

Could she get it?

The man lined up, ready to thrust into her body, and she reached for the blade, managing to pull it free before he realized what she was doing.

She didn't hesitate, because she knew if she failed, he'd rape her, kill Luca, then take her back to Storm. Her fear for Luca overrode everything, even her own terror at falling back into her brother's hands.

Aiming for whatever was body part was closest, she plunged the blade into his belly.

His eyes grew round with surprise as he swayed sideways, his hands going to his stomach and curling around the knife's handle.

Then they grew bright with rage.

He swore at her, calling her a colorful litany of names as he yanked the knife free.

She hadn't thought of that.

In her mind, once she stabbed him, it would all be over, but the blade, dripping with her attacker's blood, was swinging down toward her.

Mackenzie shrieked and grabbed at his wrists. She couldn't stop him, but she did slow him down enough that the blade scratched along her cheek, down her chin, and along her neck before sinking in just beneath her collarbone.

Obviously thinking he had her now, the man rocked back on his heels and sneered down at her. "Your brother is going to punish you for that, little girl."

What could Storm do to her that he hadn't already?

Nothing.

Never before had she fought back against her brother. He was seven years older than her; he'd always been bigger. He thought she was weak, but today, she wasn't just fighting for herself. She was fighting for Luca too.

It was that thought that had her grabbing for the knife—still embedded in her flesh—and swinging it up, burying it in the man's neck.

He spluttered, and blood immediately began to pour from the wound and dribble from his mouth. He grabbed it, pulled it free, and blood began to gush.

When he made a move to stab her again, she scrambled backward out of his reach.

The man somehow got to his feet.

Advanced on her.

But then he dropped to his knees and, a moment later, slumped sideways.

Was he dead?

She was afraid to go and look. She'd never touched a dead body before. She didn't even like picking up the dead body of a fly or a spider if one died in her house. She always used the vacuum cleaner to suck them up, but there was no gigantic, human-sized vacuum cleaner around now.

Just as she was crawling toward her would-be rapist, another man appeared through the trees. He was wearing the same clothes as the man who had attacked her, so she knew he wasn't one of Luca's team or someone else sent to rescue them.

Her fingers curled around the weapon the first man had dropped. She lifted it and fired at the approaching man over and over again until the gun wouldn't fire any more bullets.

Some of her shots had probably gone wide, but enough had hit the man that he was down on his knees, blood staining the front of his shirt.

"Mackenzie?"

Luca's rough voice broke the thin barrier of her control, and she started to sob.

Through blurry, tear-filled eyes she saw him get to his feet; fire a bullet into the second man's head, finishing him off; and check the first man. He didn't do anything to him, so she assumed she had killed him, and then he was crouching before her.

When he reached for her, she didn't hesitate to throw herself into his arms, sending him toppling backward and onto his backside. When she would have pulled back to check if he was okay, he tightened his hold on her, and she surrendered to the need to be in his arms, wrapping hers around his neck and burying her face against his chest as she sobbed.

It felt good to be in his arms—safe, better than it should—and she knew she was already more attached to Luca than was wise.

CHAPTER SEVEN

September 29th
7:17 A.M.

He didn't want to let her go.

Bear clutched the woman to him, holding her so tightly he was sure he must be hurting her, but she was burrowed so firmly against him it was clear she didn't care.

Maybe she needed to be held as much as he needed to hold her.

When he'd realized they weren't alone, the man had already been standing over him. The fever was messing with his senses and his situational awareness, and it had almost gotten him killed and Mackenzie captured.

The woman had killed to protect him.

Killed.

Sure, his team always had his back when they went on a mission, both his Delta team and Prey's Alpha team. He'd had teammates eliminate threats he hadn't been able to, and he'd done the same for them. But this was different. This woman was a civilian with zero training. She'd been brutalized and kidnapped, held captive for weeks. He'd treated her badly since the moment he found her, and yet she'd defended him, protected him, and killed for him.

The sound of gunfire had dragged him out of unconsciousness. She'd shot one of the men, not killing him, at least not outright, but he would have died from the injuries if Bear hadn't finished him off. The first man, though, had already been dead. She'd stabbed him twice, once in the abdomen and once in the neck, the neck wound being the fatal one.

Stabbing was an up close and personal way to kill, and he knew she hadn't had a knife on her, which meant she'd used the man's own weapon against him.

Pants shoved partway down his legs, it didn't take a genius to figure out that the first man had been about to rape her when she'd gotten her hands on the knife.

Or ...

Grabbing her shoulders, he dragged her backward so he could see her face. Tear-drenched eyes stared back at him, but her sobs had eased to sniffles.

"Mackenzie, did he rape you?" he asked outright. No point in beating around the bush.

She hiccupped on another sob but then shook her head. "He was about to, but I saw the knife and grabbed it."

Relief that she'd been spared that was short-lived when he saw the blood on her face and chest.

Her blood.

"You're injured," he snapped, fear making his words sound harsh when really, the sight of blood on her made him feel ill.

"Oh ... yeah ... he, uh ... he pulled the knife out of his stomach and ..." She waved a trembling hand at her wounds.

Keeping his touch as gentle as he could, he probed her wound. It appeared to be mostly one big, long one, starting on her left cheek and trailing down her chin, along her neck in a shallow line, and then getting deeper just under her right collarbone.

With a growl that had her smiling rather than looking afraid, he stood, scooped her up, and carried her back to where he'd been sleeping.

"Your leg," Mackenzie protested.

"Is feeling better. You got hurt."

"Better than the alternative," she said softly as he set her down and sat beside her.

"You did good, little siren."

She huffed a small laugh. "Siren?"

"I can't shake the feeling that your brand of stubbornness and sweetness is dragging me in against my will, and sooner or later, I'm going to get dashed to pieces on the rocks," he admitted as he found his first aid kit in his pack.

Her brow furrowed. "I shouldn't have kissed you. I don't kiss married men," she blurted out.

Now it was his brow that furrowed. "Married?"

"You had a fever. You were in and out of consciousness, but when you were awake, you weren't really awake. You said a few times that you wanted to kiss me, but I don't think you were really talking about me, really seeing me. I mean, we don't know each other," she said nervously, as though she felt that same connection he did, only it unsettled her because it was too soon to feel anything.

"I'm divorced," he said as he pulled out bandages and pressed them against her wound.

"Oh."

There was something in the way she said that one little word that made his hands freeze. "What?"

"Did um ..." She ran her tongue along her bottom lip, and damn if it didn't make him want to kiss her again. "Did you not want the divorce?"

"Why do you ask that?"

"Well, you wanted to kiss your wife ... ah, ex-wife ... while you were delirious, and you said just now that you don't want to feel anything for me, so I ... uh ... just assumed that maybe you wanted to stay married but your wife didn't."

Hell, she was cute when she was flustered. What was he going to do with her? The last thing he wanted was to fall under her spell. She was innocent—she wouldn't have killed her brother's men if she wasn't—but he wasn't looking for anything long-term, and Mackenzie seemed too sweet to be interested in one night of hot sex.

Still, the need to reassure her was strong enough that he brushed a knuckle along her lip, tracing the same path her tongue had taken. "It was you I was thinking about kissing while I was feverish."

Those expressive eyes of hers grew wide. "Me?"

"Yeah, siren, you."

"But we don't know each other."

"No, we don't."

"Then why do I keep wanting you to kiss me?" Mackenzie looked as perplexed as he felt and only a little less unhappy about it than him.

The thought that she didn't want to feel anything for him hurt, even though it shouldn't and it was the same way he felt about her. It should be what he wanted. He didn't want to want her, and if she didn't want to want him, then problem solved. They'd find their way back to his team, get her back home where she belonged, and they could both go back to their lives as though none of this ever happened.

"Why don't you want to want me? Why do you think I'll wind up hurting you?" she asked.

"You're not the only one with trust issues, sweetheart." He told her as he taped a bandage in place over the wound on her chest.

She nodded in understanding. "Your ex?"

"Amongst others."

"I'm sorry you were hurt." There was a sincerity in her words and her expression that hit him straight in the heart. This woman didn't even know him, and yet she'd shown more care and concern for him over the last few days than his own family ever had. All they had seen was a broken man who needed to come crawling back home, no job, no leg, nothing to do but cave to their pressure.

But that wasn't who he was.

Fighting to make the world a safer place for people like

Mackenzie, that was who he was. It wasn't a part of him he could shut off to cater to his family's wishes.

His gaze dropped to her lips. Damn, he wanted to kiss them so badly he ached with need.

"Luca?" she whispered.

"Yeah?"

"I want it too."

Her permission and acknowledgment that this weird thing brewing between them wasn't one-sided was all he needed.

Curling an arm around her waist, he pulled her into his lap. One of his hands dug into her hip, anchoring her against him, while his other threaded through her hair and angled her head so he could plunder her mouth.

Something inside him shifted when their lips met, something primal was awakened, a deep-seated need he didn't understand and didn't want to examine to keep this woman safe. To protect her, to cherish her, to show her what it was like to be the center of someone else's world, the sun of their universe.

This wasn't him at all, and he knew he should push her away for both their sakes, but the idea of walking away from her about gutted him. And yet he knew it was what he was going to do.

Still, when her small hands rested on his shoulders, her fingers latching on to him, clinging with the same desperation he felt as he held her to him, he wondered if it would be a mistake to walk away from her. This thing between them was there whether he wanted it to be or not, and while he didn't know what would come of it, there was a part of him that wanted to find out.

Desperately.

"Here we are, worried about you, and you're making out with the girl." The voice and muffled laughter had him jerking to his feet, one arm clutching Mackenzie to him, as he spun around and raised his weapon.

It wasn't until he saw his team—minus Brick—standing there that he realized the voice belonged to Surf.

"Luca?" Mackenzie asked, and he realized she was shaking in his arms.

Carefully, he set her on her feet and deliberately took a step back. This was it. Time to re-establish boundaries, to remind them both that she was nothing more than part of a mission, and that now his team was here, they'd be delivering her back home and moving on to the next job. "No need to worry. It's the good guys this time. This is my team, Mouse, Arrow, Domino, and Surf. There's also Brick, but he was hurt when we raided your brother's compound. Guys, this is Mackenzie."

There was no distrust on any of his teammates' faces, so he assumed the background checks on Mackenzie had shown she wasn't involved in her brother's plans. Not that he doubted that anymore. She was as innocent as they came.

"Pleasure to meet you, Mackenzie," Surf said, shooting her his most charming smile, and Bear felt a surge of red-hot jealousy slice through him. But he didn't want Mackenzie, so why should it matter if she hooked up with Surf?

She shook his hand and smiled, but Bear could see the strain of the last several weeks on top of everything that had happened the last few days beginning to take their toll.

Apparently, he wasn't the only one, because Arrow rolled his eyes and shooed Surf away. "You hurt, Mackenzie?" he asked indicating the bandage on her chest.

"Oh, I'm okay, but Luca was shot. He's running a fever. I gave him the antibiotics in his pack, and he seems to be doing better, but I'm worried about him."

"Everything is fine now," he said gruffly. "And she's not okay. That guy stabbed her."

His teammates' faces darkened as they took in the dead man with his pants around his knees. No words were needed to explain what had almost happened. When Arrow arched a brow at him, he shook his head to say she wasn't raped, but she'd come damn close to it. Much too close.

"How about we get both of you to the hospital to get checked out. Boat is only a little way down the lake," Arrow said, moving to support Bear while Mouse moved in to pick up Mackenzie.

"I can walk," she protested as his friend gathered her up.

"No offence, honey, but you look wiped out, and you're not wearing any shoes. We can move much faster if I carry you, and that means we can get Bear to the hospital quicker," Mouse said, knowing just how to gain her compliance.

As they started walking, Mouse carrying Mackenzie, Arrow helping him walk, Surf in the lead, and Domino watching their six, he knew he was going to have to get used to the idea of letting Mackenzie go. A clean break was probably best. Even though he knew it was going to hurt him as much as it would hurt her, he also knew it was the right thing to do. This was it, the last few hours he'd spend in her presence.

* * * * *

September 29th
12:34 P.M.

She should be happy.

She was alive, no longer her brother's prisoner, safe, clean, and warm. Her wounds had been tended to, she'd eaten, and she'd gotten a little sleep. All of those were good things, and yet Mackenzie couldn't get rid of the knot in her stomach.

The knot was there because Luca wasn't.

It was silly, given that she'd known him a whole forty-eight hours, but she missed him. There was something between them, something that intrigued her as much as it terrified her.

Luca wasn't the kind of man she would even think of looking twice at. He was too big, too intimidating, too powerful, too everything. And yet she couldn't deny that if he asked her out on a date or said he wanted to get to know her better, she would say yes in a heartbeat.

Enough of her life had been spent living in fear; maybe it was time to try a new approach. Her friends were always telling her she needed to get out more, but she liked her safe little life. Routines and schedules helped her feel secure. Sunday night dinners with her parents, Monday night book club, Wednesday night classes at the gym, Friday or Saturday night dates when she had a boyfriend.

The rest of the time, she was tucked away in her home, which boasted a top-of-the-line security system she tried to use to trick her brain into thinking she was safe from her brother.

But his shadow always hovered over her.

It was time to banish it once and for all.

"How's our favorite patient?" Surf asked with a grin as he and the other guys on Luca's team entered her hospital room. The men were all big like Luca, and with the four of them in her room, there seemed to be little space for anything else. While they weren't as good as having Luca here, they were the next best thing, and she smiled at all of them.

"Luca isn't your favorite patient?" she asked.

"You kidding?" Domino said as he lounged in the chair beside her bed. "He's the worst patient. At least you smile and are polite, even if you are a stubborn little thing."

She chuckled at that because if there was one thing Luca wasn't, it was smiley and polite. Still, she liked him, gruffness and all, and she wanted to see him again sooner rather than later. "Is he doing okay?"

After Luca's team had found them, they'd walked for about a mile—well, she hadn't since Mouse had insisted on carrying her and she'd agreed because Luca's health was more important than her pride—until they got to a boat. She'd fallen asleep on the boat ride but woken when they got back to shore and into an SUV. They'd driven to a small airfield and taken a helicopter to a hospital. Once they'd arrived here, she'd been taken to one room,

Luca to another, and she hadn't seen him since, although the guys had been in and out of her room.

"He's going to be fine," Arrow assured her. "Bullet went straight through. There's some muscle damage, but nothing that he can't recover from."

"I'm glad. I can't imagine how hard he had to have worked when he lost his leg. I didn't even know until I checked out his wound."

"He's a tough one," Mouse agreed.

The smiles fell off the guy's faces, and she immediately felt chilled. Pulling the blankets up to her chin, she asked, "What's wrong?"

"Nothing, darlin'," Surf told her. "We just need to ask you a few questions if you're up to it."

Interrogation time.

Luca had hinted that she was going to be grilled about her involvement with her brother, although she'd thought it wouldn't happen until she got home. She had no idea how she was going to convince these men she wasn't working with Storm when she wasn't even sure she had convinced Luca, and he'd admitted to having some feelings for her. "O-okay."

"Hey now," Surf said as he reached out and took her hands. One of them had an IV running into the back of it, which he was careful to avoid as he squeezed them gently. "It's going to be okay. We already know about your relationship with your brother. We just need to know what happened that night and if you heard anything while you were with him."

"You don't think I'm working with him?" she asked, looking from man to man as they all met her gaze squarely and shook their heads.

Feeling a little better, she wondered where to start. She guessed the beginning was as good a place as any.

"Storm's dad was in the Army. He was caught in an IED explosion and survived but had a traumatic brain injury. After

74

that, he kind of lost touch with reality and became obsessed with storms, and one day, he took Storm, who was four at the time, and went chasing after a tornado. He was killed, Storm was injured, and I guess that's where he got the obsession with storms.

"A year later, our mom met my dad, and they married. Two years later, I came along. Storm hated my father. My dad served too. He was injured as well, lost both his arms, and got into politics after he was medically discharged. When I came along, Storm decided to hate me too. He made my life a living hell."

"He hurt you?" Domino asked.

"All the time. My mom had to quit her job so she could stay home to try to stop it happening. Child protective services were regular visitors to our house. They always wanted to blame my dad, but he never laid a hand on me. It was always Storm. Mom felt torn between the two of us. She was always defending Storm, saying he wasn't responsible because he'd been through so much."

She picked absently at the blanket. Her mom making excuses for Storm had hurt almost as much as her brother's fists. Storm might have been through a lot, but that didn't mean it was okay for him to hurt her.

"Your brother was sent to military school when he was sixteen. What happened?" Mouse asked. His eyes were kind as he looked at her, and even though she didn't want to talk about it, she did.

"I was nine. My mom was held up at the store, not home by the time I got home from school, but Storm was there. He had a knife, grabbed me, twisted my arm so badly he broke it and dislocated my shoulder, then threw me onto his bed and cut my clothes off." She shivered as memories of that day mixed with memories of what had almost happened this morning. "My mom didn't get home in time to stop him."

The hand covering hers tightened, and she looked over at Surf. "I'm sorry," he said softly, and she nodded, appreciating his words, but she noticed something hidden deep in his eyes.

Something she knew he didn't want her to try and unravel.

"It was the final straw for my dad. He said Storm had to go or he was taking me and leaving."

In her mind, it had been too little too late. Her mom at least loved Storm, but her dad didn't, and yet he'd stood by and let her brother hurt her over and over again because he was too busy with his political campaign.

"I've had restraining orders against him ever since that night. He used to come around the house all the time, though, and stand outside my window and stare in at me. He'd write me letters and follow me sometimes, but then two years ago, it stopped. I didn't see him hanging around, and there were no more letters. I thought he'd finally moved on." The relief she'd felt was gone now as she realized Storm had never intended to let her go.

"What happened the night he took you?" Domino asked.

"I woke up, and he was in my bedroom along with four other men. He told me it was time, but I had no idea what he meant by that, and then he ordered his men to beat me. I passed out and woke up on a plane. After that, I was in and out, but I know we took an SUV and then a boat to the island. He had me beaten again, and then I was thrown into that hole. I didn't come out until Luca found me."

"Did Storm come and see you while you were there?" Mouse asked.

"No. Nobody did. They threw down food once a day, and that was it. I was just left down there. I knew it wouldn't last, but it was better down there than whatever Storm had planned for me."

"Did you hear the others talking?" Surf asked.

"They would run drills, and I would hear them shooting often, but I don't know anything about their plans. I'm sorry. If anyone wants Storm caught, it's me. I want to be free to finally live my life without having to worry about him and what he's going to do to me next, but I don't know anything that can help you. In fact, you all know more about his plans than I do."

When she thought of the life she might have, the future that could be brighter if the threat of Storm was eliminated, she saw Luca. It was way too early to know if there could be something real between them, but she wanted to find out, wanted to set her fears aside and see what could develop.

But that couldn't happen as long as Storm was still out there.

CHAPTER EIGHT

September 29th
2:42 P.M.

His skin felt too tight. He needed to get out of here, put some distance between himself and the woman he couldn't stop thinking about.

"Your girl is something else."

Bear glanced up as the guys entered his hospital room but merely offered a grunt at Surf's praise of Mackenzie.

As if he didn't know the woman was amazing. She hadn't run when he'd told her to when they were attacked this morning. Instead, she'd stayed and killed to protect him.

He wasn't kidding himself; he knew that if Mackenzie had run, he'd be dead right now. She was what they wanted, not him. He'd just been an obstacle in their path, one who had been weak and feverish. The blows he'd received had knocked him out, and he'd been completely helpless. If Mackenzie had followed his orders and fled, they would have put a bullet in his brain and gone after her.

Not only would he be dead, but she would be back in the clutches of her evil brother.

"You finished questioning her?" he asked.

He'd wanted to be there for her while she was questioned about her brother, not because he thought his team would go hard on her—in fact, when they learned how she's saved his life, they'd become her biggest supporters—but because he'd known how hard it would be for her. But sitting in there, holding her hand because he had no doubt that he couldn't be in the same

79

room as her and not touch her, would have given her the wrong impression.

Clean break.

That was what was best for her.

And for him.

"Yes," Mouse replied. "Reports have been sent to Eagle."

"And?" he prompted.

"And what?" Domino asked.

"And is she cleared?"

"Dude, she was never a suspect," Surf said as he dropped into the room's only chair. "I think you were the only one who ever thought there was a chance that she could be working with her brother. When you told us you found her there and we were able to relay that to Eagle, Raven had a background check on her within minutes and cleared her as a suspect. We went in after the two of you to rescue a victim, not to arrest a terrorist."

A relieved breath whooshed out of him. As much as he hated to admit it, he'd needed to hear his team—his friends, his brothers in every way but blood—say that they believed Mackenzie was innocent. It was what he believed, but he didn't trust himself anymore to make good judgment calls when it came to knowing whether someone was telling him the truth.

"You really thought she could be guilty?" Mouse asked.

"No," he answered quickly.

"You have to stop thinking everyone is like your parents and your ex," Domino said with a sigh. "Seriously, man, you have an amazing woman in there who actually seems to like your grumpy self. Don't ruin it by doubting her just because other people have betrayed you in the past. That's not fair to her."

His team was operating under a major misconception here. "She's not my woman."

Mouse frowned. "What do you mean? You guys were kissing when we found you, and we've about had to tie her to the bed to stop her from roaming the hospital halls until she finds you.

Certainly seems like there's something going on between the two of you."

"Well, there's not."

"So you don't mind if I ask her out?" Surf asked. "Because she is one impressive woman. Not only did she save your life, but she told us what it was like for her growing up, and that she's able to function at all in the world is nothing short of a miracle."

"Sure, fine, whatever, ask her out if you want," he growled through gritted teeth, refusing to get drawn into Surf's game. He wasn't going to be goaded into admitting he wanted anything with Mackenzie.

"Dude, you're about to have a coronary," Surf laughed. "Just admit you like her, because if you won't, I will seriously consider walking back down the hall to her room and asking her out on a date. One of us should be with that woman, and if you don't want it to be you, then I'm willing to step up and take the position."

Instead of answering, Bear picked up his pillow and threw it at his friend, which only made Surf laugh harder.

"For real, though, man," Mouse said, "you should give her a chance. She's strong enough to handle our lifestyle, she's sweet, and she obviously likes you. Why would you walk away from that just because your parents and Natalia were selfish and manipulative?"

Of the six guys on their team, only he and Mouse had been married before. Mouse's wife had died in childbirth, leaving him to raise their adorable daughter, Lauren, alone.

Thanks to his parents stepping up and helping him out, Mouse had been able to continue to serve in the military until an accident had left him blind in one eye; then he'd joined Prey. His situation and Mouse's were nothing alike. His friend had adored his wife, been devastated when she died, and hadn't been betrayed by the people who were supposed to love him unconditionally.

This was too much. He couldn't handle thinking about Mackenzie any longer. Nothing was going to happen between them. He wasn't going to let it, nor was he going to sit around talking about it with his friends like they were a bunch of teenage girls.

"What time are we flying out?" he asked.

The guys exchanged glances at his abrupt and obvious subject change.

"So that's it?" Arrow asked. "You're just going to walk away from her, pretend like you never met her?"

"Yes."

"You think you can do that?" Domino asked. "You think it's going to be that easy?"

No. "Yes."

"I never thought I'd call you a coward, Bear," Mouse said, and from the look in his friend's eyes, he meant it.

He and Mouse went all the way back to preschool. They'd lived in the same town, and their parents had been friends. They'd played football together, enlisted together, gone through boot camp together, and both gone on to join Delta. When Bear had lost his leg and then his wife and his family, the only friend he'd had who had sided with him was the man currently looking at him with a disappointment that filled him with shame.

But what could he do?

He was messed up, physically and emotionally. His ability to trust others was just gone. It wasn't like he was deliberately trying to be a jerk or a coward or hurt Mackenzie; he just didn't have it in him to trust anyone else again.

Without trust, there was no future for him and Mackenzie.

It was as simple as that.

"The plane is leaving in about three hours," Surf said as he shoved to his feet and headed for the door.

"Where are you going?" Bear demanded.

"To hang with Mackenzie. I don't think she should be alone right now, and since you won't step up and be there for her, somebody has to."

When Surf was gone, the others also stood and headed for the door. Guess he was in for a repeat of the Natalia situation. Once again, his friends were siding with the woman instead of with him.

Only this time, he knew he was the one in the wrong.

"Maybe nothing would have developed between you and Mackenzie," Mouse said before he left. "But it seems like such a waste not to find out."

Alone in his room, he slammed a fist into the bed. It wasn't as satisfying as punching something like the wall or preferably one of his friends who had just ditched him to go and hang out with the one person who might actually be able to heal him, but it was better than nothing. He had to do something to alleviate the ball of guilt sitting heavily on his chest.

Was he making a mistake?

Surely it was too soon to feel anything other than lust and respect for Mackenzie, but maybe that wasn't such an awful place to start.

He almost swung his legs over the side of the bed and reached for the crutches propped up against the wall but stopped himself. He had nothing to offer the woman, and she'd already been through so much.

She deserved someone who could love her wholly and unconditionally. Someone who would put her first like she deserved, who would worship her and never let a day go by where she didn't know how special she was.

That man couldn't be him.

Sagging back against the mattress, he forced himself to let it go. There could be nothing between him and Mackenzie, and he was right to make it a clean break. She'd been through a traumatic ordeal. Once she got home to her friends and family, she would likely forget all about him. After all, he hadn't exactly made their time together particularly pleasant.

His team would get over their infatuation with Mackenzie, and sooner rather than later, their lives would all go back to normal.

Only Bear knew he would never forget Mackenzie, the kisses they'd shared, or the too brief time he'd gotten to spend with her. He might not want to feel anything for her, but that didn't mean he didn't.

* * * * *

September 29th
5:38 P.M.

"Hmm?" Mackenzie said, blinking when fingers clicked in front of her eyes.

"You okay, darlin?" Surf asked.

"Sure. Sorry, did you say something?"

While she appreciated the guys hanging out with her in her hospital room so she wouldn't be alone, the person she really wanted to see was Luca. All of his friends had assured her that he was okay, his leg hadn't needed surgery, and he would recover. The infection was clearing up nicely, and he had orders to remain off it and rest, as there was redness and irritation on his stump, and he needed to let it heal.

She knew all of that, but what she didn't know was why she couldn't go and see him.

"Yeah, darlin, I said a whole lot of things while you were zoning out." The look Surf gave her had the hairs on the back of her neck standing on end. Something was wrong but she knew that none of the guys were going to tell her what.

Was Luca not really okay?

They wouldn't lie about that would they?

Even though she'd only known them for a few hours she was already getting a feel of the group dynamics. Surf was the lighthearted one, although she could see he was hiding something dark and painful behind his forest-green eyes.

Arrow was the team medic and the one who tried to take care of everyone else. Mouse was the responsible one, and she understood why when she learned he was a single dad. Surf was the fun one, easygoing and charming, but pain lurked in his green eyes. Domino was the quiet one, and much like with Surf, she could see he was hiding secrets that tormented him. She liked every single one of them, but she absolutely believed they would lie to her to spare her feelings.

"Luca is okay, right?" she asked, needing the reassurance.

"He's fine, honey," Arrow replied patiently.

She nodded, not quite believing them. "Sorry, Surf, what did you ask me?"

"Sure you can focus on me long enough to answer?" he teased. When she poked her tongue out at him, he laughed. "I was asking about your business. I think it's cool you started your own business doing what you love."

Mackenzie smiled despite the ball of tension lingering in her gut. There was no way she couldn't smile when she thought about the company she had worked so hard on. Both her parents had wanted her to follow in her dad's footsteps and enter politics, but that was the last thing she wanted.

"I always loved sewing and making things when I was a little girl. When I graduated college, I realized I had no idea what I wanted to do with my life, but I did know I didn't want to wind up in a job I hated. I thought that since I loved making things, maybe I could turn that into a job, so I started Made by Mackenzie."

That was without a doubt one of the best decisions she'd ever made. It felt like taking the first step in getting control of her own life and living on her own terms.

"It took me a few years to get it up and running, start making a name for myself, but now I make a pretty decent living. I sell handmade knitted and crocheted toys, puppets, scarves, mittens, and hand-sewn clothes for children. Pretty much all my time goes into making them, so I don't have much of a life outside of my business, but I love that I can make a living doing what I love."

"Our bosses have a whole mess of kidlets and more on the way. I bet they'd love to buy some of your things," Arrow said.

"Oh, I couldn't possibly sell them anything, but I'd love to make them something for free as a thank you for saving me. I mean, I know you didn't come for me specifically, but if it weren't for all of you, I'd still be trapped in that hole with my brother."

"Heads up, sweetheart, they're not going to let you make them anything for free, but I know they'd love to have some of your things," Domino said.

"I'd love to make something for your little girl," she said to Mouse. "What does Lolly like?"

"Mermaids, unicorns, and anything pink," Mouse said with a slight grimace.

"Hey, pink is a great color, my favorite," she said.

"Girls," Mouse muttered, but there was a joy in his eyes when he spoke about his daughter, and she knew he would gladly live in a house all decked out in pink to make his baby girl happy.

She'd never thought much about having kids of her own; she'd always been too busy trying to hide from her brother to put too much energy into anything else. Of course, there had been boyfriends along the way—she wasn't a virgin by any means—and there'd even been one guy she'd thought there might have been something with, but in the end her fears of Storm had gotten in the way.

Now, though, when she thought of the future and kids, she couldn't help but see a couple of little Luca's running around.

Crazy.

Wasn't it?

"All right, it's about time to spring you from this joint so we can go catch our plane home," Arrow announced.

Mackenzie was more than ready to get out of here and go back home. Her little cottage was her favorite place to be, the home she'd always wanted as a child, a home that felt safe. Well, it used to anyway, but now Storm had even managed to ruin that too. Maybe she wasn't so ready to go home after all.

Or maybe it was the fact that she'd be leaving Luca behind.

"Are we going to go see Luca now?" she asked. Every time she'd mentioned going to see him before now, the guys had given some vague reason why she couldn't. A doctor was checking on him, or he was sleeping, or he was going for tests. She hadn't pushed things, because she was sure all of those were true, but now she was starting to wonder.

The guys exchanged glances.

Her stomach dropped.

"What?" she demanded. Something was wrong. She knew it was. She just didn't know what exactly.

"It's nothing," Arrow said.

"I want to see Luca. Now," she added.

More exchanged glances.

Okay, now she was really starting to panic. What had happened to Luca that they didn't want her to know?

"What's going on? Why won't you let me see him?"

Surf sighed, scrubbed his hands down his face, then placed his hands on her shoulders. "I'm sorry, darlin, it's not that we won't let you see Bear. Its … he doesn't want to see you."

Her mouth dropped open.

Pain stabbed at her heart.

Luca didn't want to see her?

So they hadn't known each other long, and it wasn't that there had been time for anything to develop between them, but there was something there. She knew there was. Shouldn't they at least see if it could go somewhere?

It wasn't like she was after a marriage proposal or anything. She just liked him and thought he liked her too. He'd told her that he didn't like feeling anything for her and that he had trust issues. What had she been thinking? Of course he wasn't going to pursue anything with her.

Obviously, she'd been living in crazy town thinking that anything would happen with Luca, but it hurt that he was just going to cut her right out of his life. Not even a goodbye.

"We tried to talk sense into him," Domino said sympathetically.

"It's not that he wants to hurt your feelings or anything," Arrow explained. "He just has issues he's not willing to work through at the moment."

"It's okay," she said dully. This whole thing had been one nightmare after another. Just when she thought things couldn't get any worse, they did.

She wanted to go home.

Forget all of this happened.

It had been stupid to allow herself to feel anything for Luca. He was nothing more than the man who saved her life, and that was all he'd ever be. Luca wasn't interested in anything with her. He had his own issues, and she certainly wasn't issue-free. After what her brother had done to her, maybe she would never be relationship material.

This was for the best.

It probably wouldn't have worked out between them anyway.

"Mackenzie, we'll talk to him, make him see …"

"No, it's okay," she said, cutting off Mouse and swinging her legs over the side of the bed. "I understand. Of course he doesn't want to see me. I think I'd just like to get dressed and go home now."

As she brushed past the guys and headed into the bedroom, she tried not to let it hurt that he hadn't even wanted to say goodbye.

Tried but failed.

CHAPTER NINE

September 30th
4:14 P.M.

This was one of the worst missions he'd ever been on.

And it had nothing to do with the fact that he'd been shot.

Bear couldn't have cared less about the bullet hole in his thigh. The wound wasn't that serious. Even with it being the leg with the prosthetic, he'd be back in top shape within a couple of weeks tops.

He'd been lucky, especially given the fact the wound had gotten infected. There had been a very real possibility he could have wound up losing more of that leg, and if he had, he could have kissed his career at Prey goodbye.

Eagle was his friend as well as his boss, and Bear knew the man would have found something for him to do, but he wouldn't have been able to do what he loved anymore. If he wasn't fighting to make the world a better place, then he was nothing.

If it hadn't been for Mackenzie, that might very well have been the future he was facing.

He owed her better than what he'd given her. Bear knew that, but he also knew there was no way he would have been able to see her one last time, thank her for saving his life, and tell her goodbye. If he'd seen her, he had a feeling he wouldn't have been able to walk away.

But what other choice did he have but to walk away?

There couldn't be anything between them. He had major trust issues, and that wasn't fair to Mackenzie. Add to that that she had trust issues too, and they would be like the blind leading the blind.

There was no way that could possibly have worked. What he'd done was the best for both of them. This way, no one got any further involved, and he was sure in time that he would forget those few kisses they'd shared.

After all, that was all there had been, a few kisses, nothing more.

Wasn't like there had been time for them to really get to know one another. He'd been his usual gruff, surly self, and she'd trailed quietly along behind him as they trudged through the forest. That was it. The whole sum of their relationship.

Oh, and the whole she saved his life thing.

How could he not feel something for a woman who had quite literally saved his life and almost been raped for her troubles.

"I know that look."

Bear looked up as Eagle came breezing into his office. Because he was a coward and couldn't face Mackenzie again, he'd taken a commercial flight back to the States while the others had all flown on one of Prey's private jets. He'd arrived in New York about an hour ago and been summoned straight to Prey's offices. He had no idea what Eagle wanted with him, but he guessed he was about to find out.

"What look?" he asked as Eagle rounded his desk and dropped into his chair. The man looked exhausted, but between running one of the most successful private security firms in the country and his sixteen-month-old daughter, Luna, recently being admitted to the hospital after a particularly bad chest infection, it was no wonder.

"That one," Eagle said with a smirk.

"I don't have a look on my face," he said a little sullenly.

After spending two days in the forest, then the night on the plane, the only sleep he'd had had been the fever-induced slumber that had been more passing out than actually sleeping. He was tired and crabby, and what he wanted was to go to his apartment and crash, not sit here to apparently play twenty questions with his boss.

"Sure you do." Eagle pushed back in his chair and linked his hands behind his head, examining him with a look that made him want to squirm.

"And what look is that?"

"The look of a man smitten."

"Smitten?" Deflecting was his best option right now. His team had been disappointed in him for refusing to see Mackenzie, and they'd obviously tattled if Eagle had called him in to discuss her.

"With Mackenzie Arden."

He'd read the reports on the plane of everything she'd told his team about her brother, and he'd about lost it when he'd found out what had been the final nail in the coffin that forced their mother to finally kick her son out of the house to protect her daughter.

In fact, if he hadn't been on a plane surrounded by people, he very well may have hit something. When he got home, he might do it, because that rage hadn't faded yet. Knowing how close Mackenzie had come to being violated all over again because she hadn't wanted to leave him added fuel to the fire.

"I think that silence says it all."

"It says nothing," he insisted. There was no way he was going to voice that he couldn't get the pretty brunette out of his head. That he'd thought about her every second since he watched her be taken away to be examined by a doctor. That he was afraid he'd never be able to stop thinking about her.

"Mouse is worried about you."

"Well, he shouldn't. There's no need to."

"He said you like Mackenzie but walked away without even saying goodbye. That you wouldn't even come home on the jet."

"I paid for my own ticket," he growled.

"Yeah, that's what I was worried about, you charging the Prey account for a plane ticket." Eagle rolled his eyes. "What's going on?"

"What do you mean?"

"What happened with you and Ms. Arden while you two were out there?"

"Nothing." No way was he telling his boss that he'd kissed her. More than once.

Eagle cocked his head and studied him with perceptive blue eyes. If there was one thing everybody knew about Eagle Oswald, it was that the man never hesitated to go after what he wanted. He was accustomed to getting his way, and when he'd set his sights on his now wife, Olivia, he had won her heart despite their rocky start.

But there would be no heart winning here.

It just wasn't possible for him and Mackenzie.

"If nothing happened, you would have been on the jet with the others."

Bear sighed. Eagle wasn't going to give up on this. "When I found her and she told me she's Storm's sister, I wondered if she was working with him."

"She's not," Eagle interrupted.

"I know that now. I got shot, told her to run, but the stubborn little thing wouldn't leave my side. We got separated from the others and had to take a boat. Mackenzie's smart. She got rid of the other boats so we couldn't be followed, but they were patrolling the lake. My wound got infected, Mackenzie looked after me, then when some of her brother's men found us, she killed two of them."

"She saved your life."

"She did."

"That all you feel for her? Gratefulness?"

"Yes," he lied. He'd rather lie and let everyone think he was acting out of character over Mackenzie because she'd saved him. It was better than admitting he was too messed up to ever be in a relationship. There was nothing he could offer Mackenzie. He just didn't have it in him to give her what she needed.

Eagle nodded once. "Then it's a good thing you stayed away from her. She's been through hell with her brother and deserves peace. You're right. You have issues you aren't prepared to address, so you're not good for her, if you can't give her what she needs, then you did the right thing." Eagle pushed away from the desk and stood. "Mandatory two weeks off. You and Brick both need to recover from your wounds. Give it a few days, and I'll set you up for PT so you can start rebuilding strength in your leg."

With that, his boss left the office.

Bear stared after him. He hadn't expected Eagle to agree with him that he wasn't good enough for Mackenzie, that he would only wind up hurting her.

It was true—he knew that—and yet it hurt to know other people knew it too.

While he certainly hadn't sat around telling everyone his sad life story about how his wife had left him after he lost his leg and his parents had taken her side, it also wasn't a secret that he was divorced and estranged from his family, and Eagle and Mouse alone knew the whole story. Everyone knew he kept his emotions locked down tight and kept people at arm's length. He just hadn't realized everyone else thought he was such a screw-up.

They weren't wrong.

Then his brows narrowed suspiciously. Eagle was trying to use reverse psychology on him in an attempt to get him to do something about Mackenzie, but he wasn't going to be played.

He'd made the right choice. He just had to keep reminding himself of that.

* * * * *

September 30th
6:01 P.M.

Her house looked cold and dark as the SUV pulled up outside

it.

Mackenzie had been longing to be back here from the moment her brother snatched her from her bed, but now that she was here, she didn't get that warm, cozy, safe feeling her sweet little cottage usually gave her.

Memories of the day she'd bought this place filled her mind. She'd been so proud of herself for saving enough money to buy a home. Her business had been taking off, and she'd worked so hard. Seeing all that work pay off had been so rewarding.

As a child, she'd always wished her house had been the same safe haven her friends had, and when she finally owned her own home, she had been determined to make it just that. Every single piece of furniture in there, every paint color on the walls, every little added touch, they had all been chosen with such care, creating her own little slice of paradise.

Now Storm had ruined that like he'd ruined everything else in her life.

"You sure you don't want us to drop you off at a friend's house, or your parents' house?" Arrow asked for about the hundredth time. Mackenzie hadn't expected the guys to actually see her home. She'd thought they'd put her in a cab once the plane landed at a small, private airfield and be done with her. When she'd said as much, they'd all given her funny looks she couldn't quite interpret and insisted they would see her to her front door.

"I'm sure. I have to face this place sooner or later anyway, so may as well get it over with," she replied with far less enthusiasm than she should have used if she wanted to convince them she'd be okay.

And she would be okay.

It was just that right now, she wasn't sure how she was going to get to the okay point. She was terrified of going to sleep in her bedroom, terrified just to step inside the room, let alone get into bed and under the covers, let alone actually close her eyes and fall asleep.

But she was an expert at learning to shove away her fear so it didn't consume her. She'd done it all her childhood, and she could do it again now.

"You don't have to face it tonight, though," Mouse said. "Do you have someone you can go to tonight?"

They knew she'd called her parents from the hospital and assured them she was all right, and she'd called both her best friends as well. Her parents still lived in the same home she'd grown up in, and she'd never felt safe there, so that was out. One of her friends was married with two little kids, so she couldn't impose, and the other had moved in with a boyfriend just before Mackenzie was abducted. She didn't really know the man and wouldn't feel comfortable there either.

"I do, but I'm going to stay here." She tried to inject a bit of confidence into her tone but was pretty sure she failed.

"Mackenzie—" Surf started, but she cut him off.

"No. It's okay. I'll be fine. I appreciate everything you've all done for me, but I'm sure you're all anxious to get home." She might have only spent a short time with these guys, but she genuinely liked them.

They weren't at all what she'd thought alpha warriors like them would be. Mackenzie had always thought men like Luca would be arrogant and condescending. She'd thought they would be all cold and hard, no emotions, just killing machines, but she couldn't have been more wrong.

Luca was definitely gruff and grumpy, not a hearts and flowers kind of guy, but she couldn't forget his gentle touch as he held her after she'd killed two men, his soft kisses, and his friends had been really sweet with her.

The guys did that thing where they seemed to communicate without actually saying anything. "You want me to stay? Hang out with you for a few days, or at least tonight?" Surf offered.

That was sweet, but she couldn't expect someone to be there

to babysit her forever. Best to rip the Band-Aid right off and just get it over with. Things would get easier with time. They had to. "I appreciate that so much, but I couldn't possibly impose like that."

Surf sighed like he disapproved but nodded. "You have our numbers. Call if you need anything."

Her brow furrowed. "I don't have your numbers. I don't even have my cell phone. It was still in my room when Storm took me. I don't even know if it's still there. Maybe the cops have it."

Arrow shot her a grin. "Raven might have hacked your phone and entered all our numbers. And she made sure it was returned to your place since the cops no longer need it."

"Oh, that's … sweet." Maybe she should be angry that her phone had been hacked, but since they'd done it to help her, so she had someone to reach out to if she needed it, she couldn't find it in herself to summon any anger.

There was no point in dragging it out any longer. Undoing her seatbelt, she opened her door and climbed out of the car.

This was it.

Time to say goodbye.

Time to face the new wave of pain her brother had inflicted.

"Thank you again for …"

"Stop with the thanks," Mouse said mildly.

"And call if you need anything," Arrow added.

"You got this, Mackenzie," Surf encouraged.

"We'll wait until you're inside," Domino added from the driver's seat.

She nodded, resisted the urge to say thank you once more, and instead just gave them a small wave before closing the car door and hurrying down the path to her front door. Someone had gotten her keys for her, so she unlocked it and gave a last look over her shoulder at the guys, who all waved.

Since she knew they really wouldn't leave until she was inside, she opened the door and stepped inside her house, locking the door and setting the alarm behind her. Her alarm had been top of the line, yet it hadn't stopped her brother from getting inside without her receiving an alert. If she'd known her brother was coming, maybe she could have found a way to do … something.

Flicking on the light in the hall, she glanced around. Everything looked the same as it had when she'd tidied up and gone to bed that night, but it felt different. Her place was small— a kitchen dining room on her left, a lounge room on her right, and a small laundry room with attached powder room at the back.

Upstairs, there were two en suite bedrooms, the spare set up as her home office with her sewing machine and supplies of wool, cotton, and material. It might be small, but she'd loved this place and didn't want Storm to ruin that, didn't want him to take anything more away from her.

Turning on both the kitchen light and the lounge light, she then headed up the stairs. Mackenzie hated that she crept, tentative and scared, because she knew Storm was on the other side of the world, and his men were with him.

No one was here.

Just her.

Alone.

She'd always enjoyed her own company because it was safe, free of fear, but tonight, she felt lonely.

At the top of the stairs, she couldn't not go to her office and flick the light on, just to reassure herself that there was nobody there.

Then she had no more excuses.

It was time to face her biggest fear.

Mackenzie moved to her bedroom door, switched on the light, and surveyed her room. It looked the same as it had when she'd been taken, only someone had cleaned the blood from her floor and remade the bed. She knew a crime scene unit would have gone through the house when she was reported missing, but whoever had cleaned up had also cleaned away the powder used to dust for prints.

On the bedside table was her phone. The cops had returned it to where they found it. Mackenzie walked over to it, picked it up, and touched her finger to the screen to unlock it.

Curious, she opened the contacts app and scrolled through the list, looking for each of the guys. They were there, Arrow, Brick— who she hadn't met yet but had heard a lot about—Domino, Mouse, and Surf. Almost afraid to look she scrolled back up to B, but she didn't see Bear there. Did he hate her so much that he hadn't wanted her to have his number?

Of course he didn't.

If he couldn't even face her to say goodbye, then the last thing he'd want was for her to have a way to contact him.

Because she couldn't help herself, she scrolled down to L, not expecting to see his name there, but for some reason she had to know for sure.

Luca Jackson.

That had to be him.

Mackenzie smiled, her racing pulse slowed a little, and she no longer felt about ready to jump out of her skin at the slightest of sounds. It wasn't much, and she knew Luca wouldn't want her to call him, likely didn't even know that she had his number, but having his name in her phone soothed her and gave her the strength to face her fears and once again do damage control for the destruction her brother had caused in her life.

CHAPTER TEN

September 30th
7:43 P.M.

Storm drummed his fingers on his elbows.

Anger simmered inside him as he sat in his room waiting for news. Anger he was determined to keep a lid on, but it wasn't easy. There was just something about his sister that managed to get his blood boiling, stealing from him the ability to think straight. He did things he didn't understand when she was around, things he felt no need to do with other people. She possessed the ability to disrupt everything, and that wasn't something he could afford right now.

Not when he was so close to getting what he wanted.

Storm had worked so hard to learn to control his anger, to learn how to use the cadence of his voice to sway people into listening to what he had to say. Anger turned people off, but people had done studies on different voice timbers, speeds, and levels, and he had learned everything there was to know about it.

It had worked too.

He had successfully taken over the survivalist compound, turning the men and women who lived there, who were already suspicious of the government and out to rid their lives of its controlling forces. It hadn't taken him long to convince them that his plans to destroy the government were within their grasps if they all worked together.

There were certain words you used, much like a salesman had buzz words to try to convince you to buy that car you couldn't afford and didn't really need. Only what he was selling wasn't cars, or houses, or expensive clothes. It was selling your life and your soul to the cause.

A worthy cause, though, and one that required complete dedication.

He had given all of himself to this, to creating a new world, to removing the system of government designed to keep them down and oppress those without money. It was only fair that he ask those who joined him to make the same sacrifice.

"So?" he asked Ezra when his second-in-charge set the cell phone down. He'd been waiting patiently—or not that patiently—for answers.

Answers he needed.

Everything fell apart if he didn't get Mackenzie back.

Without the child the two of them would create, the new world order couldn't come to being. He couldn't deprive the entire world of the one being that would create a utopia that would bring happiness and joy to all.

No more rich and poor. No more classes, putting down others because they didn't have what you had. No more benefits for the wealthy while the poor missed out. The world would finally become the even playing field it was always supposed to be.

But to bring in this perfect world he needed the child only he and his sister could create.

"Mackenzie entered the US a couple of hours ago," Ezra replied.

That wasn't what he wanted to hear.

It had been a mistake to keep Mackenzie in the hole. He'd done it because he was being petty, because he hated his perfect sister and her perfect little life. Although he supposed he ought to thank her, because if their mother hadn't kicked him out of the house when he was sixteen, then he would never have been set on this path.

Military school had given him plenty of contacts he was now able to use to make his plans a reality. It had also helped him to harness his anger. Of course, he wasn't cut out for the military, and after the way they had abandoned his father when he needed them the most, it hadn't been what he wanted to do with his life.

Still, he harbored resentment toward his sister, and he'd wanted to punish her. Show her what it felt like to be alone, abandoned, and trapped in a world you didn't chose and didn't know how to escape.

His experiences had made him stronger, but when it came to his sister, he felt like the same angry little boy who had been shoved aside when a new, better baby came along.

"Was it Prey Security?" he asked.

Ezra nodded. "Our source said she left on one of Prey's jets along with four men who have been identified as part of Prey's Alpha team. Another member of the team took a commercial flight back Stateside. We're assuming they were the team who raided the island. Mackenzie and the man who flew back commercially were both admitted to a hospital. They must have been separated from the rest of the team. They were the ones who killed Ezekiel and Phil."

Ezekiel was Ezra's twin brother, and he'd lost it when they'd discovered the two men's bodies. Once Mackenzie had given him the son he needed, he intended to give her to his men to use. Perhaps he'd give her to Ezra as payment for Mackenzie's role in the death of Ezekiel.

"We need to find out if Prey will be providing security for Mackenzie," he said. While he was confident his men could take a team from the renowned security company, it would make things so much easier if Mackenzie was alone and unprotected. Once he got her back, he would be keeping her with him at all times. That way, he wouldn't have to worry about losing her again.

Nothing could mess with his plans.

"We'll get eyes on her as quickly as we can. We still have a few men over there who can do a little recon, and then we can come up with a plan to get her back. You can't go back, though. Not now. We can't let them get their hands on you," Ezra said.

As much as he hated to admit it, Ezra was right. He would have to allow his men to retrieve his sister and bring her to him, but once he got his hands on her, she was going to pay for causing him this much trouble.

"What do you want to do about the Prey team? Do you want us to go after them too?" Ezra asked, anger and a desire for revenge burning brightly in his dark eyes.

While part of him would love to make Prey pay for the hassle they had caused him, the last thing he needed was to escalate things with people who were possibly able to destroy what he was trying to create.

"No. Prey are too powerful. They're already looking for me because of Dove. We don't need to be doing anything to draw more of their attention our way," he replied.

Ezra glowered, opened his mouth to no doubt offer a rebuttal, but then snapped it closed again. "What do you want to do next?"

"Have our men in the States focus on Mackenzie while the rest of us keep doing what we've been doing. Mackenzie is important, but she is part of the second phase of the plan. For now, we need to continue working toward destroying the government. That is what's most important right now. My sister can't run forever, and even if Prey is watching her, they won't indefinitely. She's nothing to them. She's nothing to everyone but me, and one day, she'll realize that. That I need her as much as I hate her."

It was an odd dichotomy, but then again, he supposed sibling relationships were always complicated. The forced friendships of youth, forced to live together, play together, survive together, everything changed once you reached adulthood. There was no longer that element of parental control over your lives, and you either found a way to form a genuine bond, or you drifted apart.

Now he envisioned a world where there was no control.

No government.

No parental figures.

No military with more weapons than anyone could ever need.

A true utopia. No control, no wealthy to grab and hoard cash, no imbalance of power because one person possessed the ability to destroy you with weapons.

Everyone equal.

That was the world he wanted, the world he was determined to bring into existence, and he didn't care what he needed to do to make it happen. No sacrifice—his or someone else's—was too great.

CHAPTER ELEVEN

September 30th
8:28 P.M.

Bear hated using the crutches, but his leg needed a break from the prosthetic, so for the next couple of days, he was stuck with them. Which meant he was also stuck at home, and his team was grounded until he was healed. Which sucked mostly because it would give him too much time to think about things he should be forgetting.

Still, at least he had his leg, and he had one stunning brunette to thank.

With an irritated sigh, he shoved away thoughts of Mackenzie.

No matter how hard he tried not to think about her, he couldn't seem to stop. In fact, it seemed the more he tried not to think of her, the more he did think of her.

It was like he was possessed, only it was the worst kind of possession because he didn't want to be having feelings for a woman he barely knew.

That was what was eating at him the most.

For going on a decade, he had prided himself on not allowing anyone to get close. He didn't form attachments unless it was with the guys on his team.

Cold, hard, standoffish, that worked for him. It was the man he had become, hardened by betrayal, and he didn't want to change. He had zero wish to fall in love, to risk himself like that, and a tiny piece of him resented Mackenzie for making him feel when it was the last thing in the world he wanted.

The rest of him couldn't deny that he'd like to get to know her, find out what made her smile, what made her laugh, find out how she liked to spend her time, what she did for fun. He definitely wanted more kisses and to know what it felt to be buried so deep inside of her that he forgot everything but the sweet woman slowly healing his soul.

Could Mackenzie really heal him?

Was he stupid for thinking so much about a woman he didn't even know?

There was something there, but he had no idea what. It had been so long since he'd even thought of allowing anyone to get close, and now he felt so out of his depth, something he despised.

The only thing he knew was he didn't want to hurt Mackenzie.

His apartment buzzer went off, and he grabbed his crutches and moved to the door to let the pizza delivery guy in. After eating, he was going to crash. His body needed rest, proper rest. He was sure this weird obsession with Mackenzie would be gone by morning. Adrenalin, infection, and lack of sleep were probably responsible for the unnamed feelings he had for the woman.

When he brought up the image from the camera at the building's front door, he groaned.

So much for his pizza and bed plan.

Surf grinned and waved, holding up a stack of pizza boxes. Domino's expression was more disapproving, Arrow was fussing over Brick, and Mouse looked vaguely apologetic.

His team. He loved them, but in this moment, he hated them too. Why couldn't they just let it go?

There wasn't a doubt in his mind that they'd come to discuss Mackenzie, but it was the last thing he wanted to do. What he wanted was to forget all about her, the stubborn glint in her eye when she'd tried to look out for him, the gentle way her fingers brushed across her forehead when she checked his temperature, the sweet taste of her lips. He wanted it all out of his head, and he wanted it out now.

If he thought there was any chance his team would leave if he ignored them, he would have done just that, but they were a stubborn bunch, so he pressed the button that would open the front door, then unlocked his apartment door and went to sit on the couch. Two minutes later, his friends were bursting through the door, pizzas in hand.

"What are you doing here?" he grumbled, but when Surf set one of the pizzas down on the coffee table, he immediately reached out to snag a slice.

"Thought you'd want to know that Mackenzie made it home safely," Mouse said, clear rebuke in his tone. What was it about the woman that his whole team enamored with her? Probably the same thing that had him, a man who *wanted* to spend the rest of his life single, unable to get her out of his mind.

Bear grunted. What did they want him to say? Ask for her number and tell them he'd call her? He wasn't going to do that.

"She was scared to go into her house alone," Domino said as he and the other guys lounged around his living room, taking their own slices of pizza.

His heart clenched at the thought of her hurting and alone, facing her fears without anyone to watch her back. As much as he hated the thought of her afraid, he wasn't going to call her up or hop on a plane and fly to Virginia to see her.

"Faced her fears like a champ, though," Surf added. "I offered to stay with her, but she turned me down."

Even though Bear knew Surf was just trying to goad him—the ladies' man went through women like he was worried they were about to drop off the planet—he couldn't help the surge of jealousy that took hold inside him. He didn't want Mackenzie, but he didn't want anyone else to touch her either. It made him a jerk and very selfish, but he couldn't help how he felt. He might not want to be attracted to Mackenzie, but he was, and he wanted to get to know her even as he rebelled against the notion.

"Raven put our numbers in her phone," Arrow told him. "So she can reach out to us if she needs anything."

Again, his chest constricted at the idea of her having his team's phone numbers. He should be grateful that she had a support system if she needed it in addition to her family and friends, but it was jealousy that ate away at him. If anyone was going to be there for her, he wanted it to be him.

Any doubt that he wasn't good for Mackenzie was evident in his thought process. He ached for a chance to find out what could develop between them but wasn't prepared to take that risk, yet he also didn't want anyone else—even his team—getting close to her.

"She won't, though," Mouse said, his gaze much too assessing.

Bear focused on his pizza to avoid meeting his eyes. Of everyone, Mouse knew the most how much his parents' betrayal had hurt him. Growing up together meant he knew just how to read Bear and just what buttons to press.

"She won't reach out to us even if she needs us because you hurt her when you wouldn't see her, wouldn't even say goodbye."

As if Bear needed Mouse's direct hit to feel bad.

There wasn't any way he could feel worse about the entire situation. He wasn't trying to hurt Mackenzie on purpose. He respected her, admired her, and was proud of how she'd handled herself. She was caring and compassionate and had managed to see past his gruff exterior to the pain he hid underneath. But none of that changed the fact that he had been betrayed too many times to risk giving his heart to a woman.

"What do you want from me?" he demanded, setting the slice of pizza down, no longer hungry. How could he eat when his stomach was churning with the knowledge that right at this second, Mackenzie was alone and scared in the house her brother had abducted from. She was stubborn, and he suspected she wouldn't reach out to her friends or family either. As much as he wished things were different, they weren't, and Mackenzie wasn't his problem.

"To let go of your trust issues," Surf said like it was the easiest thing in the world.

"You think I wouldn't do that if I could?" he growled.

He wasn't exaggerating the betrayals he had. After losing his leg serving his country, his wife served him with divorce papers before he was even out of rehab because he wouldn't return to his parents' ranch, and they'd taken her side and cut him out of their lives. How was he supposed to trust after that? And that wasn't even including the betrayal of one of the men on his team that cost him his leg and almost his life.

"I think sometimes it's easier to hold on to the past than it is to let it go," Domino said with an undertone to his voice that said he wasn't just talking about Bear and Mackenzie.

While he didn't necessarily disagree, he'd been perfectly happy with his life up until a couple of days ago. "I'm not going to be calling Mackenzie, so let it drop."

"She deserves better than for you to just pretend she doesn't exist. You were kissing her. It's clear you're interested. There's no harm in just seeing where things could go. They might not go anywhere," Arrow said.

His friend was so very wrong.

There was harm in seeing where things could go with Mackenzie.

He could let himself fall in love with her, and she could wind up shredding all that was left of his cold, dark, shriveled little heart.

"You're right," he said, reaching for the crutches and standing, "Mackenzie does deserve better than someone like me. That's why I won't be calling her."

With that, he left the room. There was no point in rehashing it anymore. Bear got it. His friends liked Mackenzie. He knew why; she just had that alluring mix of strength and vulnerability that made protectors like them stand up and take notice.

But they were right. Mackenzie deserved better than a man who didn't know how to trust, who would inevitably ruin anything that could be between them.

Which was why he'd walked away and why he wouldn't be calling.

* * * * *

October 1st
2:52 P.M.

Mackenzie couldn't keep still, squirming in the hairdresser's chair.

She was so unsettled and balancing precariously, right on the edge, of falling apart completely.

When she'd been in Uganda, she'd done such a good job of keeping it together. It wasn't until she was alone in her bed, in the dark, that the tremors had come.

The first crack in her shell.

In her mind, she kept reliving the moment one of Storm's men climbed between her legs and shoved his pants down. Every time the images played out in her mind, her fear intensified.

It had been so close. Mere seconds away.

Then there was the blood.

So much blood.

The look of the man's eyes when he realized he was dying was something she would never forget, no matter how much she wanted to.

She was a killer.

Perhaps not a murderer since what she had done was in defense of herself and Luca, but she had still taken a life.

That made her a killer.

Her hands clenched into fists so tightly it was painful, but she couldn't make herself uncurl them no matter how hard she tried.

Those hands had been responsible for shoving a knife into a man's neck and for picking up a gun and shooting another man.

While it might have been Luca who finished off the second man, her shots had hit her target, and he would have died from the wounds even if Luca hadn't delivered a kill shot to the head.

Two lives.

Over because of her.

Even though her brain knew they were bad men who had chosen to side with her brother the terrorist and help him with his plot—the details of which she was still a little hazy on—and they would have killed Luca and then abducted her, taking her back to Storm, she couldn't get over the guilt she was feeling for killing them.

It wasn't like she didn't have other things she should be thinking about. Her business relied on her keeping in regular contact with her clients and delivering their orders on time. There were a whole bunch of emails and messages she had to respond to; plus, she'd have to work almost round the clock to even make a dent in catching up on all the orders she'd missed during the six weeks she'd been missing. Given that she'd been abducted, she was sure her clients would understand, but this was her livelihood, and she relied on customer reviews and them recommending her to their friends.

Once again, Storm had managed to mess with everything important to her.

"Mackenzie," her hairdresser, Sasha, said, exasperation heavy in her tone. "You're not okay. You need to talk to someone."

Yep, she did.

Problem was the person she needed to talk to didn't want to talk to her.

She'd given Sasha the cliff notes version of what had happened to her when she came by in the morning. While she had always loved her ▓▓▓▓ American heritage, including her corkscrew curls, six weeks trapped in a hole in Uganda had sent her hair into a wild, tangled mess she would have had no hope of remedying on her own. So, making an appointment to see her hairdresser had been top of her to do list today. She'd also hoped that it might calm her to be around people and doing something that was a part of her regular routine, but it hadn't.

"All done?" she asked Sasha, ignoring the woman's comment about talking to someone.

Sasha sighed but nodded. "Yeah, sweetie, all done."

"Thanks for fitting me in," Mackenzie said.

"Of course, sweetie. No way I wouldn't have when you told me what you'd been through." There was obvious concern in Sasha's eyes, and Mackenzie internally begged her friend not to bring up the kidnapping again.

While she knew she was going to have to address it at some point, for now, everything was just too raw. And what could a therapist possibly know about what it was like to be tormented your entire life by your brother, then have to kill two people to survive? The only ones who could understand and help her cope with taking a life were Luca and his team, but she could hardly reach out to any of them given how Luca ended things with her.

Thankfully, Sasha didn't bring it up again, and Mackenzie paid her bill and hurried out of the salon. There were a couple of other errands she needed to do before she headed home, including stopping by the pharmacy to get painkillers and something to help her sleep, then the grocery store to pick up as much chocolate as she could fit in her basket. Her parents had stopped by to visit this morning and brought groceries for her, but they hadn't included any chocolate, and that just wasn't okay. Chocolate was her comfort food, and she needed all the comfort she could get right now.

The grocery store was unusually quiet, and although the young man serving her gave her a curious look as he studied the cut along her face, he didn't mention it, and she soon had her medicines and her chocolate and was heading to the parking garage.

Predictably, her parents had wanted her to come and stay with them, at least for a few days, but she could already see the guilt in her mom's eyes that Storm had gone after her again, and Mackenzie knew she couldn't do it. Right now, she was having a hard enough time dealing with her own emotions, let alone having to cope with her mom's too.

As hard as it was being in her house alone, it was the only option she had, so she had to suck it ...

Mackenzie's steps slowed as she felt someone watching her.

The urge to stop walking and look around was strong, but if she was being watched, she didn't want to tip them off that she was on to them.

Instead, she continued toward her car as she pulled her cell phone from her purse and dialed 911.

No sooner had the call connected than she caught movement out of the corner of her eye.

A man dressed all in black jumped out of a van parked a few spaces down from her car and ran toward her.

Automatically, her mouth opened, and she screamed at the top of her lungs.

The parking garage was mostly full of cars, but there didn't seem to be any people about.

There wasn't a doubt in her mind that this was another of her brother's men, just like there were no doubts about what Storm would do to her when he got her back.

No way was she going to let herself get abducted this time.

Throwing her shopping bag with way too many chocolate bars in it at the man approaching her gave her enough of an opportunity to run toward her car. All she had to do was lock herself inside and drive away if she could. Even though she hadn't gotten a chance to tell the 911 operator what was going on, her screams should be enough that they would send a patrol car to her location anyway.

Thank goodness for GPS trackers in phones so they would be able to locate her.

Just as she reached her car, arms wrapped around her chest and yanked her backward.

She didn't hesitate.

Slamming her head back into the man's face, she ignored the pain that blasted inside her own skull and put her hand between his legs, grabbing hold of his penis and squeezing as hard as she could as she yanked down.

The man howled in pain and released her.

She threw her door open, jumped inside the car, and slammed the door closed to lock the car.

Her hands shook so badly she almost didn't get the key in the ignition, but once she did, she turned the engine on and threw the car into drive. The van had pulled up behind her, and there was a car in front of her.

She couldn't get out.

She pressed the horn over and over again, hoping the sound would draw someone's attention.

The man outside her door slammed something against the driver's side window, and she watched as the glass splintered.

He hit it again and again until it shattered, raining glass shards down upon her.

He reached inside the car. Grabbed hold of her hair. Yanked.

She scratched at his arms.

Sank her teeth into his hand when he tried to grab her shirt.

As hard as she'd fought, she wasn't going to get away. The man would get her out of the car and into the van. It was already a forgone conclusion.

Would Prey come for her if they learned she'd been abducted again?

Would Luca care?

The man was opening her door when she heard it.

Sirens.

The man obviously heard it too, because he swore and doubled his efforts to pull her out of the car, swinging a fist at her head and connecting solidly with her temple.

Mackenzie kicked out, managing to connect with his groin. He swore again, but the sirens were getting louder, and he released her and returned to the van, whose tires screeched as it took off.

She sagged back into her seat, breathing hard, shaking, her head pounding with pain, but she was okay. Safe.

For now.

The thought slammed into her as if from outside herself. Yes, she'd manage to escape Storm's men. They hadn't taken her this time. But one truth was painfully obvious.

They'd be back.

And she was a one-woman army with no backup, left alone to fight for her life.

CHAPTER TWELVE

October 1ˢᵗ
7:11 P.M.

Bear's heart hammered with an uneasy beat as he moved slower down the hall than he'd like thanks to his crutches as he made his way to the conference room at Prey.

He had no idea why this evening meeting had been scheduled, but when Eagle summoned you, you didn't ask questions. You just showed up.

Since he'd all but thrown his team out of his place last night because he couldn't tell them what they wanted to hear, he hadn't asked any of them to pick him up, and he couldn't drive, so he'd had to take a cab here.

That delay had caused him to be last to show up. When he hobbled through the door, he found the rest of his team sitting around the table. Eagle was also there along with his wife, Olivia. Olivia had been an employee at Prey before she and Eagle got together. After a very rocky start, the two were now happily married, and Olivia helped Raven Oswald—one of Eagle's sisters—run Prey's cyber division.

From the somber looks on everyone's faces, Eagle had already told them what was going on.

Since he and Brick were out on medical for at least another two weeks, they couldn't be here about a mission, so what was going on?

Had Prey found Storm?

Even though he wasn't physically up to a mission, he would make sure he was in on bringing Storm in, even if it was in a support role. The man had caused his sister so much pain and heartache, and while Bear couldn't be there for Mackenzie, he could at least ensure that she didn't have to worry about her brother anymore.

"What's going on?" he asked as he eased himself into a chair, resting his crutches against the table beside him. There was something in the way everybody was looking at him that put his nerves on edge. Not that it took much these days. Bear could barely remember the last time he'd actually slept, not since before the mission to raid Storm's compound. Now any time he drifted off, he dreamed of Mackenzie being assaulted and killed, and he kept waking in a cold sweat.

Eagle cleared his throat, and seeing a man who was never nervous using delaying tactics amped up his anxiety.

"Is this to do with Storm?" he demanded.

"Partly," Eagle said. Then he raked his hands through his dark hair and met Bear's gaze squarely. "There's no easy way to say this, so I'm just going to say it. First of all, I don't want you to panic until I finish, and I don't want you to interrupt until I—"

"It's Mackenzie, isn't it?" he asked as he did indeed panic and interrupt.

"What did I just say?" Eagle grumbled. "Mackenzie is okay. All right? She's fine, but there was an incident earlier this afternoon."

An incident?

There was zero doubt that Eagle was downplaying things, and since he already knew that Storm had abducted his sister once, he had to assume the incident was actually an attempted kidnapping.

"I was concerned about her brother making another attempt at abducting her, so I pulled a couple of members of Bravo team and had them watching her house. This morning, she went down to a local shopping mall, got her hair done, and ran a couple of errands. I didn't want to spook her by having her see two men she didn't know following her, so I told Tank and Rock to hang back. They parked on the street outside the parking garage so they could follow her home."

Eagle paused to take a breath, but Bear held his, knowing what came next wouldn't be good.

"On her way to her car, Mackenzie was attacked. Two men in a van tried to grab her. She called 911 and fought them off. Luckily there was a patrol car right nearby, and they got to her quickly. By the time the cops arrived, the men had fled, likely scared off by the sirens. Mackenzie didn't see their faces, so she couldn't give a description."

Fear felt like a living being inside him. It crawled through his bloodstream, making him feel sick. His head practically vibrated with images of Mackenzie fighting for her life after everything she'd already been through.

Once again, she had been forced to face her brother's wrath all on her own. Her parents had failed her every time they had allowed Storm to remain in the family home, knowing he was a threat to her.

He'd failed her too.

She was alone because he had been too afraid to admit to her or to himself that a spark had been lit between them in Uganda. A spark she had been prepared to acknowledge while he had run like a coward.

Just because he was afraid of getting hurt again.

Bear was disgusted with himself.

Wasn't he already hurting? Wasn't denying that there could be something between the two of them causing him pain anyway? Surely risking falling for her and losing her couldn't be any worse than the constant sick feeling that had plagued him since he'd watched Mackenzie be taken away at the hospital knowing it would be the last time he'd see her.

"You okay, man?" Arrow asked.

Despite the way he'd gone off on his team when they'd just been trying to help him, every single one of them was currently watching him with a mixture of sympathy and concern. He didn't deserve it, but he appreciated his brothers caring enough about him to try to convince him to pull his head out of the sand and see what was standing right in front of him. A chance at finding peace, at healing the wounds to his heart, at happiness.

That chance was wrapped up in a five-foot-two, curly-haired package of stubbornness.

"Was she hurt?" he asked in a tight voice.

"A couple of bruises, but she's okay," Eagle replied.

"Cops took her statement?" Bear wasn't sure the cops could do much to stop Storm, but the more people watching over Mackenzie, the better.

"Yes," Eagle answered.

"Did she go to the hospital?"

"She said she was okay. Medics did need to restitch the wound on her chest; stitches must have pulled while she was fighting off her assailant," Eagle informed him.

Of course she refused to go.

Stubborn little thing.

Despite the fear crashing in waves through his body, he couldn't stop one corner of his mouth lifting in a small smile. He could just picture Mackenzie insisting she was fine and didn't need a trip to the hospital. Given how much time she'd spent in and out of them as a child, it was no wonder she avoided them at all costs now.

The smile faded as he realized he could have sat with her at the hospital in Uganda, maybe distracted her a little, taken her mind off where she was and why she was there, but instead, he'd been doing his best to pretend she didn't exist. He might not like that the woman had managed to make him feel something in a matter of days, but it didn't change the fact that she had done just that.

"Prey won't leave her alone and unprotected. Her brother isn't going to get his hands on her," Eagle said fiercely, and Bear could tell the man had already adopted the woman in his mind and made her part of the Prey family. "What I need to know is whether I should pull in the rest of Bravo team and have them watch Mackenzie or if you want Alpha team to fly to Virginia."

All eyes turned to him, but he didn't look away from Eagle.

"I know you and Brick aren't cleared for duty, but since this is Mackenzie and we all know that you like her, whether you admit it or not, I'm prepared to let you take this mission. It's personal to you—to all of you, I think—but it's up to you. If you want to go, she doesn't have to know you're there. You can just watch over her and make sure she's safe. Or if you're sure you don't want to see her again, then I can send in Bravo team. They can watch over Mackenzie and hopefully capture alive whoever comes after her next. We need information on where Storm is so we can end this once and for all before anyone else gets hurt."

Guess it was time for him to make up his mind.

Was he prepared to let a chance at happiness slip through his fingers because he was afraid Mackenzie would betray him like everyone else had?

He'd survived the betrayal of his Delta brother, his wife, and his parents. He'd lost his ability to trust and hardened his heart in the process to protect against more pain, but if he could survive all of that, then he could survive a betrayal by Mackenzie if he had to.

Life was a risk, he understood that. Every time he left on a mission, there was always a chance he wouldn't make it back home. He accepted that risk like it was nothing because to him, it *was* nothing to lay his life on the line to protect his country. Yet the idea of laying his heart on the line left him near paralyzed.

* * * * *

October 1st
11:35 P.M.

Mackenzie rolled over onto her back and stared up at the

ceiling.

After the day she'd had, she had hoped that she would be tired enough to go right to sleep, but she'd been in bed for over an hour now and, so far, hadn't even drifted off once.

Every time she closed her eyes, she was back in the parking garage.

It had been lucky she'd gotten the call off to 911 before the man in black had grabbed her, because if she hadn't, she'd be back in her brother's clutches right now.

"Everything worked out okay," she reminded herself.

Yeah, maybe if she said that enough times, she'd believe it.

Because even though it hadn't worked this time, her brother would keep sending people after her until he got her back. There was no way to stop it from happening. When she'd explained everything to the cops, they had promised to up patrols in her street, but it wasn't like they were going to post someone outside her house.

But Storm's men weren't stupid. They'd just wait until the cops did a sweep of her street before making their move.

Maybe she should have stayed with her parents.

If she was honest, it was probably just her being stubborn. It was a bit of a problem for her, but she'd spent her entire childhood being unable to depend on the adults in her life. When you didn't have anyone around to take care of you, you learned how to do it yourself. And that's what she'd done.

Only sometimes, she took it to the extreme.

Then again, she still hadn't ever had anyone step up for her.

Her brother had scared away any man she dated longer than a couple of weeks. Whether he somehow managed to get to the man and deliver threats, or whether it was just Storm stalking her that scared them away, she didn't know, but the end result was the same. They chose themselves and bailed.

Of course she didn't want anyone to get hurt because of her, but for once, it would be nice to be someone else's number one.

At least Luca hadn't run because of her brother.

Nope, he'd run because of his own issues.

Sitting up, she reached over to switch on the lamp on her nightstand and picked up her cell phone. She unlocked it, then pulled up the contacts app and found Luca's name. As she'd already done a dozen times since being attacked this afternoon, she hovered her finger above his number but didn't touch it.

He didn't want to hear from her.

It wasn't like he could have made it any more obvious. He hadn't even bothered to say goodbye. Mackenzie hoped that was because he had felt the same little spark between them that she had and it terrified him, but maybe that was just wishful thinking on her part.

Maybe she'd imagined the whole thing because she'd been afraid and needed comfort and reassurance. Those kisses they'd shared, maybe that had been his way of trying to keep her calm because dealing with a hysterical woman would have made his job that much harder.

She wanted to pretend that she wasn't hurt by his rejection, but she couldn't.

It was okay if he didn't want to see what could have been between them. It wasn't like he owed her anything, and they hadn't spent more than a few days together and shared only a couple of kisses. She absolutely could have handled it if he'd just told her he wasn't interested, but instead, he'd deliberately ignored her as soon as they were safe.

Setting the phone down, she threw back the covers and stood. She was making way too big a deal out of this. He *had* told her he didn't like feeling anything for her. It was just that she had at least needed the closure of telling him goodbye.

"You know he was right, Kenz," she reminded herself. "It would have been even harder to walk away if you'd seen him again. A clean break was best. You're already more attached than you should be."

It was true; she was.

But Luca was a man who wouldn't have been scared off by her brother. And he was one of those alpha protector types. If they were together, she knew he would never allow anyone to hurt her. Who knows? Maybe that was why she had gotten attached so quickly. He was what she'd always dreamed of having in her corner. She could take care of herself, but it would be so nice not to have to fight all on her own all the time. It got exhausting.

"Pretty pathetic, Kenz," she told herself as she reached for her robe and wrapped it around her.

Sticking her feet into a pair of cute unicorn slipper boots her friend had given her for her last birthday, she walked to the door. Sleep obviously wasn't going to come no matter how exhausted she was, so she may as well turn her attention to the mountain of work she had to do.

At least after she'd given her statement, been checked out by the medics, and made it back home, she'd gotten on her computer and replied to all the messages there. Thankfully, people had been super nice about it and very understanding. Every single one of them had been happy to reschedule a date to get their items, and none of them made her feel bad about it.

There was more than enough work to keep her mind occupied, and that was exactly what she needed right now. She needed to do something that came naturally to her, that she could lose herself in. Hopefully after she worked through the night, she'd be able to finally get a little sleep.

Mackenzie crossed her bedroom, closing the door behind her automatically. As a kid, she'd always kept her bedroom door closed, a barrier between herself and Storm even if it was a ridiculously flimsy one. A door had never kept him out, and now being on different continents wasn't even enough to keep her safe from him.

Big brothers were supposed to protect you, look out for you, scare away boys who hurt you, but her big brother was the one who had caused her more pain than anyone else ever could.

With a sigh, she padded across the hall and was just reaching for the doorhandle to her work room when she heard the unmistakable sound of her front door opening.

She'd know that sound anywhere.

No matter how many times she oiled the hinges, they continued to squeak. She'd even gone and bought new ones, spent an entire Saturday afternoon taking the door down and replacing them, and still, they continued to squeak.

Now someone was opening that door.

They'd come up the stairs, find her, knock her out, maybe beat up on her first, and take her right back to Storm.

She heard the beep of the alarm code being entered.

Footsteps sounded on the stairs.

She had to hide.

It wasn't much of a plan, but there were only so many places she could hide up here. It wouldn't take the man—or men—all that long to search them and find her, but she wasn't just going to stand here and wait.

She slipped into the craft room. There was no time to ease the door closed behind her, so she ran to her work desk by the window and climbed underneath it, pulling the chair in to hide herself as best as it could.

As far as hiding places went, it wasn't a great one, but it was better than nothing.

She could hear him opening the door to the bedroom; no doubt the fact that her lamp was turned on made him expect to find her in there.

A muttered curse floated through the otherwise quiet house.

Followed a moment later by the sound of something in her room being thrown; her mattress, maybe?

Then she could hear the bang as he obviously threw open her bathroom door.

Another curse followed as he found the bathroom empty.

She could hear him tossing furniture around in there as he probably checked inside her antique wardrobe and behind her rocking chair.

Then she heard more footsteps.

His partner was obviously coming to help search for her.

Two against her one.

They would be trained and armed, and she was just her. After the way she'd fought in the parking garage, they'd be expecting her to do that again, so she couldn't assume her attempts to strike out would do any good. They might even just shoot her and be done with it. Storm only needed her alive; he didn't need her in one piece.

Mackenzie curled herself into as small a ball as she could, knees pulled up to her chest and her face buried face against them, and wrapped her arms around her legs, holding herself together, doing her best to keep her tears quiet as she prayed for a miracle.

CHAPTER THIRTEEN

October 2nd
12:09 A.M.

Mackenzie's sweet little cottage looked peaceful enough on the outside, so why did Bear have such a pit growing in his stomach?

A sense of foreboding, accompanying an eerie silence, felt like a black cloud swelling over the sweet little cottage with a pretty little garden. He could totally picture Mackenzie living here. It was the safe haven she'd missed out on as a child when her home had been terrorized by her brother. This place would have made up for all of that.

Until Storm managed to ruin that for her as well.

If he'd kept in contact with her, could the abduction attempt have been avoided?

The part of him that was consumed with guilt said of course it could have, while the more logical part of him said even if they'd kept in touch, he still would have had to go back to Manhattan, and Mackenzie still would have come here. While he might not have been able to stop her brother from making another attempt at kidnapping her, he could have at least been there to support her afterward. If he'd been smarter, at least agreed to talk on the phone, get to know each other, then she would have called to tell him what had happened.

Instead, she was left dealing with it alone.

Again.

"Anything to report?" Bear asked Gabriel "Tank" Dawson, the leader of Prey's Bravo team. Tank and Sebastian "Rock" Rockman, Bravo team's medic, were watching Mackenzie's house from an RV parked in the driveway of the house across the street. The house's owners were currently away overseas on vacation, which made it the perfect place to keep watch on her without her knowing.

For now, he wasn't going to let Mackenzie know he was here. Knocking on her door at midnight would only scare her given what had happened the previous afternoon. Tomorrow morning, he'd let her know he was here and that he and his team were moving in until they had this situation under control.

There was every chance Mackenzie would fight him on that, and he couldn't blame her. It had been a mistake not to give her a chance. In his mind, he'd overplayed it. All or nothing. What he should have done was ask for her number, and they could have gotten to know each other, then gone from there.

In life, there were no do-overs. He had to accept with what he'd done and deal with the consequences, but he hoped Mackenzie accepted that he wouldn't be walking away until he knew she was safe.

Or maybe he just wouldn't be walking away.

"Nothing so far," Tank replied. As his nickname implied, the man was built like a tank, quite possibly the largest man Bear had ever seen, and he himself was a big guy.

"Once she got home, she stayed there. No visitors. She switched her lights off around ninety minutes ago," Rock elaborated. "And looks like she's back up."

When Rock nodded at the house, Bear turned his attention back to it as well and saw that one of the upstairs bedrooms had a light shining from it. The idea of Mackenzie being too afraid to sleep had him curling his fingers into fists and wanting to fix things for her even as he knew he was likely part of the problem.

"We got a van approaching," Mouse's voice announced through the comms.

"Black van. Same as the attempt on her earlier?" he asked.

"Affirmative," Mouse replied. Mouse, Arrow, and Brick were

stationed on the west end of Mackenzie's block; Surf and Domino on the east. Now that he and his team were here, Tank and Rock would be leaving later in the morning to rejoin their team.

As much as he wanted to go running inside, if he moved now, it would alert the men that Mackenzie was being watched, and they would bail and come back with a whole team if that was what it took for Storm to get his hands on his sister. They needed to get the upper hand, and the only way to do that was to get one of Storm's men alive.

To do that, he had to be patient and make sure these men were after Mackenzie. With an entire team of former special forces operators outside her house, there was no way she was in any real danger.

He just wished Mackenzie knew that.

Because all she would know was that someone was breaking into her house and that they were there to take her to her brother.

As he, Tank, and Rock watched, they saw the black van come to a stop outside Mackenzie's house. The driver stayed in the van while one man dressed all in black climbed out and headed for the front door.

If someone noticed the man at the front door—and it was unlikely anyone would since it was after midnight and the street was otherwise quiet—he would look like a man arriving home and unlocking the door. It took the intruder only seconds to pick the lock, and Bear wondered if the man actually had a key he'd stolen from somewhere.

Waiting was hell, but they needed to split the men up if they wanted to take them down quietly. The last thing he wanted was to have the whole neighborhood woken by gunshots. That was a sure-fire way to get innocent people killed.

Once the first man was inside the house, he started moving.

Tank and Rock followed behind him, and he had no doubt that the rest of his team was moving in as well.

The man in the van had music playing, and it was clear he wasn't expecting any trouble. He didn't even appear to notice them as they approached.

Leaving the Bravo guys to take care of him, Bear headed for the house. That man was alone in there with Mackenzie, and he had no idea where she'd been or if he already had her. Back in Uganda, one of the men who'd attacked them had tried to sexually assault her, and there was every chance this man might try to do the same thing.

As he picked Mackenzie's lock just as the intruder had, he could hear someone trashing the place.

Or was it Mackenzie fighting for her life?

Her ability to hold it together under pressure only made him like her that much more. She'd fought off and killed the men in Uganda, and she'd fought off the man in the parking garage. He had no doubt in his mind that she would fight to the death tonight as well.

But this time, she wouldn't have to, because he was here.

Bear took the stairs three at a time, desperate to get to Mackenzie, and found a man exiting her bedroom just as he hit the second floor.

"She's hiding somewhere, little b—"

"You don't want to finish that sentence," he warned as he launched himself at the man. No way was he allowing anyone to say anything even remotely disparaging about Mackenzie.

It wasn't until he spoke that the man seemed to realize he wasn't the partner from the van.

By then, it was too late.

Bear knocked him down, narrowly avoided the fist that came swinging at his face, and delivered a blow of his own to the side of the man's head. This guy wasn't your average kidnapper. He was over six feet of pure muscle, obviously well trained, and Bear had to assume the man had served in special forces before going to the dark side and joining Storm's army.

Out of the corner of his eye, he spied something moving and reacted just in time to avoid a syringe plunging into his leg.

He grabbed the man's wrist and turned his own weapon against him.

The drugs must have been to knock Mackenzie out so she could be more easily transported acted quickly, and before the man could fight back, his eyes were fluttering closed, and he passed out.

At least they had one of Storm's men now.

"I got the man inside. He's drugged unconscious, I need someone in here now to secure him," Bear said into his comms as he pushed to his feet and scanned the hall. The man had said Mackenzie wasn't in the bedroom, and if she had been downstairs when he broke in, there would have been lights on, or she would have fled out the back door once the man was distracted upstairs.

That meant she had to be up here somewhere.

His gaze landed on the open door to the other bedroom, and he headed for the room. It was set up as her work room. Material and boxes of wool and cotton were everywhere. Partially done projects covered a couple of worktables, and there was a large bookcase stuffed with small boxes of what he assumed were various supplies for her creations and folders likely filled with patterns.

There was also a desk by the window with the chair pulled in tight.

A perfect hiding place.

Bear went straight to it, pulling back the chair to reveal Mackenzie huddled in a ball, her face buried against her knees, tucked tightly into the back corner.

He reached for her. "Mackenzie."

She startled at his touch and his voice and came out swinging. Her small fist managed to connect with his jaw, the blow hard enough to hurt but not enough to do any real damage. Still, he couldn't be prouder of her. Mackenzie was the very definition of survivor. No matter how scared she was, she didn't give up, she fought with everything she had.

"Whoa, babe, easy," he murmured as he took hold of her forearms and pulled her out from under the table. "Stand down, little siren. No need to mess up my pretty face."

Her body went completely still, her eyes clearing, and he could see she was looking at him now, seeing him and not a random man there to abduct her.

"Luca?"

"Right here."

As much as he wanted to pull her into his arms, bury his nose in her hair, and breathe in her soft scent, he had no idea if it was an appropriate response. He'd been the one to put an abrupt end to what could have been between them. He could hardly expect her to throw herself at him now.

Add to that two abduction attempts in twelve hours, and being touched by anyone she didn't really know probably wasn't going to be reassuring. So instead, he dropped and stood there awkwardly, waiting to see what she did next so he could figure out what he was supposed to do next.

"But you … I don't … why did you … what are you … you saved my life. Again." There was gratefulness in her gaze, but there was also wariness. She didn't trust him, and he had no idea how he could earn her trust, if it was even possible.

* * * * *

October 2nd
1:50 A.M.

This was weird.

Her quiet, empty little house was now so full of people she barely had enough chairs for everyone to sit in. The eight massive men seemed to take up all the space in her living room. They were sprawled out along the three-seater couch, sitting on the two armchairs, and had pulled in the four chairs from her kitchen table.

Although there was a spare chair for her to sit in, Mackenzie was on the move. Back and forth between the kitchen and the living room, making coffee, finding snacks, anything to keep her mind occupied so it didn't wander to the man who had been dragged out of here an hour ago.

Anything to avoid Luca.

She had no idea what he was doing here. He'd told her that Eagle Oswald, the oldest of the six siblings who owned and ran Prey Security, had been concerned her brother would come after her again and had put two of his men—Tank and Rock, who apparently were part of a different team who worked for Prey—on her. They hadn't been able to get to her quickly enough when she'd been attacked in the parking garage because they'd been trying to keep an eye on her covertly.

That all made sense, and she greatly appreciated Eagle Oswald caring enough about her to keep someone on her, but what didn't make sense was why Luca was here now.

"Come sit, darlin," Surf said, patting the spot beside him on the couch. "You've been fussing around taking care of everyone, but I think you're the one who needs a little care right now."

Luca shot a glare at his friend but didn't comment as Mackenzie reluctantly went and took a seat on the couch, wondering whether he didn't like the idea of her cozying up next to his friend, even though she wasn't really cozying up to Surf. Now that she didn't have anything to do, her nerves started to get the better of her. Her hands began to tremble, and she pressed them together between her knees, not wanting the guys to notice. They were all warriors, heroes, and here she had hidden like a coward when that man broke into her house.

"Here." Luca thrust a mug of steaming tea at her, and she took it, wondering how he knew she liked tea and not coffee.

"Can you tell us what happened tonight, Mackenzie?" Arrow asked gently.

All the guys had been so nice to her, taking care to make sure she was all right. She would have bet anything upon seeing them that they didn't a sweet bone in their bodies, and she was sure people thought that about them all the time, but really, they were like great, big, kind of scary-looking, ridiculously hot and attractive teddy bears.

"Umm, yeah, I guess," she said, not really wanting to go over it again. How was she going to stay in this house knowing she would never be safe here? "I don't really have much to tell you, though. I couldn't sleep. Lay there for a while, tossing and turning, then decided it was pointless. I have a whole ton of orders to catch up on since it's been weeks since …"

She trailed off, not wanting to think about those weeks as Storm's prisoner because it only reminded her how close she had been to being back in that situation.

"So, uh, I decided I may as well get some work done, hoping I might be tired enough to sleep once it was light. I was just in the upstairs hall when I heard the front door open. It squeaks. No matter what I try, it keeps doing it. Guess this time, it saved me. When I heard him come, I, umm, I hid."

Her gaze was fixed on the floor, unable to meet their eye and see that they thought she was weak and pathetic.

"Look at me." There was a clear command in Luca's voice, and for some reason, that made her obey even though she dreaded looking at him. His brows were drawn into a deep V. "What's with the attitude?"

"Attitude?" she asked.

"Subtle, man," Mouse muttered under his breath.

Luca ignored his friend. "You seem embarrassed about something. Ashamed. I know it's not because you hid when your house was broken into."

"You wouldn't have hidden," she said in a small voice.

"I'm also trained and armed," he reminded her. "You did the right thing."

"He would have found me." Try as she might, she couldn't stop a shudder rippling through her body.

"You did the right thing," Luca repeated.

"Did you hear him say anything?" Mouse asked.

"He was just angry I wasn't in the bedroom," she replied.

"Can you positively identify him as the man from the parking garage?" Arrow asked.

"I didn't see the man at the parking garage." Subconsciously, her hand moved to brush across the bandage just under her collarbone. "I didn't see the man tonight either, so I'm not sure they were the same, but I guess it's a safe bet."

"Can you tell us what happened at the parking garage?" Mouse asked softly.

"I already gave a statement to the cops." The last thing she needed when her nerves were so fried was to relive that moment when she'd been so sure she was going to be taken again.

"The cops aren't equipped to go up against a man like your brother," Surf said.

"They didn't even post a cop on your door after you were nearly taken," Luca muttered, and she could tell by the way his hands were clenched into tight fists that he was furious about that.

"You guys are equipped to go up against Storm?" she asked, wanting to believe it was so, but her brother seemed to have a lot of highly trained men on his side.

"Darlin', it's only a matter of time till we get him," Surf said like it was a foregone conclusion.

Time.

Maybe that was true, but the fact was she might not have that much time.

Storm wasn't giving up on her; he'd made that plain to see. Still, she trusted these men and kind of did believe they could take her brother.

"I was walking back to my car when I realized I was being followed. I pulled out my phone and dialed 911. That saved my life. I didn't get a chance to say anything because one of the men ran at me. I screamed and ran for my car, but he grabbed me before I could get into it. I slammed my head back into his face, then grabbed him between the legs and yanked hard," she said and almost reached up to rub the back of her head.

She didn't want the guys to see how much she was shaking just retelling the story. Even though she was feeling better now, the hit had left her with a lasting headache.

"He let me go, and I got inside the car. I was going to drive away, but the van blocked me in. The man was banging on the window. He managed to break it and grabbed me. I was so sure he was going to get me out of the car, but then I heard the sirens. He did too, because he cursed and let go of me, jumping back into the van and taking off."

Mackenzie got the summary of the parking garage incident out as quickly as she could so she didn't have to think too hard about what she was saying.

"Both men cursed. Did they say the same thing?" Brick asked.

"Uh, yeah, they did actually."

"Did you see the van?" Surf asked.

"It was black. I don't think there were any logos on the side."

"Could you tell anything about the man who tried to grab you?" Mouse asked.

"He had on black jeans and a black hoodie, black sneakers too, and black gloves. He was wearing a ski mask." She concentrated on being in the car, trying to fight off the hands grabbing her. "The skin around his eyes was white, and his eyes were gray. Not blue, or blue gray, but gray, kind of like silver. Is that him? The man who broke in here tonight?"

"Yeah, that's him," Luca told her.

There was no real relief at his words, and she knew that even though that man might not be a threat to her anymore, her brother still was.

Always would be.

Unless he was dead.

She'd worry it made her a bad person to wish her own brother dead, but given the way he'd tormented her since birth, she didn't think anyone would blame her.

"What are you going to do with him?" she asked, almost afraid of the answer. They hadn't called the cops and had bundled the unconscious man into the back of an SUV but hadn't told her where he was being taken.

"Get answers," Luca replied darkly, and he didn't need to elaborate for her to realize that meant through whatever means necessary. Including torturing them out of him.

"And until then?"

Storm wouldn't care about the loss of the man. He'd just send another in his place.

"You get roommates," Luca replied.

Her eyes widened in surprise, and she looked around at the men lounging in her living room. "Wait. What?"

Surf grinned at her. "We're moving in."

"What? All of you?" How were six big men and herself going to live in her little house?

How were she and Luca going to live in her tiny house?

"All of us," Arrow agreed.

"Even …?" She trailed off and looked at Luca, who was watching her with an expression she couldn't read.

"Even me," Luca confirmed.

Great.

Just great.

Not only did she have to deal with her brother and his violent obsession but also the man she liked who didn't like her back.

Talk about uncomfortable.

Still, at least she wouldn't be alone. That did offer her some measure of comfort. At the moment, though, that felt like a small consolation to the awkwardness of temporarily living with Luca.

CHAPTER FOURTEEN

October 2nd
7:24 P.M.

Enough was enough.

Bear was ready to call Mackenzie to the floor for her behavior. This nonsense of avoiding him needed to stop. He wanted to put her over his knee and paddle that sweet behind of hers. That was sure to lock her attention onto him. Plus, she really did have the most perfect rear end he'd ever seen, and his fingers itched to touch it. To touch her, claim her, imprint himself on her so she could never forget him.

Focus.

She could barely even look him in the eye. Any time they were in the same room, which was pretty much the entire day since he couldn't seem to let her out of his sight, she'd pretend he wasn't there, look at anything but him, ignore him if she could.

The way she smiled at his friends, who he was beginning to hate more with each soft look she sent their way, but couldn't bear to even acknowledge him was slowly eating away at him. Bear knew it was his own fault—he was the one who had refused to see her once they'd been rescued instead of at least giving them a chance—but he still hated it.

If he'd given Mackenzie a chance, he suspected she could actually heal the broken pieces of his heart, but convincing her to give him that chance after he'd acted like such a jerk wasn't going to be easy.

Mackenzie gave another sweep of the room, asking his guys whether they needed anything. It didn't matter how many times they'd told her that she didn't need to serve them, that they could get their own drinks and food. She couldn't seem to help herself.

She'd spent most of the day up in her office, working. He'd spent it up there with her, sitting on the floor in the doorway, not wanting her to be alone. There was no way to miss the looks she kept stealing his way. She didn't want him to know it; she thought she was being subtle, but he was trained to notice everything. So, he'd caught every one of the confused glances she'd snuck at him, and he'd wanted to explain, but he didn't know what to say.

Was he supposed to tell her everything?

Why he'd left things without a goodbye, why he didn't like that she made him feel things, why a relationship was the last thing he wanted?

Or was he supposed to wait for a better time? One when she wasn't being hunted by her psychotic brother.

Problem was, he was pretty sure if he waited, he'd lose any chance he had to explain.

And he was going to explain to her.

Bear didn't know why, but he felt compelled to tell her everything, as though perhaps that could somehow make up for the fact that he'd caused her pain.

"I'm going to go up and do a little more work," Mackenzie announced to no one in particular.

He pushed away from the kitchen table and followed her.

Her steps slowed, and she threw a quick glance over her shoulder, her brow furrowed. It was clear she was trying to figure out what angle he was working by following her. But that was just it; he wasn't working any angle. He honestly just liked her and wanted to explain himself.

"You, uh, don't need to come up," she said, averting her gaze.

"I know." He waited until she shrugged her shoulders and headed up the stairs, then followed after her.

She walked into her work room and went straight to the sewing machine. Mackenzie sat, lifted up the material, then set it straight down and bounded back up. "I'm going to the bathroom."

If that was a hint for him to leave, it wasn't one he was going to take.

He wasn't going anywhere until they talked.

Bear leaned against the wall by the bathroom door, crossed his ankles, and locked his hands together behind his head. He owed her more than just an explanation. He also owed her an apology, one he hoped was enough to make up for hurting her.

"Oh, you're still there," she said when she opened the bathroom door a minute later. When she tried to pass him, he moved to block her path, and she looked up at him with exasperation. "I have work to do."

"We need to talk."

"No, we don't."

"Yeah, we do."

Mackenzie heaved a sigh. "Look, Luca, you don't owe me anything. I'm the one who should probably apologize."

"Yeah?" He arched a brow in invitation for her to tell him how she was going to twist his mistakes into her own.

"You told me you didn't want a relationship, that you'd been hurt in the past and were worried I was going to hurt you too. I'm the one who read more into the kiss than what it was. Just a kiss. Nothing more. We don't know each other, so you don't owe me anything, and I'm sorry if I've made you feel like you do."

How was it possible for her to be this sweet?

His brain warned that it was some sort of trick, but his heart said it was anything but.

Despite the fact her parents had done little to protect her from her brother and she admitted she had trust issues, she hadn't lost her softer side. He respected that, admired it, and wondered if it was possible for her to show him how to do that, to not let bitterness and anger twist everything good left in the world.

"I shouldn't have left without saying goodbye," he admitted.

Surprise widened her eyes, and her gaze snapped to meet his. "Why did you?" she asked, vulnerability in her voice.

"Because I was scared that if I saw you again, I wouldn't be able to walk away, and I believed that was the best thing for both of us."

"Because of your ex?"

Bear took a step back and dragged his fingers through his hair. He wanted to be honest with her, he really did, but that didn't mean this was easy to talk about. "Come sit, please."

When he reached for her hand, he wasn't sure she wouldn't snatch it back out of his reach, but she didn't. She allowed him to take her hand and guide her over to the desk, where he pulled out the chair for her, then grabbed the chair from the table with her sewing machine and pulled it over so he could sit facing her.

Her expression was grave as she studied him, but she'd sat and was prepared to listen, and that was really all he could hope for at this point.

"My family is quite wealthy. They own a huge ranch in Montana. At school, I played football, star quarterback. It was cliché but almost expected that I date the head cheerleader. So, I did. She was hot and willing to have sex, so it wasn't like it was any great sacrifice, and I did care for her. Our families wanted us to get married, so I proposed just after graduation. My parents wanted me to work on the ranch, learn the business, but it wasn't what I wanted. I joined the military instead. My wife didn't like it, but she couldn't do anything about it."

Betrayals by his family were nothing new, he'd been used to them for as long as he could remember. Joining the military was supposed to be different. The brotherhood. It was what had happened next that had cemented his determination never again to put his trust in someone who hadn't earned it in blood, sweat, and tears.

"Around nine years ago, not long after I'd joined the elite Delta Force, a guy on the team betrayed us all. We weren't supposed to survive the ambush, but somehow, I did."

"That's how you lost your leg?"

"Yes. My wife and parents saw it as a given that I would have no choice now but to return to the ranch. After all, I was a cripple, and the military wouldn't want me anymore. They didn't, but Eagle Oswald offered me a job at the security company he was starting up. When I told my family I wouldn't be returning, my wife gave me an ultimatum. Prey or her."

"You picked Prey."

"Didn't have a choice. This is in my blood. When I said I wasn't returning to Montana to run the ranch, she left me. I was still in rehab at the time. My parents took my ex's side, and I haven't spoken to them in nine years. That's why I don't trust anyone outside my team. It's why I don't want a relationship, why part of me resented you making me feel things I didn't want to feel. I don't know if I have it in me to trust someone again, which means any relationship we had would have no chance at working out."

"So, if you thought you could trust, you would want a relationship with me?"

Bear moved off the chair and dropped to his knees in front of her. "I know we don't know each other, but I can't deny that I feel something between us. Can you?"

She shook her head.

A fluttery breath escaped her lips when he lifted a hand to palm her cheek. He met her gaze, silently asking her permission, and when her head dipped slightly, he leaned in and feathered his lips across hers.

"Luca, wait." Her hands on his shoulders stopped him when he went to deepen the kiss, and he pulled back. "I have to ask you something first." From the look on her face, she already knew the answer to whatever question it was and didn't like it. "Did you ever intend to see me again? If I hadn't been almost abducted, would you have come for me?"

It broke his heart to answer, but he owed her honesty.

Dropping his head, the word felt ripped from his soul. "No."

Tears shimmered in her pretty brown eyes. "Then I can't do this."

She all but ran from the room, leaving him staring after her, shattered inside. A second later, her bedroom door slammed closed, and with the sound, any chance he might have had at healing disappeared.

* * * * *

October 3rd

1:44 A.M.

A scream died on her lips as she jolted awake.

Why did dreams feel so real sometimes?

Mackenzie could have sworn it was really her brother standing before her, laughing maniacally as his hands reached toward her throat. As his hands had wrapped around her neck, squeezing the life out of her, he'd mocked her, reminding her that she would never be free of him.

Shivering, she touched her fingers to her neck, the feel of her brother's hands lingering there even though she knew they hadn't really been there.

Not tonight, anyway.

Ice-cold, she reached for the blankets, which she'd thrown onto the floor somewhere in her sleep, probably as she battled her dream brother and once again came out the loser, and wrapped them around herself. Sleep wasn't going to come again tonight, although she was surprised she'd managed to get in almost five hours.

Mackenzie had hoped with a house full of former special forces operators and knowing she didn't have to worry about Storm's men getting to her tonight, she might sleep through the night.

Obviously, that wasn't going to happen.

Maybe she'd get dressed and go and do some more work. It had helped her avoid Luca yesterday, at least until he'd cornered her and forced her to listen.

Okay, so he hadn't had to try too hard to force her because she wanted to understand where he was coming from. *Had* understood why he wouldn't want to feel anything for her and even why he had left things the way he had.

What she couldn't deal with, though, was that the only thing that had brought him to her now was the fact that she was in danger. Luca was a protector; he couldn't help himself. If she was in danger, he couldn't stay away, but if that was the only reason he'd come, then she knew how this would end.

With him walking away again once Storm was caught or, hopefully, killed.

Kissing him had been a mistake. Well, letting him kiss her, she guessed, but still a mistake regardless of who initiated the kiss.

Still ...

The kiss had been nice, and she did wish they could do it again, but just because she wanted to kiss Luca didn't mean it was a good idea.

Mackenzie hated feeling so confused and conflicted. At least when she was dealing with Storm, she knew that she hated him for the way he had tormented her for a lifetime, but Luca gave her that sense of security she had craved forever, and it was making her see things that weren't there.

"You don't know him. He doesn't know you. He doesn't owe you anything. It's all in your head," she repeated to herself as she got up, grabbed her robe, and put it on.

"He wants to get to know you."

The words spoken as she opened her bedroom door made her shriek, her hand flying to her chest in a vain attempt to still her wildly beating heart.

"Bear?" someone called from downstairs.

"All good," Luca called back, but his attention was focused solely on her, his brown eyes holdings hers captive.

What was happening here?

How was it possible to form an instant bond with someone?

Was it just because he'd saved her life? Because he'd risked his own to get her to safety? Because she'd saved his life in return?

She didn't know but couldn't deny that the bond was there. She felt it every time she was near him, every time she looked at him, every time he touched her. Despite her best efforts to avoid him yesterday, she'd found herself unable to properly concentrate with him sitting in the doorway of her room, keeping watch over her.

"Can't sleep?" Luca asked

There was a warmth in his eyes that hadn't been there before, and her body responded to it.

Not just her body, her heart responded to it too.

"Nightmares."

"You okay?" There was genuine concern in his eyes, and it made her smile despite her confusion and fear.

Even though it had hurt when he'd left things between them the way he had and when he admitted that if Storm hadn't come after her again, he wouldn't have come to her, she wanted to understand. But maybe she did understand a little. They'd both been betrayed by people that were supposed to love them unconditionally.

"You want to come into my room?" she asked.

Desire flared in Luca's eyes, and she realized how that had sounded.

"Oh, umm, I didn't mean, umm, I just thought … I meant just to talk," she stammered. "Not to do, umm, anything else."

Luca chuckled, and the sound warmed her. There was a rusty quality to it like he didn't have much practice with laughing, and given the betrayals he'd suffered, it was no wonder. "That's okay, sweetheart, I knew what you meant."

Flustered, all she could do was nod. When his large hand settled in the small of her back and he guided her back into the bedroom, a different kind of warmth rushed through her. She was crazily attracted to Luca. Who wouldn't be? He was insanely hot, and his body ... even his muscles had muscles ... and he was tall, and the scruffy beard was so sexy.

Mackenzie wondered what it would feel like against the sensitive skin on her inner thighs as his mouth did wicked things to her.

"Do I want to know what has that look on your face, siren?" Luca asked, although from the smug look on his face, he already had an inkling.

Knowing her cheeks were beet red, she shook her head.

The last thing she wanted to do was tell him she couldn't stop imagining kissing him.

"So, you wanted to talk," Luca said, relaxing into her rocking chair, looking far too sexy for anyone's good.

"Umm, right."

She sat on the edge of her bed, fidgeting with the blankets. Now that he was here, she didn't really know exactly what it was she wanted to say.

"Is this about the kiss last night?"

Mackenzie shook her head.

"Then it's about what I told you, that I wouldn't have come if you hadn't been in trouble." Luca dropped his head into his hands, but the look in his eyes was disappointment. She didn't have to ask to know it was at himself, not at her.

An urge to wipe away all his pain hit her, and she moved without questioning the need. Dropping to her knees in front of the rocking chair, she reached up and wrapped her hands around his, tugging until he dropped them and looked at her.

There was so much pain in those deep brown eyes of his that she felt her own grow misty.

"I understand why you pushed me away, why you left the way you did," she assured him. "I … I can't say it didn't hurt, but since you explained, I do get it. We both have some trust issues. Did you … think of me at all when you got home?" Try as she might, she couldn't keep all the vulnerability out of her tone.

"Oh, honey, yes." He pulled her up and onto his lap, circling her with his arms. "I thought about you. I second-guessed my decision to leave things the way I did. I moped, I felt awful, I yelled at my team, and I itched to see you again."

At least she wasn't the only one who had been miserable.

"It doesn't make sense, does it? I mean, we barely talked in Uganda, and I thought you hated me, but I couldn't stop thinking about you either."

As much as part of her would like to leave this conversation at this point, it wasn't enough to know they'd both missed one another. She needed to know if he was leaving again as soon as this was over. Nothing might have changed for him; he could still resent the fact she made him feel things he didn't want to feel.

"It doesn't make sense," he agreed.

"Are you going to leave as soon as this is over, when you know I'll be safe?"

"Do you want me to?"

He was scared; she could feel it. To look at him, you wouldn't think he could possibly be hurt by anything. But even hero warriors like Luca could hurt. Could have their hearts broken. And that was exactly what his ex and parents had done to him.

Like she had needed him to be strong and save her in Uganda, right now, he needed her to be strong for him. She could do that.

"I hope you might be willing to give us a chance. I'm not asking for any sort of commitment. I know we don't know each other, but I'd like to get to know you. I know you have no reason to trust me, but I won't hurt you, Luca. I know what it's like to be betrayed, to be alone, to ache for someone to be in your corner."

He squeezed her like he could take all that pain away, and she let him pull her closer. It gave her the strength to keep going.

"Maybe I can be that person for you. Maybe you could be that person for me. I don't know. Maybe it won't work out. Maybe this spark I feel will fade in time. Or maybe it won't. I just want a chance to find out. But you can't leave the way you did before. Please. I don't think I could take that." Mackenzie dragged in a breath, determined to be honest. "No. I know I couldn't."

CHAPTER FIFTEEN

October 3rd
2:02 A.M.

Her words gripped his heart, tightening around it like a vice.

It wasn't until that moment that he realized just how badly he'd hurt her when he'd tucked tail and run like a coward.

A chance.

It was all Mackenzie was asking for, and damn if he didn't want to give her that and so much more.

His mouth opened to say the words, yet Bear found they wouldn't come out. Like his heart—so very wary of being hurt again—had forced his throat to close, preventing the words from being said.

As though sensing his internal battle, Mackenzie gave him a sad smile and went to move off his lap.

Immediately, he tightened his hold. "Don't go." Those words felt raw, but he meant them in a way he knew she would understand because she'd been betrayed too. The words came from a primitive place inside him, a desperate need not to be abandoned, to have someone finally stand with him, to not be alone. "I'll give us a chance."

"I don't want you to do it for the wrong reasons. I ... I can't handle you telling me what you think I want to hear if it's not true. When this is over, if you leave because you were only here to protect me from Storm ... I'm not sure I'll be able to deal with that on top of my brother's games," Mackenzie admitted.

Her honesty hit him hard.

She had never once lied to him. She'd been upfront and told

him how she felt, what she could handle and what she couldn't, and his respect for her grew.

"I'm not telling you what I think you want to hear," he assured her. After all, that's why he'd come, wasn't it? To give them a chance. If he'd just wanted her safe, he would have allowed Bravo team to watch over her, or he would have come but not let her know he was here. "I came for you."

"But because you were worried about me getting hurt." There was no judgment in her eyes. She'd accepted his reasoning and was just doing the same thing he was, trying to protect herself from more pain, from trusting the wrong person.

"That gave me the kick I needed to get my head on straight, but I came for you. Just for you," he told her honestly.

"So you really want to give this thing between us a chance? See where it can go?"

Bear got what she was leaving unsaid. *Are you going to be here when this is over, or are you going to break my heart?* Lifting a hand—because he was sure she wasn't going to flee the moment he released his hold on her—he cupped her cheek in his palm. "I want to see where this goes."

It was the weirdest thing, but he felt her relief as surely as it was himself experiencing the emotion, and with her relief, he felt a lightening of his own feelings. His thumb swept across her bottom lip almost of its own accord, and he saw a fire of desire light in her eyes.

Was it too soon to do anything more with her?

While they both acknowledged there was some sort of elemental spark between them, the universe's way, perhaps, of attempting to show them the future, the thread joining them together was still tenuous. Both of them had major trust issues. Those wouldn't go away overnight, but once he committed to something, he was committed. He wasn't walking away.

Mackenzie's gaze was locked on his lips as his thumb continued to brush across her lips, and from the pink staining her cheeks he had a pretty good idea what was running through her head right now.

The same thing that was running through his own mind.

"What are you thinking, siren?" The expression on her face was the same one that had been there when she'd asked him to come into her room and then flustered herself when she'd realized the underlying sexual innuendo that had been so innocently implied.

"I'm ... umm ..."

Damn, she was adorable when she was flustered. "You can tell me. Maybe it's the same thing I'm thinking."

Her gaze flitted to the bed and back, and he could see indecision in her eyes. She wanted him, and she was okay with kissing, perhaps even wanted more, but she wasn't ready to do anything yet.

That was okay. He could be patient when he had to be.

He stood with Mackenzie in his arms, then he set her on her feet. "Think you can go back to bed?" When her eyes grew almost impossibly wide, he chuckled. When was the last time he'd laughed? Mackenzie had him chuckling several times in a matter of minutes. "Don't worry, siren, I wasn't intending on joining you."

"Oh." That was clear disappointment in her tone.

Maybe he'd been wrong.

Maybe she was ready for more.

"I don't want to pressure you. I didn't come to Virginia to get you into bed."

"I see," she said slowly.

Okay, he just heard that how she had heard it. This woman messed with his head, made him feel like an inexperienced teenager all over again. Although, he guessed when it came to anything other than sex, he *was* as inexperienced as a teenager. What did he know about romancing a woman? At reading one? When had he even cared about a woman's wants or needs beyond getting her off?

"That didn't come out right. Don't ever think I don't want you." He dipped his head, and she followed his gaze, looking at the tent in his pants. "I just don't want you to feel pressured."

"I don't," she said quickly.

"No?" Bear stepped closer, wrapping an arm around her waist and lifting her. "What do you want, siren?"

Her pupils were dilated; desire was clear in her face and the way she leaned into him. "I want ... I need ..."

"Tell me what you need, baby," he said as he ground her center against his hard length. He could feel her sweet heat, feel that her panties and the sleep shorts she was wearing were already soaked with her desire.

"I want ..."

Someone to tell her what she needed, if the mix of confusion and indecision in her eyes was anything to go by. Looked like his siren wasn't very confident in reading her body and knowing what she needed.

"This, baby?" he asked as he ground her against his erection again. "Is this what you want?"

Her fingers clutched at his shoulders, and her head tipped back as she gasped.

"Tell me, siren. Tell me it's what you want."

"I ... I want this," she said on another gasp as he carried her to the bed.

Setting her on her feet again, he grabbed the hem of her oversized t-shirt and pulled it over her head, revealing those stunning pair of breasts. "You want me to touch these, siren?" he asked as he palmed one breast and rubbed his palm over her tight little nipple.

"Oh." She sounded surprised that she liked the feel of a man touching her breasts. What kind of jerks had she dated in the past if she had no idea what her body responded to?

"What about this?" His fingers found her nipple, and he rolled it between his thumb and forefinger before tweaking it. "You like this, siren? Answer me, sweetheart," he ordered when she didn't say anything, giving her nipple another tweak. "You like this?"

"Oh, oh," she murmured, her chest thrusting forward, seeking more. "Y-yes."

"You want my mouth on them?"

Her gaze flew to his, and she nodded. A shaky nod, but he suspected it came more from uncertainty over things she hadn't experienced than actual fear.

Closing his lips around her pert little nipple, he sucked hard, and Mackenzie moaned, shoving her chest forward again, pushing her breast deeper into his mouth. Bear feasted on first one breast, then the other, sucking, licking, nipping, drawing moan after moan from Mackenzie's sweet mouth.

"Not enough," he murmured against her chest. "I want to taste all of you." His fingers went to the waistband of her shorts and panties. "You ever had anyone taste you down here, siren?"

Cheeks red, she said, "No, I … what if I don't like it?"

"Then I'll stop."

Clearly embarrassed, she looked away but then resolutely met his gaze again. "How will I know if I like it?"

His brow furrowed. "What kind of men have you been dating? Haven't they taught you what you like and what you don't?"

Mackenzie shook her head. "They umm, they just knew what they wanted to do. I mean, it felt good, but they never asked what I liked, so I never really thought about me. They made me, umm, you know … orgasm, so I never thought about me. About what I liked."

Of course she didn't.

Because to her, it was never about her, always about someone else's needs.

"You don't touch yourself, siren?"

Shame stained her cheeks this time. "I used to, but then I found out Storm had cameras in my bedroom. He watched me with, umm … toys … and I … I couldn't do it after that."

That was something he intended to help her overcome. He didn't want her ashamed of her body, of touching herself, of making herself feel good, because her brother was a sick, twisted pervert.

"We'll find out what you like, sweetheart," he told her as he eased her sleep shorts and panties down her legs. Then he guided her back and onto the bed, laying her down and taking her hands, moving them above her head and curling her fingers around the iron headboard. "These stay here," he ordered.

"But …"

"No buts, baby. Hands stay there, or I tie them there," he warned. Once he got her more comfortable with her body and what turned her on, he'd love to tie her down, be able to feast on every inch of her, and bring her pleasure unlike anything she had experienced before.

There was a flame in Mackenzie's eyes that said he wouldn't have to do much convincing to get her to agree to trust him to bring her pleasure and not pain and tie her up. Settling himself between her legs, he kept his eyes locked on hers as he swept his tongue across her center.

Her pelvis lifted off the mattress, and he grinned. "I think we can safely assume you like this."

Placing a hand on her stomach to hold her in place, he went down on her, lapping at her, capturing her hard little bud between his lips and suckling. He could feel the pleasure building inside her. She mewled and squirmed against his hand.

"Come for me, siren," he ordered, then drew her bundle of nerves into his mouth again and sucked hard, setting off an explosion of pleasure inside her.

He licked and sucked as she rode out the wave and knew as she came all over his tongue that he was already addicted to this woman who was both strong and uncertain.

* * * * *

October 3rd
2:28 A.M.

Mackenzie couldn't form a coherent thought.

That was …

Wow.

Just wow.

None of her previous lovers had ever made her come like that.

It was just …

Words to describe the power and strength of the orgasm Luca had just given her didn't even exist.

She blinked lazily and looked down her body to see Luca smiling smugly at her, still nestled between her legs.

"You were a good girl, siren," he said as he kissed his way up her body. "Kept your hands where I told you, came when you were told. You were a very good girl." His lips found hers, and he nipped lightly at her bottom lip before kissing her thoroughly. "Good girls deserve a reward."

Mackenzie never would have believed in a million years that an alpha male like Luca dominating her in the bedroom would actually turn her on.

Yet the orgasm she'd just had and the growing wetness between her legs told a completely different story.

Luca seemed to be giving her exactly what she needed. She'd always had trouble reading her own body and had never had a lover who cared to help her find out what she liked. They'd always just done their own thing and assumed she would like it, and since she'd gotten off, she'd never really thought beyond that. But now she knew how good it could be with a man who cared more about making her feel good than he did about himself and his own needs.

"You ready to come again?" he asked as his fingers slipped

between her legs.

"I don't think I can come again after that."

She didn't think she'd have trouble sleeping later either. Luca was giving her his own brand of sleeping aid, and it was better than any pill she'd ever taken. He was going to wear her out with orgasms to the point where she'd pass out from exhaustion, the most delicious kind of exhaustion.

"Sounds like a challenge, siren." He slid a finger inside her, and she hummed her appreciation against his lips when he kissed her again.

She didn't even realize her hands had moved until Luca pulled back and wrapped his hands around her wrists. "What did I say about moving these?"

His lips touched a kiss to the tip of one of her fingers before drawing it between his lips and swirling the tip of his tongue against her fingertip.

"I want to touch you," she begged. As much as she loved what he was doing to her body, she wanted to touch him too and watch him loose control in her hand, maybe even use her mouth. She'd never done that before.

"And you will, but not yet. It's my turn to play now."

"Luca," she said on a breathy moan when he slid two fingers into her this time. "I want you inside me."

"I am."

"You know what I m-mean." Her breath hitched as he hooked his finger around inside her and touched a spot she'd only heard about and doubted it existed.

"No condoms, siren. Told you I didn't come here for sex."

"I have some in my bathroom. They've been there for a while, but they're probably still okay. Condoms don't expire, do they?"

Before Luca could reply the world around them exploded.

The bang was deafening, and they were both thrown off the bed.

The room seemed to be falling down around them.

It was raining glass and chunks of plaster. Dust filled the air like a thick fog. Her ears were ringing.

She couldn't see.

Couldn't hear.

Mackenzie lay there, wheezing, pain vibrating through her body, unable to process what had just happened.

One second, she was living in bliss, and the next, the whole world felt like it had been tipped upside down.

Someone was calling her name, but it sounded so far away.

Luca?

Where was Luca?

Was he okay?

Hurt?

It felt like the house had been blown up, but that couldn't be. Right?

Could it?

Storm.

Her brother must have done this somehow. Sent more men after her. Only this time, they'd risked the lives of everyone inside her house. Luca and his team ... what would she do it they were all dead because of her?

"Kenzie." Luca's face appeared above her, dusty and dirty. There was blood there too. She tried to lift her hand to touch him, to make sure he was okay, but this time, she couldn't move for a whole different reason than earlier in bed. "It's all right, baby, I got you."

He wrapped her in a blanket, scooped her up like she weighed nothing, and then they were moving. Mackenzie tried to rouse herself, tried to get up so at the very least he didn't have to carry her, but for some reason, she couldn't seem to summon enough strength to move. Instead, she just hung limply in Luca's arms as he carried her through the bedroom and out into the hall.

"Bear?" one of his team called up.

"We're coming. Anyone hurt?"

"Damage down here is minimal," Mouse said, appearing beside him. "He must have thrown the explosives into the upstairs window. Heard glass shattering a moment before it went off. You guys okay?"

"We got thrown off the bed. Bumps and bruises. Mackenzie is in shock," Luca rattled off.

Okay, so it seemed they weren't keeping the fact that they'd been in her bed making out a secret from his friends. She'd be mortified that he'd so casually blurted it out to Mouse, but the fact that he wasn't hiding from his friends that they'd been together did convince her he was serious about giving them a chance.

Some of her strength returned, and she pushed lightly at Luca's shoulders. "I'm okay now. You can put me down."

"No can do, siren," Luca said as he started down the stairs. "Unless you've forgotten, you're naked beneath the blanket. No way am I letting the guys see anything."

She had actually forgotten that.

Probably would have made a fool out of herself by accidentally letting the blanket slip and giving Luca's entire team a peep show.

"Was it Storm?" she asked once they got down to the living room.

"Clothes," Luca barked out, and one of his team handed over a black long-sleeve t-shirt and black sweatpants.

"Yeah, it was likely your brother," Surf answered.

"But an explosion? He could have killed all of us." She thought Storm wanted her alive, but maybe his plans had changed.

"He knew what he was doing. That was meant to flush us out, not kill us," Domino explained what the others all obviously had figured out for themselves, but she didn't know anything about explosives.

"Flush us out?" she asked. Maybe it was the explosion, but she was having trouble figuring out exactly what was going on.

Luca set her on her feet and gave her the clothes, holding the blanket out to block her so she could change without the guys seeing her even though they had all turned their backs.

As she pulled the clothes on, he explained. "Your brother's men know that the two who were here earlier were taken. Your brother is smart and likely expects Prey is protecting you. He knows we're good, so instead of having his men come in and take us, he's trying to flush us out of the house. Plan is probably to shoot all of us on sight and take you with them. The house is on fire. They know cops and fire will be here soon. They're expecting us to rush out without thinking.

"But we're not doing that, right?" she asked as she pulled the shirt over her head and rolled up the sweatpants, which were way too big.

"Course not, sweetheart," Surf said breezily.

"We have two cars in your garage," Arrow said. "We'll split up. They can't go after both of us."

"But won't the cops want to talk to us?" she asked.

"Eagle will explain we're taking you somewhere safe and that they can talk to you later," Luca told her.

Mackenzie froze. "Wait. What?"

What did he mean that they were taking her somewhere safe? Storm would find her wherever they went. She was beginning to believe she would never be free of her brother's evil clutches. But she couldn't just disappear. Her clients had been understanding, but she'd just lost the half-started projects along with all her supplies. Would they still be understanding when she asked for more time?

"Not risking you getting hurt," Luca said like it was that simple.

"Well, where are we going?" she asked as the guys began bustling her toward the garage, all dressed and in full on warrior mode with their weapons in their hands. Even though she was afraid, her house was smoldering around her, smoke and dust thick in the air, and she knew she could never come back and live here again. She also knew Luca and his team wouldn't let anyone hurt her.

Luca grabbed her hand and pulled her along with him. "We're going to my parents' ranch in Montana."

She stared up at him, her mind shutting down any words before they could leave her throat. He'd told her about his parents and how they had taken his ex-wife's side in the divorce because he wouldn't go back home. Now he was prepared to go back there just for her, to keep her safe.

Never before in her life had someone sacrificed so much for her benefit. It was exhilarating and, to be honest, a little frightening. Having someone go so all in with her meant they could be hurt too. They were fighting for her life here, and the last thing she wanted was to wind up safe, only to lose Luca in the process.

CHAPTER SIXTEEN

This was surreal.

Was he really going back home?

Well, the ranch didn't feel like his home, but it was the house he had grown up in. While it hadn't been a horrible childhood— nothing like the hell Mackenzie had been forced to live in—it hadn't been a warm and loving environment either. His father was busy with the ranch, and his mother had been more interested in her social circle and cultivating the right people. At least, that was her excuse as to why she was never around.

Bear had played football because it was expected of him, although he had enjoyed it. He'd dated the head cheerleader because it was expected of him, although there had been perks to that relationship. And he'd worked hard to maintain a straight-A academic record because again, it was expected he would get good grades, go to college, then come back and make the ranch more successful than it already was.

The first time in his life he'd ever made his own choice and broken out against the mold was when he'd joined the military right after high school. His parents had freaked, his girlfriend had freaked, but he had refused to budge. He was pretty sure his family had thought it was a phase he would eventually grow out of, but he hadn't. Serving his country was what he was supposed to do with his life. It was his purpose.

And it had led him to the woman sitting quietly in the passenger seat of the rental.

When he'd needed a place to keep Mackenzie safe, he hadn't hesitated to volunteer the ranch. It had never been in his plan to return to this place. The decision to stay away had been made when his parents and ex made it clear they were glad he had lost half his leg and been betrayed by someone he thought of as a brother, because it meant he would return to the plans they had for his life.

There was no one else he would come back here for. No one but Mackenzie. Because keeping her safe meant more to him than the pain of returning.

How had he ever thought he could pretend he'd never met her?

In such a short time, she'd made a big impact on his life, and after spending most of the flight from Virginia to Montana talking, he felt like he knew almost everything about her now. She'd been subdued at first after they'd fled her destroyed house, but once they'd settled in on the plane and he'd started asking her questions, he'd seen that spark reignite inside her. Mackenzie was nothing if not resilient and persistent.

"Luca, are you sure about this?" she asked, reaching out to rest her hand on his thigh. It looked good there, felt good too, and he couldn't resist covering it with his own.

"Wouldn't be here if I wasn't, siren."

She gave a small smile at the nickname but quickly sobered. "You haven't seen them in nine years. And given the way they treated you, I completely understand that, but I don't want you to hurt by going back there because of me."

Which was exactly what drew him to her like she really was a siren.

It was what made him willing to risk getting dashed against the rocks as he circled closer to her. Mackenzie genuinely meant it when she thought of others, when she worried over them, when she set them above herself.

Now it was time for her to learn what it was like to be put

first.

"I wouldn't be here if I didn't want to be," he assured her. "You should know I don't do anything I don't want to do."

"Yeah, I got that," Mackenzie said, a teasing note in her voice now. "Stubborn should be your middle name. Oh, what *is* your middle name?"

He grimaced. That wasn't a question he usually answered. Still, whatever Mackenzie wanted, she got, including an answer to a question even the guys on his team didn't know the answer to. Thankfully, the others were in two other SUVs, one in front of them and one behind, so they weren't going to hear the answer. "It's Chadwick Desmond."

Mackenzie snickered. "That's nice."

"It's a family name," he grumbled. "Every firstborn son gets those middle names."

Her fingers tightened on his thigh. "I'm sorry they hurt you. I wish I could take that pain away for you."

"I know you do, babe, because that's the same way I feel about your pain."

"This is weird, isn't it? How quickly we've grown close. I didn't know instalove existed in real life. I thought it was just a trope for romance books and movies."

Her eyes grew wife as saucers, and she quickly pulled her hand back.

"Not that we're in love. I mean, yes, we like each other, and I know I care for you, I just ... well it's not ... I mean instalust, maybe? No, more than that. I'm not just attracted to you. I'm developing feelings for you, but it's not love ... well, not yet. It might be someday."

She looked up at him helplessly, and as cute as it was when she rambled, he took pity on her and reached out to reclaim her hand. "It's not love, but it is something, definitely more than lust. I wouldn't come back here for anyone but you, and that should tell you all you need to know."

"It does. Thank you. Thank you for doing this for me."

Bear lifted their joined hands and touched his lips to the back of hers. "You're welcome. And we're here. Home sweet home."

As he turned into the long driveway that would lead up to the main house, he felt his stomach cramp. He might be prepared to do this to keep Mackenzie safe, but he wasn't happy to be back here. When he'd made the vow to himself never to return, he'd meant it, and while he didn't regret doing whatever necessary to keep Mackenzie safe, this was the last place on earth he wanted to be.

"Wow," she whispered as they approached the main house. "This place is amazing."

Yeah, from the outside the place looked impressive. It was lacking inside, though. Exactly how he'd always felt. He knew women liked the look of the package, but inside, he had nothing of value to offer them. Mackenzie made him want to find pieces of himself to offer to her.

The front door of the house was thrown open as he parked the car. Both his parents stormed out, and even from here, he could see the shock on their faces as they crossed the porch.

"I'll get the door," he told Mackenzie as he turned off the engine, then climbed out of the car and walked around to help her out.

His team's SUVs were also in the driveway, and as he took Mackenzie's hand and went to meet his parents face to face for the first time in almost a decade, he didn't miss that his friends all moved to stand behind him. They had his back like a real family was supposed to. Not like his parents, who had thrown a childish tantrum because he hadn't followed the path they wanted him to take.

"Luca, what are you doing here?" his father asked, while his mother frowned as her gaze went from him to Mackenzie to their joined hands.

"Who is she?" his mother demanded.

From the haughty expression on her face, he knew his mother wasn't pleased to see him holding any woman's hand but the one they had chosen for him. But he didn't love Natalia, never had, and wasn't interested in a reconciliation, even if it would make his parents happy. They'd never once cared about his happiness, so why should he live his life in misery just to go along with what they wanted?

"This is Mackenzie, and this is my team. We're going to be staying in the cabin for a while."

He wasn't asking for their permission. Technically, he was the owner of the ranch. In an attempt to convince him not to join Prey but to come home and stay married, they'd signed over the deed to him. Since he didn't want to come home, he'd never done anything about taking ownership of the property, but if they pushed him, if they said one nasty word to or about Mackenzie, he might very well do just that. Kick them off the land, hire someone to take over and run things.

"You brought another woman to stay in the home you shared with your wife?" His mom's voice was dripping with disapproval.

"That was never my home," he reminded them.

"Because you were never here," Father said, sounding every bit as disapproving as his wife.

"I was serving my country."

"But you had a wife—"

"Who *you* wanted me to marry," he interrupted his mother.

"Natalia deserved better."

"No, Mother. *I* deserved better. She left me while I was still in rehab after losing part of my leg defending my country."

"She was your wife, and this was where you lived with her." Mother sneered at Mackenzie like she was a bug that needed squashing. How would she feel if she knew Mackenzie was the daughter of a war hero and well-known politician who came from more money than he did? "And now you bring this—"

Tucking Mackenzie behind him, he felt his team move to stand protectively around her. The whole lot of them had pretty much already adopted her as a baby sister.

He took a menacing step toward his parents. "You don't want to finish that sentence," he warned in a growl. "I've put up with the way you treated me for the last decade when I wouldn't bow to your will, but I will not allow you to speak to Mackenzie that way."

With that, he turned his back on his parents, reclaimed his grip on Mackenzie's hand, and led her away. Fury had his heart thundering in his chest and his pulse racing as his body itched to do whatever it took to put his parents in their place. But it wasn't anger at how they treated him; it was anger at their treatment of Mackenzie that had him riled up.

No one would speak to her in a disparaging way.

No one would hurt her again.

He wouldn't allow it.

From the fierce protectiveness swirling inside him, he had to admit that maybe there was something to this instalove after all, because he couldn't find another way to explain his feelings for her.

* * * * *

October 4th
7:54 A.M.

"If you're hungry, we can go to the main house to grab some food for breakfast," Luca offered as she padded through into the living room after taking her shower.

Mackenzie immediately shook her head as she pulled her foot up to her backside and stretched her hamstrings, finishing her morning yoga routine. The last thing she wanted to do was risk running into Luca's parents. Not that she expected them to like her. If they'd picked their ex-daughter-in-law over their own son, then there was no way they would support any other woman being in his life.

But aside the fact that she wasn't his ex, she'd also gotten the feeling they didn't like the color of her skin.

Not something she was unaccustomed to.

There had been plenty of times when people had ignored her, treated her badly, or even followed her around a store like she was going to steal something. She'd been mostly fortunate—gone to a school with a lot of black kids, had friends from many different racial backgrounds, and dated boys who didn't care about her skin color rather what was in her pants.

That didn't mean there hadn't been threats against her father and, by extension, her and her mom during his years in politics, but mostly, she didn't feel like she was being judged based on the color of her skin.

Yesterday evening, when she'd arrived and Luca's parents had seen her, they'd been judging her. She was pretty sure she was about as far away from what they would choose for their son as you could get, so yeah, she wasn't in a hurry to see them again.

"I'll wait till the guys get back," she replied.

After they'd arrived yesterday, while she and Luca had gotten things settled in the cabin, the rest of the guys had gone out to sweep the property. Apparently, it was important to make sure you knew the lay of the land, possible entry and exit points, problem areas, and black spots. While that all made sense, she never would have thought of it.

By the time they were done, Surf and Domino had gone into town to grab dinner, and this morning the guys had gone back to buy groceries.

"Hey." He reached over and took her chin between his thumb and forefinger. "We're not hiding indoors because of them."

He was right. They didn't know how long they were going to be here, but did she really want to spend all her time inside instead of exploring the gorgeous place Luca had grown up? The best part of the plane ride here—okay, the *only* good part of the plane ride here—had been getting to know him better.

She'd learned that he actually preferred vegetables over meat, that he was rebuilding a Harley from scratch, that his favorite movies were westerns, and that if he hadn't joined the military, he probably would have become a vet because he loved animals. Her huge, grumpy, growly guy was a marshmallow on the inside. He just didn't want anyone to know it.

"Okay, I'd love a tour of the ranch."

"How about we take a bit of a look around, and then when the guys get back and we've eaten, we'll pack a picnic and take the horses out for the full tour."

"Horses?" Mackenzie froze. She'd never been on a horse before, and they were so big. To be honest, she was a little afraid of the animals.

"It's a ranch, and this is Montana," Luca replied with a grin as he took her hand and led her to the door.

"I don't know how to ride," she told him as she shoved her feet into boots. Since her house had been blown up, they'd stopped at the mall before heading to the airfield to fly to Montana. She'd stocked up on jeans, shirts, and boots, plus a couple of warm jackets since the weather here was much cooler than it had been in Virginia.

"I'll teach you."

"They're kind of big," she said doubtfully and slipped her arms into the sleeves of her jacket when he held it out for her.

"You scared, siren?" he asked, and she could hear the taunt in his voice.

If he thought he could goad her into learning to ride, then he … was probably right. She'd cave to the challenge.

"Smug," she muttered, fighting a smile.

She was having fun with Luca. If you'd asked her a week ago when they were traipsing through the trees in Uganda whether she would ever have fun with the big, grumpy guy, she would have laughed. Now, she was excited to spend the day with him.

Hand in hand, they walked across the porch, and she stopped to breathe in the fresh, crisp air. It was so beautiful out here. The sky was a soft blue with large white and gray clouds floated lazily across it. Huge, majestic mountains ringed the horizons, gorgeous purples and darker grays against the softer colors of the sky.

There were stunning fall trees a brilliant display of golden yellows and bright reds, and wildflowers and knee-high grasses dotted the wide-open spaces. There was something beautiful and almost magical about this place. "Big sky country," she'd heard before but had never really understood what it meant until she stood here on the porch of the adorable log cabin and saw it with her own eyes.

"It's so pretty out here. I feel so free, like everything else has faded away because there's so much beauty, so much nature," she said, her voice soft.

"It is beautiful," Luca agreed, but she suspected, for him, some of the beauty of the landscape was tainted by the memories of the way he'd been treated by his family.

"Did you used to play out here when you were a kid?" she asked as they walked along a dirt path that ran down toward the house, then weaved off to the right toward a huge red-and-white-painted barn.

"When I was really little, my friends and I would fly kites in the fields. One summer, when I was ten, we built a treehouse down by the river." He pointed off to their left, where she could see a thick grove of trees and assumed they stood guard around the river. "It was a lot of fun until my best friend fell out of a tree and broke his arm. I tried to work on it on my own after that but almost cut off my finger using the saw."

She lifted their joined hands and searched for a scar. "This one?" she asked when she found a jagged white line.

"That's the one."

Mackenzie touched a kiss to the pale scar. "All better now."

"Yeah, babe, all better."

"How old were you when you learned to ride?"

"Three."

"Wow, so little. What other pets did you have? I mean, I know this is a ranch, and I assume you had dogs, but did you have any other animals?"

"Chickens. We had goats for a while, cats too, and we used to have a huge aviary that belonged to my grandfather, but after he died, my parents got rid of it."

"I didn't have pets growing up." Mackenzie suddenly regretted asking the questions. "I had a bunny when I was six, but Storm …"

"I'm sorry, Kenzie, it sucks your brother ruined so much for you, but soon he'll be out of your life for good."

Shaking off the bad mood that threatened to ruin what could be a lovely day, she couldn't not smile as Luca opened the heavy barn door and she saw the most beautiful light brown horse with a silvery tail and the cutest foal standing beside it.

"Aww," she gushed as they walked over to the foal. "It's so cute."

"Want to feed her some carrots?"

The foal was adorable and much smaller than its mother, who was watching them with hopeful eyes as Luca walked over to where the mare obviously knew the carrots were kept, but Mackenzie never fed a large animal before and was worried about getting bitten.

"I know you're not too scared to feed a foal, siren," Luca teased, dangling the piece of carrot in front of her.

Rolling her eyes, she grabbed it and knelt down, eyeing the foal and its mother somewhat warily. She did want to feed them, and she was even a little excited about Luca teaching her to ride, but she didn't want to lose a finger. Could horses bite off a finger? She had no idea.

"Like this." Luca took her hand and uncurled her fingers so

her hand was flat and then placed the piece of carrot on her palm. "Keep your hand flat, and they won't be able to bite you."

He kept his hand circling her wrist as he guided it between the bars of the stall and toward the foal. A soft little nose snuffled near her fingers, and then it took the piece of carrot.

Mackenzie giggled. That was much easier than she'd thought it would be. "Can I feed her another one?"

"Of course." He gave her another piece, and she fed it to the foal. "You ready to feed mama here?"

There was still a little bit of trepidation as she straightened and took in the horse who was around the same height as her. It was beautiful and looked so calm standing there beside its baby, but it was a big and strong animal.

"Here you go." Luca placed another piece of carrot on her palm and stood behind her, his front flush against her back, one arm snaking around her waist to hold her to him, as she reached her hand out toward the horse. There was no hesitation on the mama's part. She knew what carrots were, and she knew she wanted it, her mouth moving immediately to snatch up the treat.

"Can I pat her?" she asked.

"Of course."

The horse was smooth and softer than she'd thought she'd be as she stroked the side of its head.

"That wasn't so scary, was it?" Luca asked as he nuzzled the side of her neck.

Mackenzie tilted her head to give him better access and leaned back against his sturdy body. "No, it wasn't so scary." Certainly not scarier than risking her heart by trusting Luca. He wasn't the only one with trust issues and the fact that they both had them meant they were building this relationship on a shaky foundation.

As his lips kissed a line along her jaw before he turned her to kiss her properly, her fears and doubts all faded away. How could she not believe in finally finding peace, security, and a place where someone would finally put her first when they were standing in his family barn, a place he'd never wanted to return to but had for her, with his lips making love to her mouth?

CHAPTER SEVENTEEN

October 4th
9:12 A.M.

"Wow, that's a lot of grocery bags," Mackenzie said as they opened the backs of the two SUVs.

"Hey, we're big guys. We eat a lot," Surf teased, making her smile.

Bear liked watching the way the team had taken her under their wings, wanting her to feel comfortable and part of them.

Because she *was* part of them now.

"Ooh, chocolate," Mackenzie said as she picked up one of the bags. "And more chocolate, and more chocolate. How do you guys stay in such amazing shape if you eat this much chocolate?"

"Chocolate is for you. We had orders from the gruff guy to get you as many bars of chocolate as we could find," Domino said.

"Aww, you're all such sweethearts," she said, shining her smile on all of them.

"Cool it on the sweetheart talk, Kenz," Brick said with a grimace. "We have images to maintain you know. Keep the sweetheart talk for the gruff guy."

She laughed. "Noted. And he's not so gruff." She walked over and stood on tiptoes to kiss his cheek. "Thanks for the chocolate," she whispered so only he could hear.

She'd told him that when she was stressed, she binged on chocolate. Being here on his parents' ranch was an added stress on top of everything else she was dealing with, so he'd told the guys to make sure they got her plenty.

"You're welcome." He kissed her properly, then took the bag.

"And you don't carry anything. The guys have it."

"You're right. He's not so gruff, at least not anymore." Arrow shot him an understanding look as he took the grocery bag.

"Luca Chadwick Desmond Jackson not gruff. I don't believe it."

All seven of them turned at the sound of the voice and approaching footsteps, and there was Natalia. She was dressed in white jeans that molded to her long legs and a blue cashmere sweater that matched the color of her eyes as though it was designed to do so. Her long blond hair was twisted into some fancy knot on the top of her head, and she turned her delicate nose down as she took in him, his team, and Mackenzie.

It was one of the things he liked the least about Natalia. She always thought she was better than everyone else. Her father had been a successful businessman when they'd been in high school, so she'd been spoiled, had everything she ever wanted, and had been horrible to the girls who weren't as fortunate. That trait had continued while they were married. He was sure it was the main reason she hadn't wanted him in the military. In her mind, there was no social standing in that, but a successful ranch owner was right up her alley.

"So you finally came home," Natalia said, turning her attention back to him. "You wouldn't come home when I begged you to, when I pleaded and told you it was the only thing that would save our marriage, but now you came home for her."

"Guys, can you take Mackenzie inside?" he asked, never taking his eyes off Natalia. The guys hadn't commented on his middle name, so he knew they were as tense as he was with his ex's sudden appearance. Although he was sure they'd be making their jokes later. Once he heard the cabin door close, he asked, "What do you want, Natalia?"

"To talk to my husband," she snapped as she stepped closer. "The husband who refused to come back here when I asked but would come for some other woman."

"You said that already. And I'm not your husband. We've been divorced for a long time."

Her glare slowly morphed into a smile, the seductive one she'd always used when she was trying to convince him to do what she wanted. Natalia took a few more steps toward him until she was close enough to reach out and run her fingers down his chest.

Bear took a step back. Not only did he not want his ex-wife touching him, but it wasn't appropriate for another woman to put her hands on him now that he and Mackenzie were working on figuring out this thing between them.

Natalia looked shocked at his reaction. Never before had he turned her down when she offered sex, and he knew an offer of sex from her when he saw one. But sex had pretty much been the only perk of his relationship with her, it was all they'd had. They didn't have anything in common. They didn't talk. They didn't enjoy one another's company. They didn't want the same things out of life.

He already felt closer to Mackenzie in a matter of days than he ever had to Natalia, and he'd known her most of his life.

"I never really wanted the divorce, you know. I just wanted you to realize that there were consequences to your actions. I wanted you to see what you had to lose."

If Natalia thought that, then she didn't know him at all.

He'd made his choice and decided what he couldn't lose was his purpose in life.

"Now that you're back here, maybe we could have a second chance, a chance to fix things, make them work this time."

When she reached out to touch him again, her hands lower this time, brushing just above the zipper for his jeans, he snapped out a hand and caught her wrist in a grip just shy of bruising. While he didn't want to hurt her, he did want her out of here. There was nothing between them, never really had been, and now he had something worth fighting for, worth risking his heart for.

"I don't want to make things work. I never did. And if you

touch me again, you won't like the consequences," he warned, releasing her and taking a step back.

Natalia pouted, her ice-blue eyes shooting darts of rage at him. "Because of her?"

"Her has a name, and no, not just because of Mackenzie, although that's part of the reason."

"But a politician's daughter?" Natalia sneered. "Really, Luca? You wouldn't come back to your own parents' ranch to make things work with your wife, because you weren't going to waste your life doing something that wasn't important enough, but you'll date the daughter of a politician?"

Maybe he shouldn't be surprised that his parents had called Natalia to tell her he was here and had brought a woman with him and that they had obviously gone digging into Mackenzie to find out who she was, but he was. His family would try anything to control him and manipulate him into doing what they wanted, but it wasn't going to work.

"Do you *love* her, Luca?"

"She's important to me."

Could he fall in love with Mackenzie? Absolutely. But it was too early to tell what was going to happen with her. All he knew was that the woman was special and that she saw him, the real him. That was something he wasn't going to let go of. It was something he knew didn't come along in everyone's lifetime.

"Of course you don't love her," Natalia scoffed. "You don't know how to love, do you?"

The jab caused the desired sharp pain in his chest.

There hadn't been any love between his parents, and they'd had nothing to give him. There had been no love between him and Natalia, and part of the reason he'd been afraid to acknowledge this thing between him and Mackenzie was fear that he didn't know how to love.

Natalia's gaze shifted briefly behind him before she grabbed his shoulders and kissed him hard on the mouth.

As he shoved her off him, he heard a gasp and turned to see Mackenzie standing at the open cabin door.

That was why Natalia had kissed him. If he wouldn't give her what she wanted, then she'd try to take away what he wanted.

"Never do that again," he snarled at her, then snapped to his team, who were standing behind Mackenzie, "Get her out of here," he said to his team. He strode up the porch steps and tossed over his shoulder, "And Natalia, you're the one who doesn't know how to love. Any woman who leaves her husband while he's in rehab after losing part of his leg knows nothing about love."

Leaving his team to deal with his ex, he took Mackenzie's hand and led her into the cabin. There was pain in the brown eyes that stared up at him, and he prayed Natalia hadn't gotten what she wanted and driven a wedge between him and Mackenzie, as though that might bring him running back to her.

"She kissed me, not the other way around. She saw you and wanted to hurt you. I would never cheat, never betray you. You know that, right?"

Tentatively, Mackenzie reached out to place a hand on his chest, above his heart. Her touch, unlike his ex's, warmed him in a way that had nothing to do with sex. "I know you wouldn't cheat on me. And I saw her look right at me before she kissed you. I know why she did it. I just wasn't ready to see another woman's lips on yours."

"You're the only woman I want to be kissing," he assured her.

"That's good, because I want to be the only woman kissing you."

He dipped his head, but Mackenzie stopped him before he could kiss her. "You better brush your teeth first. Clean that woman off you. She had her chance with you and threw it away. Her loss, my gain."

Wrong.

His gain.

From where he was standing, he was the one who had come out on top. He'd lost a family and a wife who cared nothing for him to gain a woman who was so much more than he deserved.

* * * * *

October 4th
8:31 P.M.

"You've never had s'mores before?" Surf looked at her like she had suddenly grown three extra heads.

"Nope, never," Mackenzie repeated as she held the stick with a marshmallow on the end in the fire.

Although the day had started out awkward with Luca's ex making an appearance, it had turned out to be a lot of fun. He'd given her a riding lesson before they'd taken the horses out for a tour of his property. They'd gone down to the river, and he'd taken her out in an old canoe he'd built as a kid; then they'd hiked for a while through the gorgeous fall foliage.

Dinner had been hot dogs and burgers cooked over the flames in the fire pit. The guys had joined them, and she enjoyed seeing how Luca and his team teased and laughed each other. She could feel the genuine affection they had for one another.

They were a family and had all made it clear in their own ways that she was part of that family now.

"You don't know what you're missing out on," Surf said as he held out a cookie with a few blocks of chocolate on it.

Mackenzie took the cookie and chocolate and lifted her marshmallow out of the flames, placing it on top of the chocolate. She used the other cookie Luca held out and pulled the marshmallow off the stick. Sandwiched between the cookies, with the chocolate melting from the heat, she lifted the s'more and took a bite.

"Well?" Mouse prompted like he was eagerly awaiting her

response.

At the sight of the five former special forces operators all excited over gooey, chocolatey snacks, she laughed. "You guys and the s'mores, you're like little kids."

"They're a great snack," Arrow said enthusiastically.

"The best," Brick agreed.

"We take them on missions when we can," Domino added.

She looked over at Luca, who was sitting behind her on the Adirondack chair, his knees on either side of her hips, and he shrugged. "I don't get their obsession either. I like them, but I don't love them like these bozos do."

"So do you like them?" Surf asked.

"I do. It's yummy."

"Told you you'd love them," Surf said as he grabbed himself another couple of cookies and another marshmallow.

"Like them, not love them," she corrected, hiding her grin. "Chocolate on its own is better."

"That's it. You got to dump the girl, Bear," Arrow teased, making her laugh. It felt so nice to just sit around, laughing and having fun. She felt safe with them, all of them, but Luca in particular.

Leaning back against his chest as she ate her s'more, she snuggled closer when he wrapped his arms around her waist. When was the last time she'd felt this relaxed?

Mackenzie couldn't even remember.

The shadow of her brother had *always* been hanging over her head.

Even after he'd been kicked out of the house, even when she'd moved out on her own, when she'd been out on a date or hanging with her friends, she had always felt the weight of her brother's obsession.

Always.

Except now.

Now she had a whole team of protective alpha warriors who

would do whatever it took to keep her safe. Luca and his team were stepping up and doing what her parents should have done for her when it first became clear her half brother was a threat to her. It felt so good to have people at her back. Not just at her back, they were all around her, surrounding her, making sure she was protected.

The guys were talking, ribbing one another, and she curled her legs up underneath her and rested against Luca and listened to them. The wide expanse of sky above them soothed her in a way nothing else had before. The cold air wafted around them, the odd star peeped out around the clouds, and every now and then, they were bathed in thin moonlight.

She hadn't even realized she'd gotten chilled until Luca's arms tightened around her. "You want to go in?"

Part of her did, but the other part was enjoying this too much. Luca didn't talk a whole lot, only adding the occasional comment to the discussion. In fact, most of the talking was done by Surf and Arrow, with Mouse chiming in more often, and Brick, Domino and Luca obviously the quieter ones. Still, it was obvious that despite their different personalities, all six of the guys were like brothers, and she couldn't help but envy them just a tiny bit.

"I'm okay. Don't want to take you away from your friends."

"We're going to head in. Kenzie's cold," Luca announced, and she smiled at his mile-wide protective streak.

"We'll hang out here for a while, give you guys some privacy." Surf winked at her, and her cheeks heated, leaving her glad no one would notice in the firelight.

"We'll have you covered tonight, though," Mouse assured her. "We'll take turns getting some sleep, so there'll always be at least two of us awake at all times. No need for you to worry."

"Thank you," she said, not feeling like that was enough to communicate just how much everything they were doing for her meant. They'd all dropped everything to come out to Montana just for her, and it meant a lot.

Luca stood and scooped her up before she could stand, and instead of protesting, she just looped her arms around his neck and rested her head on his shoulder. He carried her into the cabin and through to the master bedroom. It was at one end of the cabin with its own bathroom, and the other two bedrooms were on the other side with their own bathroom. In the middle was the living space.

Once they came inside, a couple of the guys would sleep in the beds in the spare bedrooms while the others kept watch. She felt completely safe.

Actually, she felt a whole lot more than safe.

Tilting her face, she touched a soft kiss to Luca's jaw, then another, edging closer to his lips.

"Mackenzie," he warned.

"What? This isn't what you want?" She knew it was because at the touch of her lips, he'd started to grow hard. She could feel him prodding against her bottom.

"Last time we almost had sex, things didn't end well," he reminded her.

Yeah, it had ended with her brother having her house blown up while she and Luca were in bed. "You think that means I don't want to have sex with you again?"

He set her on her feet and brushed his knuckles across her temple with a gentleness that belied his large size and gruff exterior. "This is a hard time for you. I don't want to pressure you for anything you don't want to give."

Her heart warmed in her chest, and tears blurred her vision. "Then it's a good thing I want to give you this."

Her hands went to the zipper of his jeans, and she unzipped him and shoved aside his boxers so she could take him in her hand. He was big—huge—and she wondered how far he would allow her to go before he took control.

Slowly, she moved her hand closer and curled her fingers around him. He jerked at her touch, and it seemed like he got bigger and harder. Mackenzie tightened her hold and began to slide her hand from his base to the tip, pausing to swirl a finger over it before sliding her hand down again.

She looked up to find Luca watching her, his eyes dark with desire, his arms hanging by his side, fingers curled into fists, and she knew he was restraining his dominating tendencies for her sake. To give her power and control when for most of her life so much had been out of her control.

He was giving her a gift, and her heart warmed more.

This was what it felt like to have someone put you first above all else. He'd just given her something she would treasure for the rest of her life.

As though reading in her eyes that she knew what he had given, he snapped his control, grabbed her hand, and tugged it away.

"I can't wait any longer to have you," he growled.

Since her body felt like a burning inferno of need, that was a very good thing.

"I need you, hard and fast," Luca said as he yanked on her jeans, snapping the stud, then shoving them down her legs. Her sweater was next, then bra and panties, before he turned his attentions to removing his own clothes.

Wow.

She'd hadn't seen him in all is naked glory yet.

Mackenzie hadn't even known men who looked like Luca existed. He was every woman's fantasy, all muscle, hard lines, and smooth planes, strength and dominance. Perfection.

As her gaze roamed his body and then rose again to meet his, she saw the tiniest flicker of doubt hidden deep in those soulful dark eyes. She wouldn't have noticed it if she wasn't learning to read him.

Was he self-conscious about his leg?

In Uganda, he'd freaked when she'd made the "lose a leg" comment, so she had to assume he was.

Dropping to her knees before him, she touched her lips to his bare skin, right above where his prosthetic was.

If he thought this made her think less of him, he was crazy.

Of course she wished he hadn't suffered through the loss of a limb, but she didn't care beyond his pain. To her, he would always be her strong, powerful savior. The man who had pulled her out of the darkness—physically and metaphorically—taken bullets for her, almost died for her, and faced his deepest fears just for her.

Reaching down, he grabbed her and lifted her up, hooking her legs around his waist.

"Thank you," he whispered in her ear before he slipped a hand between them, his fingers sliding easily inside her. "Need you ready for me."

As his fingers thrust in and out of her, his mouth closed over one of her breasts, sucking hard, making her body shudder as the first sparks of her impending orgasm shimmered through her.

His wicked tongue flicked her pebbled nipple in time of his fingers thrusting, and his hard length was between them, pulsing, teasing her with what was coming.

"Please," she begged. "Luca, I need …"

"What, siren?" He added another finger inside her as he kissed her breathless. "Tell me what you need."

"This." She grabbed his length, squeezed it, and tried to guide it to her entrance. She'd probably die if he didn't get inside her in the next half a second.

"Hold on," he ordered, and her hands found his shoulders, clutching them as he moved her and speared her on his length.

"Oh," she hummed, squirming as he filled her in a way she'd never experienced before. He was big, but he'd prepared her, and there was only the tiniest of twinges as her body quickly accommodated his size.

Luca's hands gripped her hips as he began to thrust into her harder and faster with each movement of his hips. "Touch yourself."

Her fingers obeyed his command. One hand still braced on his shoulder, the other moved to where their bodies were joined, and she found her hard little bud. It had been so long since she'd touched herself. Shame over her brother watching her had ruined it. There had been no pleasure left to get out of it.

But here and now, there was nothing but pleasure.

Their mouths found one another's, his thrusts grew more urgent, and her fingers moved faster on that bundle of nerves that was seconds away from setting off an explosion inside her.

It hit her hard, pleasure firing through her body, her internal muscles clamping down on him and setting off his own explosion of ecstasy.

When all that were left were small aftershocks, he rested his forehead on hers. "We didn't use protection."

Huh.

The thought had never even occurred to her, and she was always careful.

"I'm clean," he told her.

"Me too, but I'm not on any contraception." She was all prepared for him to freak out. They both had trust issues and had only known each other for a few days. An unplanned pregnancy was the last thing they needed.

But he didn't freak.

Instead, he merely lifted his head and met her eyes. "If you got pregnant, we'll deal."

"We will?" For some reason, the idea of carrying Luca's baby didn't freak her out either.

"I never used to believe in forever."

"And now?" She already knew what he was going to say but needed to hear the words. Needed to believe she wasn't alone in this crazy ride.

"Now I think anything is possible. Including forevers."

Forever.

With a man who would always put her first. It was a dream

come true, and yet that dream could be shattered by her brother in a heartbeat.

CHAPTER EIGHTEEN

October 4th
11:14 P.M.

Bear's hand moved from covering one of Mackenzie's bare breasts to resting on her stomach.

Had he really told her he didn't care if they'd made a baby?

He was never irresponsible like that. Ever. When you had no plans of trusting a woman with your heart, you weren't looking for a relationship. And when you weren't looking for a relationship, the last thing you wanted was to get a woman pregnant. Bear always used protection. Even when a woman told him she was clean and taking contraception, he still made it clear he was going to use a condom.

Yet he hadn't even considered using one when he'd carried her into the bedroom and she'd started kissing him. It had never occurred to him. All he'd been able to think about was Mackenzie and how badly he wanted her.

She really was a siren calling him in, only instead of dashing him against the rocks, breaking him into a million pieces, she was taking the pieces his family had broken and helping him put them back together.

Beneath his hand, her stomach was flat and smooth, her skin soft like silk. What would it feel like to put his hand there and feel their baby inside her? To feel his child kicking and moving in there? To know he had created a new life, a person who would love him unconditionally and never betray him?

He might have learned nothing about what it meant to be a parent from his own, but he'd watched his best friend raise a child

189

all on his own, watched as, one by one, the Oswald siblings fell in love and started families. He'd seen what it meant to love with your whole heart.

Maybe that was something he could learn to do.

Maybe it was something he was already learning to do.

Mackenzie shifted in her sleep, snuggling closer against him. He had her spooned against him, her back flush against his front, one arm snug beneath her neck, his other holding her close. As she moved, her backside grinded against him, and of course his member immediately took notice.

He should let her sleep. She'd been through so much in her life but especially over the last few days, and she needed the rest. Last night, she'd had nightmares. They'd slept together in the bed— just slept—and she'd thrashed and moaned in her sleep. She'd been reluctant to tell him what haunted her dreams but had admitted after some prompting that her dreams were about the man she'd killed.

That she'd been put in that position was his fault. He'd been stubborn, immediately attracted to the gorgeous woman but not willing to admit it. That had made him extra surly, and because of that, he hadn't taken the gunshot wound seriously. If he had, maybe he wouldn't have ended up delirious with a fever and unable to protect her.

"Never again," he whispered, his lips against her neck. "From here on out, I will *always* be there to protect you."

As though his words somehow registered even though she was asleep, she shifted again, pressing back until there wasn't even a millimeter between them.

Waking her up for another round of lovemaking wasn't wrong, was it?

Around her, he was insatiable. Sex, of course, had always been enjoyable, but it had always been lacking an emotional connection. He felt that connection with Mackenzie. It was why he hadn't been upset when he realized they'd forgotten the condom earlier. Whatever was between them had the propensity to grow into something amazing, and that made taking the risk of trusting her that much easier.

His hand swept lower, across her stomach, and down to settle between her legs.

At the first stroke of his finger across her little bundle of nerves, she moaned and arched her back. "Mmm, Luca," she murmured sleepily as his finger circled her entrance.

"You awake?"

"I am now." She sucked in a breath as he teased her entrance and slipped just the tip of his finger inside her before withdrawing it and tracing down to swirl over her hard little bud. "You wake me up to tease me?"

"Yes." He was somewhat surprised by his own answer.

It was always important to him that the woman he was with enjoy herself, but he had never cared before about dragging things out and making them last. Foreplay was always just a way to make sure the woman got off; it wasn't something he'd found particularly enjoyable, although he'd never hated it either. It had always just been part of the process.

This was different.

He wanted sex with Mackenzie to last as long as possible.

"Luca," she moaned, a mixture of swelling desire and impatience in her tone that made him wonder how long he could keep her like this—desperate, needy, hovering on the edge—before he finally let her fall over it.

How many times could he make her come in a row? That sounded like a question he wanted to find the answer to.

"Patience, siren," he said as he curved up his free hand to palm her breast.

"I love when you do that," she said as he took one of her nipples between his thumb and forefinger and rolled it, giving it a gentle tweak.

"Good, because I can't get enough of touching you."

Never did he think he would ever feel this way about a woman. Nor had he ever thought he'd actually enjoy or want to spend time with anyone outside of his small circle, yet the idea of Mackenzie not being near him gave him an odd batch of anxiety.

How the woman managed to have such an impact on him in such a short time, he had no idea. Maybe she really was a siren. It seemed to be the only explanation that made sense.

"Oh," she moaned as his finger dipped deep into her tight, wet heat, and he could feel her internal muscles quivering. For a woman who hadn't known much about her body, what she liked and didn't, what turned her on and what didn't, she was surprisingly receptive. It didn't take much at all to have her orgasming.

"Come for me, siren," he ordered as he added another finger, then turned them so he could find that spot inside her he knew would make her come hard. He pressed his thumb against her bud, rubbing small circles over it in the way he'd seen her do when she was touching herself earlier.

"I-I'm close," she gasped as her hips began to rock.

"I know, babe. Come now."

He gave her nipple another tweak and felt her fly apart. Her body undulated, her internal muscles clamped around his fingers, and his name fell from her lips in an uneven cry. Bear didn't let up stroking her, touching her, until he felt her ride the final wave of her orgasm and collapse in his arms.

"That was definitely worth waking up for," she sighed like a content cat and threw a sexy smile over her shoulder.

He was about to flip her onto her back and sink inside that delectable heat, but one of the guys hammered on the door.

"Bear, get up," Domino called out.

"Did they hear us?" Mackenzie asked, but he'd caught the tone in his teammate's voice and knew that while yeah, the guys probably had heard them, that wasn't why Domino was hammering on their door.

"Get up, babe," he ordered, "and get dressed."

"Something's wrong?" Mackenzie asked as she hurried to do as he'd said.

"I'm guessing there is."

He quickly threw on jeans and a shirt, not bothering with the buttons, pulled on socks, and shoved his feet into his boots. By the time he was dressed, he looked over to find Mackenzie on the other side of the bed, pulling on her own boots.

They certainly had bad luck when it came to making out. Last time, Storm had ordered his men to blow up Mackenzie's house, and now they'd made out again, and something else had happened.

Grabbing her hand, he led her out into the living room, where he saw Domino and Brick standing, weapons in their hands, and knew whatever was happening wasn't good.

"Two men set off sensors at the back of the property," Brick told him before he could ask.

"They found me again?" Mackenzie asked, and her fingers tightened around his.

"They won't get you," Bear reminded her, the vow he'd made earlier while she was still asleep echoing in his mind. He'd promised her he would always be there to protect her, and it was a vow he intended to keep.

"But if they found me here, they can find me anywhere. I'll never be safe."

Her voice wobbled on the final word, and the sound pierced right through his heart. A heart he'd thought was cold and hard, devoid of the ability to love and care about another person. A heart he was learning had the capability to be huge and full of emotion when it came to the right person.

"No one is going to hurt you," he told her, pulling her into his arms and crushing a quick kiss to her mouth. "We need to get her out of here. Once she's safe, we can figure out a plan. We need to get these men alive. The guys from her house wouldn't talk. We need these ones. We need to know where Storm is."

Keeping an arm around Mackenzie's shoulders, he led her out of the cabin and across the porch, heading for the SUV. Once he had her inside, they'd drive back into town, grab a couple of rooms at a hotel, then contact Eagle and ask him to send the jet.

Just as they approached the vehicles, the ranch house suddenly burst into flames.

* * * * *

October 5th
12:09 A.M.

As the main house exploded into a fiery mess, Luca grabbed her and shoved her up against the side of the SUV, covering her body with his own.

Mackenzie curled her fingers into his shirt and clung to him. Why was this happening to her?

Why couldn't Storm just leave her alone?

It had to be her brother, right? Who else would have blown up Luca's house while she was staying in the cabin just half a mile away?

No way it could be a coincidence, but how had Storm found her here? He shouldn't have been able to. This place had no links to her, which meant he had figured out Luca was connected to her and had tracked him to find her.

How was he doing that? It wouldn't be easy to find out the names of the men who worked with Prey, and that would assume that he knew they were the ones who had found his island and taken her. Then he had to be able to access information on the men's pasts, because Luca had grown up here but hadn't lived here in almost a decade.

"We have eyes on the tangos?" Luca asked, his entire demeanor now screaming special forces operator. His body was hard and tense, a muscled wall of rock standing between her and the rest of the world, but one of his hands was curled around the back of her head, and his fingers gently massaged her scalp.

She didn't hear the reply and assumed he was wearing a comms unit to communicate with the rest of his team. Domino and Brick were standing just behind Luca but were facing away from the SUV as though keeping watch for possible threats. They all knew Storm had found her, his men obviously assuming she was staying at the ranch house, so they'd set off another explosion.

What was it with her brother and explosives? He'd had a thing for them when he was younger too. She remembered when he'd set one off in their backyard, killing her bunny and blowing up most of her toys, which he'd brought down from her bedroom.

Now it was Luca's family home that had been blown up, his parents no doubt inside at the time. Had they been injured or killed?

How would she ever look him in the eye again if they were dead because of her?

"I'm sorry," she whispered when he pulled back and looked down at her. Mackenzie found she couldn't look at him and instead fixed her gaze firmly on the ground.

He merely hooked a finger under her chin, tilted her face up, and feathered his lips across hers. "Not your fault."

"Are your parents okay?" she asked, not willing to let herself off the hook.

"They're not hurt. Arrow is with them."

"What about Storm's men?"

"Mouse and Surf have it handled."

She took that to mean that they'd caught the two men who had broken onto Luca's family's property and that those men would be interrogated to find out what they knew. Mackenzie couldn't find it in her to summon much hope they'd get any answers. They hadn't from the men who had broken into her house the other night, so why would this be any different?

"We need to get you out of here." He reached around her to open the car door and ushered her into the backseat.

"We can't leave yet. You need to see your parents, make sure they're okay," she protested. Even though he wasn't close with them, for good reason, surely he wanted to make sure they really were okay after his house had been blown up.

"We should stop by and see if they saw anything," Brick said as he climbed into the passenger seat.

Luca grumbled but didn't protest as Domino got into the driver's seat. They drove down the winding track toward the main house, which wasn't quite as badly damaged as she'd thought now that they were closer. It looked like whatever explosive they'd used had caused damage to the front part of the house, but the back looked relatively unscathed.

As soon as they stopped, Luca's parents hurried toward the SUV. Even in the dark, with just the flames to light the night, she could see that they looked furious.

Before they even were out of the car, his mother started screaming at them. "This is *her* fault, isn't it?"

Not letting her out of the car, Luca blocked the open doorway. "Don't," he growled in his gruff bear voice.

"Did you know?" his mom shrieked, ignoring her son's warning. "Did you know she was dangerous? Did you know bringing her here would put all of us in danger? Your own parents? You care so little about us that you were willing to risk our lives for this woman you don't even know?"

"Stop it. Now," Luca ordered.

"Stop it? You act like we were marginally inconvenienced by what happened. Instead, our home, a house that's almost two hundred years old, that's been in the family for five generations, has been destroyed. Your father and I could have been killed. Do you even care about that?"

His mother's barbs were hitting their intended targets.

Mackenzie was feeling worse by the second. She never should have agreed to come here. What had she been thinking allowing anyone else to get drawn into her mess. She should have known better, should have known Storm would lash out and do whatever it took to get her back.

"Enough!" Luca roared.

"You get angry at me, your own mother, when *she's* the one responsible for this." His mother waved a hand at the burning house. "I thought when you came back here, you might have finally decided to have some respect for your family and the hard work that has gone into building this ranch. But instead, you brought a woman you knew would bring trouble right to our door and flaunt her in our faces, in Natalia's face. The woman you pledged to love forever, that's how you respect her? How you respect us?"

"Enough," Luca said again, only this time, his voice had dropped low, carrying the same dangerous undertones he would have used when talking to a dangerous terrorist. It was the same voice he'd used on her when he thought she was working with Storm. "Take Mackenzie back to the cabin. Call the others and let them know you'll be there with her, then call Eagle and ask him to send the jet," Luca told his team without turning his glare off his mother.

When Luca closed the door, Domino started the car back up again and headed up the road they'd just driven on to the cabin.

"It's going to be okay," Brick assured her, twisting in his seat to face her.

She nodded and mustered a smile for him, but it was half-hearted at best because they all knew it wasn't going to be okay.

Far from it.

Coming here had been a mistake. She'd allowed the fact that she liked Luca, that he made her feel safe and protected, that he cared for her, that he was big and strong and always in control, to let her lower her guards.

A mistake.

One Luca and his parents were paying for.

Their beautiful home, which had been in their family for generations, was now burning, and it was all her fault. Now that Storm knew she'd been here, he would likely send more of his men to retrieve her. Even if she left, it didn't mean Luca's parents would be safe. Next time, they might wind up hurt or even murdered.

If that happened, she'd never be able to look at Luca again without being crushed by guilt.

Pulling her knees up to her chest, Mackenzie wrapped her arms around them and buried her face in an attempt to hide the fact that she was perilously close to falling apart. It was bad enough her brother had made it his life mission to torment her, which apparently wasn't enough for him, and also had plans to kill thousands of innocent people, but now he was hurting people she cared about.

She more than cared about Luca.

A lot more.

She knew he was capable of handling the threat against her; she trusted him and his team. But what price would he be forced to pay to keep her safe? This house? The ranch? The lives of his parents?

It was too steep. How could she ask him to risk all of that for her?

What if his team were hurt next? His family might have betrayed him, but these men were his brothers, and Brick had already been hurt in the initial raid on Storm's island compound. But without Prey's support, she didn't stand a chance at surviving her brother.

Which left her in an impossible situation.

Leave, and she may as well hand herself straight to Storm on a silver platter.

Stay, and she risked the life of the man she was falling for and everyone he cared about.

CHAPTER NINETEEN

October 5th
6:53 A.M.

The need to escape the claustrophobic hotel room had him standing out here alone in the early morning.

Too bad he couldn't escape his emotions as easily.

Anxiety—no, *fear*—was like a living, breathing entity inside him. At any second, it felt like it could become real and snatch Mackenzie away from him, making his worst fear a reality.

"Breakfast is here," Surf called out, but Bear didn't turn around.

After waiting for the cops and fire department to show up at the ranch, he and his team had given their statements, referred the local cops to the ones in Virginia to confirm the fact that someone was after Mackenzie, then packed up their things and driven into the city to find a hotel to stay at.

Eagle was sending his jet to pick them up, but it couldn't get in until later in the day. Since Bear hadn't wanted to remain at the ranch, they'd decided hanging out at a hotel was the safest place for Mackenzie, and that was all he really cared about.

Right now, he was standing on the balcony, staring out across the city to the mountains in the distance, watching as the sky slowly changed from the inky black of night to a lighter gray as the sun prepared to rise.

It was already busy out, people walking along the sidewalk, traffic busy, tourists with cameras all excited to explore, locals less enthusiastic about spending the day at work. The cacophony of sounds was giving him a headache, yet he found he was reluctant to head inside the hotel room and face the quiet.

He couldn't run from his problems forever, and he couldn't hide from them and pretend they didn't exist, he was beginning to realize.

"Bear." Mouse's calm voice coming from right behind him on the balcony finally tore his attention away.

"Yeah, I'm coming," he said as he turned around to meet his friend's concerned brown eyes. "I'm good," he assured Mouse, answering the unasked question.

"Yeah?" Mouse looked skeptical, and Bear couldn't blame him.

He wasn't doing well and hadn't been for a long time. As a kid, it was easy to bury his head in the sand and forget about the fact his parents didn't love him. He was wealthy and good looking, which meant he was popular, and the adoration of his fellow classmates had made up for the lack of love at home.

Then there had been the military. In and out of one dangerous mission after another, training when he wasn't sent out, the brotherhood that developed between him and his team. There was no time to worry about much else.

Losing his leg, then his wife, then his parents one after the other after the other had been a series of devastating blows, but he'd buried his head in the sand and focused on the new family he was forming at Prey.

While he would never regret the choices he'd made or the men who'd dropped everything to help Mackenzie not because she was a mission, but because he cared about her, he hadn't dealt with what had gone down with his family. Something he was going to have to rectify if he wanted a real chance at happiness with the woman sound asleep in the hotel suite.

"I'm good," he repeated, and it was partially true. He was determined to lay his demons to rest once and for all.

"Your phone's been going hot," Arrow said as Bear closed the sliding glass doors behind him and Mouse. It was chilly out, and while he'd been enjoying the cool, fresh air, he couldn't expect the others to freeze just because he was wound tight.

Bear merely grunted, dropped down onto one end of the sofa, and eyed the breakfast the guys had ordered. They had enough food to feed an army, which he supposed was a good thing since they had a small army. Eagle was also thinking of bringing in one of the other teams to help, since it was clear Storm Gallagher was a bigger threat than they had originally believed.

For the man to have tracked Mackenzie down at his ranch meant Storm had contacts, lots of them, and ones who were prepared to help him break the law.

"She woken up?" he asked, nodding at the closed door to one of the bedrooms, where Mackenzie was taking a nap. He'd wanted to stay with her, but when they'd arrived at the hotel, she'd said she needed some time alone to process, and while he hadn't wanted to agree, he could hardly deny her that when he was someone who needed time alone to process.

The explosion at his ranch had shaken her more than the one at her own house, and he felt a gap developing between them, one he didn't know how to cross. She blamed herself for his family home being destroyed, and he didn't know how to help ease her mind.

"No, not a peep," Arrow replied, and Bear saw echoed in his friend's blue eyes the same concerns he had. Mackenzie was struggling but wasn't used to having a support system, so she likely wasn't going to reach out to any of them including him.

As he reached for a plate of scrambled his eggs, his phone, which he'd left on the coffee table when they got here, began to buzz. His mother's name was on the screen, so he reached out and touched the screen, declining the call.

"You don't think you should talk to them?" Brick asked. He was one to talk given his relationship with his family was every bit as contentious as Bear's.

"No." There was no point in elaborating, because it was as

simple as that. He'd get in contact with the insurance company since, as the owner of the property, he was the one who would be stuck dealing with them, but right now, his priority was Mackenzie.

As he looked around at his team, he felt a swell of appreciation for them and the unconditional support they'd given him over the last nine years. He wasn't an easy man to get along with; he knew that. He was more often than not surly and grumpy; the nickname Bear had come about for a reason.

Yet these men never complained. They joked and teased him and followed his orders on a mission without question.

They were good men, more than he deserved, and he wished he'd been a better friend to each and every one of them.

"If any of you want to bail, I won't hold it against you," he announced.

This mission was personal to him now. He wouldn't allow Storm to live, because as long as he was alive, Mackenzie wasn't safe. There wasn't anything he wouldn't do to end this for Mackenzie. While Prey sometimes operated in gray areas, he was prepared to jump right into the black. Mackenzie was his priority, but he couldn't ask his friends to make that same choice.

Storm was a dangerous man. He'd kill anything stopping him from getting to his sister, and Brick had already been injured by his men. It was one thing to ask them to risk their lives for Mackenzie; it was another to ask them to wade into the black alongside him.

"Bail?" Arrow asked with a frown.

Setting the untouched plate of scrambled eggs down, he stood, paced over to the closed bedroom door, and placed a hand on it, wishing he could go inside and offer Mackenzie the comfort she needed. But she'd asked for space, and he was trying to respect that. Raking his hands through his hair, he turned to face his team. "I'm going to do whatever it takes to keep her safe. I can't ask you to cross that line with me."

"You really think Eagle is going to put you on a leash?" Surf demanded. "He wants Storm Gallagher almost as much as you do after the man almost got Dove killed."

"Even if he did try to put you on a leash, you really think we wouldn't have your back?" Mouse looked offended at the suggestion.

"I'm prepared to move out of the gray area we operate in for this," he warned them. Mackenzie was too important to allow her to live in constant fear of her brother and what he was going to do to her next. This wasn't an option for him. It was something he had to do.

"We've got your back," Mouse assured him.

"Both your backs," Surf added with a glance at the closed door behind him.

"She's important to you," Arrow said, a statement, not a question, but Bear nodded anyway. "Then that makes her important to us."

"Plus, we do actually like her, and she's been through more than enough," Surf said.

"So, I'm going to say this once more, and then we're going to pretend that this conversation didn't happen, that you didn't actually think we'd let you handle this alone. We've got your back," Mouse said, overenunciating each word.

All the guys were looking at him, their expressions solemn but fierce, and he wondered why he had ever thought they would let him walk this road alone. It was why they were so close. They were a family and, unlike his own family, didn't walk away when one of them needed something.

They supported each other unconditionally, which was something Mackenzie was going to have to get used to. She was part of the Prey family. He wasn't walking away, and he wasn't letting her push him away.

* * * * *

October 5th
12:14 P.M.

Mackenzie moved the fries around her plate without really eating them.

She didn't know why she bothered. It wasn't like all six guys at the table couldn't tell she had done little more than nibble at her lunch, but for some reason, she felt like she had to keep up pretenses.

Luca and his team seemed to be under the impression she was this strong, capable woman who laughed in the face of danger but that couldn't be further from the truth. Her entire life, she'd felt afraid, like all she wanted was to find a hole deep enough and dark enough to finally hide from her brother and find herself some peace.

Sure, she'd taken self-defense classes and had learned how to shoot so she could protect herself. And yeah, she'd killed that man in Uganda, but that was just because she'd had no other choice. When her back was up against a wall, she could do what needed to be done, but the rest of the time, she just hid.

There was nothing strong about that.

The guys were talking in hushed voices at their table in the hotel's restaurant, but she wasn't paying any attention to what they were saying. They'd wanted to order room service, but she was sick of being cooped up in the hotel suite. It felt too much like being in that hole on Storm's island on Lake Victoria.

Trapped.

She was so tired of feeling trapped.

"You okay?"

Mackenzie looked up at Luca and did her best to muster a smile for him. She wasn't being fair to him. She was withdrawing emotionally because she was so afraid he would wind up hurt—or worse, dead—because of her. That fear was paralyzing her, taking her heart and squeezing it in a vice until it felt like her ribs had been broken all over again.

"Fine," she replied, and although they all knew it was a lie, thankfully, none of the guys pushed.

Reaching into the center of the table, she grabbed a bottle of ketchup and squirted some onto her plate. It was time to buck up, find a way to help Prey figure out where Storm would be hiding out, and take her brother down once and for all. She didn't want to lose this chance at happiness with Luca and was so afraid that with Storm still out there, that's exactly what would happen.

Picking up a fry, Mackenzie touched the end of it in the ketchup, and just like that, her mind threw her back to Uganda.

Red.

Blood.

Blood spilling from the neck of the man who'd tried to rape her.

She dropped the fry and shoved away from the table. "I need to go to the bathroom," she mumbled, not making eye contact with anyone as she hurried away from the table.

"Kenzie, wait." Luca was behind her, but she couldn't look at him either. She just needed to get the blood out of her head.

A hand gently circled her wrist, stopping her, and he turned her to face him. He waited so very patiently while her eyes took a slow journey from the floor to his face. There was no pity in his gaze, nothing that said he felt sorry for her. There was just admiration and understanding.

"I can't stop thinking about the blood … the man I … Maybe I'm not as okay with what I did as I thought I was," she admitted, not sure why she'd told him the truth. Maybe because she knew he deserved it. He was putting everything on the line for her; at the very least, she owed him the truth.

His large hand palmed her cheek, and instinct had her tilting her face to get closer to absorb more of his soft touch. "You need to speak to someone about it. I'm here any time you need me, but

I think you need a professional as well."

Pride had her wanting to refuse, to claim she could deal with it on her own, that time would help, but that would be a lie. One she didn't think he'd let her get away with. So instead, she nodded.

"It will get better, all of this, I promise."

Instead of reassuring her, his words sent a jolt of panic through her. Luca was prepared to do anything to keep her safe, including risking his life, and the thought of losing him ... she couldn't even go there.

"You ready to go back to the room?"

"I just need a moment," she said, voice strained as she nodded toward the bathroom.

"All right."

When it looked like he intended to wait right there outside the bathrooms, she said, "I'll meet you back at the table. I'll be okay," she said cutting off his protest before he could utter it.

Luca touched a kiss to her forehead, then went to rejoin his friends, and she entered the bathroom, turned on the tap, and scooped up cold water to splash on her face.

A brother who abused and tortured her.

A mother who put her son above her daughter.

A father who loved his career more than his child.

Her family was such a mess, and because no one had gotten Storm help, now he had turned into a terrorist.

The bathroom door opened, but she didn't bother looking over to see who had entered. She scooped up more water and splashed it on her face as though she somehow might be able to wash away her problems. If only life was that easy.

"Do you know who this is?"

Mackenzie startled at the furious voice and lowered her hands to find Luca's ex-wife standing beside her, a photograph in her hand. She had no idea the woman was even here at the hotel. From what she'd gathered, Natalia lived in a cabin on the ranch, just another way Luca's parents had hurt him, allowing his ex to stay on his family's land.

Natalia was gorgeous, tall, and blond with big breasts, but Mackenzie didn't feel any jealousy toward her. Luca had never been in love with Natalia; he'd married her because it was what his parents wanted, and she had betrayed him.

When she turned her attention to the photo, a picture of Natalia with a brown-haired little boy of about nine, her stomach plummeted.

Could it be …?

"No," she murmured, forcing the word out past the lump in her throat. He would have told her, wouldn't he?

"This is Luca's son," Natalia announced triumphantly.

She was going to be sick.

Why wouldn't he have told her he had a kid?

She knew Mouse had a little girl, had even seen pictures of Lolly, but Luca hadn't mentioned anything about a son. There was no way he would have a child and not be part of their life, especially given how his family had treated him, but why didn't he tell her?

Her being here hadn't just put the ranch, his parents, and ex in danger, but his son as well.

"That's right," Natalia said, and she had to assume her thoughts were written clearly on her face. "You're putting Luca's son in danger by bringing your problems to his doorstep. Do you want to be responsible for my son's death?"

This couldn't be happening.

Why did Luca lie to her?

"I-I didn't know. H-he never s-said anything," she stammered, clutching at her stomach, which was cramping painfully. Her selfishness had endangered a child, and not just any child, but the son of the man she was falling for.

"He doesn't know," Natalia said, and there was no shame in her blue eyes at her admission that she had kept the man she supposedly wanted to be married to from his own son. "And I won't tell him as long as you stay here. Luca wasn't ready to be a father to my son if he couldn't even do the right thing and come back home. But he is home now, which means he's ready to face his responsibilities."

Fury gripped her. She wanted to slap the woman.

How dare Natalia believe that because Luca was unfit to be a father because he dedicated his life to protecting the innocent and taking down terrorists.

But her fury didn't change the fact that she was putting a child's life in danger just by being here.

"If you pack up and leave right now, then I'll go and tell Luca about his son," Natalia said.

Blackmail.

Now on top of everything else, she was being blackmailed. Either she backed off Luca, or Natalia would keep her secret. She could tell Luca herself, but that didn't mean the woman would let him be part of his son's life so long as she was around. Mackenzie hated being put in this position, but she didn't see a choice.

"If you don't tell him, then I will," she threatened. She'd suffer anything, including walking away from Luca, to make sure he got to be part of his child's life.

"I wanted to tell him—I always did—but he made his choice, and it wasn't us, maybe now he's ready to make the right choice. You leave right now, and I'll go out there and tell him."

Leave without saying goodbye?

Maybe that would be best.

After all, it had been Luca's original plan.

With trembling hands, she pulled out her cell phone and brought up Tank's name. After meeting him at her place before they left to come to Montana, the huge man had given her his number and told her to use it if she was ever in trouble and couldn't get hold of Luca or one of his team.

She'd never really thought that day would come, but here it

was.

She typed out a text to Tank, who was right upstairs in the hotel, having flown out with his team on the jet to deal with the men from the ranch and take her and Alpha team to a new location, to come down and meet her round the back of the hotel outside the restaurant. She'd noticed a door leading outside further down the hallway the bathrooms were on. If she snuck out there, the guys wouldn't see her, and she wouldn't have to explain to Luca why she had to leave him.

It made her a coward, but she wasn't sure she could walk away if she saw him. She wasn't going to come between him and his son.

No one had followed them to the hotel—the guys had been careful to make sure of that—so she should be safe enough for a couple of minutes while Tank took the elevator down and met her outside.

"You won't keep Luca from his son?" she asked as she put her phone back in her pocket.

"Of course not. It's what I always wanted, the three of us to be a family."

How could she deny Luca that? It would be selfish to make him pick her over his child.

There was no choice but to walk away.

With a last look at the photo of Luca's son, she turned and left the bathroom, only to walk into two large men.

Men with guns.

Just when she'd thought her life couldn't possibly get any worse, fate decided it could.

CHAPTER TWENTY

October 5th
12:56 P.M.

Bear stared at the hallway that led to the bathrooms, waiting for Mackenzie to come back.

Was she okay?

She was struggling, totally normal given everything that had happened to her. No one could be okay after all of that.

What she needed was some down time. Time to start processing what she'd been through, time to relax and let go of the need to live on a constant adrenalin high, time to heal. Instead, what she got was an insane brother who just kept coming at her. No wonder she couldn't eat and needed to escape to the bathroom. She needed an escape from her life. A temporary one, at least.

What was taking her so long?

She was still putting emotional distance between them. He understood it was because she was afraid, same reason he hadn't contacted her when they came home and made such an abrupt disappearance from her life, but he hated it just the same.

How had he gone from the guy who wanted no personal attachments outside of his team to a guy who would do anything to make sure his girlfriend felt safe, protected, and cared about?

Girlfriend?

They hadn't discussed titles yet but this one felt ... right.

"I'm going to go fine Mackenzie," he announced, shoving away from the table.

"You sure? Thought she wanted some time to gather herself,"

Arrow said.

"She's had time."

"She doesn't want you to see her fall apart," Mouse said gently.

Panic struck him. "You think that's what she's doing? Falling apart?"

Space to pull herself together was one thing, but if she was in the bathroom falling apart, then he wasn't sitting here at the table waiting and leaving her alone. She was helping him put the pieces of himself back together after what his family had done; surely she had to know he would do the same for her.

"Not *falling apart* falling apart, she just wants you to think she's strong," Surf said.

"I already do." Leaving the guys at the table, he headed for the bathroom. No more of this hiding from him. The two of them needed to sit down because apparently there were a few things he had to make clear to her. At the bathroom door, he hammered on it. "Kenzie?"

He paused, waiting for an answer.

Got none.

"Mackenzie, you in there?"

She wouldn't leave, would she?

No, she wasn't stupid. She knew she was in danger. Just because they hadn't been followed to the hotel didn't mean Storm couldn't find her here. After all, her brother had found her at the ranch.

"Mackenzie, I know you said you wanted time, but I need to know you're okay."

There was still no response.

A stirring in his gut told him something was wrong.

"Kenzie, if you don't answer me, I'm coming in," he warned.

Walking into the woman's bathroom wasn't what he wanted to do, but he needed to know that she was okay.

If something had happened to her on his watch, he'd never

forgive himself.

"If anyone else is in there, I'm sorry. I need to come in and check my girlfriend is okay," he called out before pushing open the door. The bathroom was large, comprised of a small seating area, two basins in a large granite counter, and three toilet stalls, two of which had the doors open, but one was closed.

Was it Mackenzie?

Was she hiding from him?

That didn't seem right. Why would she do that? She was upset and overwhelmed, but really, she was doing a pretty good job of holding it together, all things considered.

"Kenzie? You in there?" he asked softly.

No answer.

It wasn't Mackenzie. She wouldn't ignore him while he was standing right here.

"Sorry to be in here. I'm looking for my girlfriend. I'm worried about her. Have you seen her?" If Mackenzie had left the bathroom, why hadn't she rejoined them at the table? She knew they were waiting for her and that it wasn't safe for her to be alone.

Whoever was in the toilet stall didn't answer, and the stirring in his gut grew.

Something was going on. Mackenzie was upset, but she wasn't reckless, and she was someone who cared about others. She wouldn't leave him to worry.

Maybe he was overreacting. The person in the stall was probably just afraid to have a man hammering on the women's bathroom door, then coming inside. Maybe she even thought he was the one who had given Mackenzie cause for concern.

"Sorry, for bothering you," he said, retreating to the hall. Where had Mackenzie gone? If she'd left, he'd have seen her. The hallway opened right up into the restaurant dining room. There was literally no way she could sneak past, because he'd been watching. Unless …

That thought died in his mind when the door to the women's bathroom opened and Natalia stepped out.

Her blue eyes grew wide when she saw him, and she took a small step back.

Looked like he had his answer.

His ex had done something to scare Mackenzie away.

"What did you do?" he asked, advancing on her.

"I … umm …" her eyes darted about as though searching for an escape, and he knew he was right.

"What did you say to Mackenzie, Natalia?" he demanded. She had something in her hand, something she tried to slip into her pocket.

Reaching out, he snagged her wrist and lifted it so he could see what she was trying to hide. When he saw it was a photo of Natalia and a boy of about nine, his stomach dropped.

No.

Natalia wouldn't do that, would she?

Keeping hold of her wrist, he dragged her along with him, ignoring the looks they were getting.

"Mackenzie is gone," he announced when he reached the table. The guys all stood, eyes moving from him to Natalia.

"What's going on?" Tank asked, appearing out of nowhere. "Mackenzie texted me to ask me to meet her down here. I told her I would, but no way wasn't I checking in with you guys first."

"Natalia showed her this." Bear snatched the picture from her hand and thrust it at his team.

Mouse took it, his mouth dropping open in shock as he passed it to the others. "Is that your son?"

"No," he growled. Red-hot fury bubbled inside him, making it difficult to cling to his composure. "But I bet she made Mackenzie think he was."

"You know about him?" Natalia asked, obviously not expecting that.

"That you were pregnant with another man's baby when you

served me with divorce papers while I was in rehab?" he sneered. "Yeah, I knew. Eagle knew about what happened, found out you were pregnant, and asked me if the baby could be mine. I knew the timing was wrong. You did too. I'm betting it's why you waited till you got Mackenzie alone before showing her this. What did you say to her?" Whatever it was had to be enough to have her asking Tank to come and get her and leave without facing him.

"He could be your son," Natalia huffed, refusing to look embarrassed over what she'd done.

"No, he couldn't. Before I left on that last mission, the last time we were together, I never got off. I knew something was going on with you and suspected you had been cheating. There's no way that kid is mine, because the last time I was with you was six months before I lost my leg. If the boy was my son, you would have already been showing when you visited me at the hospital."

Mackenzie had such a big heart. If Natalia had told her the boy was his son and threatened to keep him away from the child or not tell him about the boy, then she would have done anything to make sure that didn't happen.

Including walking away and surrendering her chance at happiness.

The woman was too sweet and kind for her own good.

"Tell me what you said to her, Natalia." The dangerous tone of his voice had her trembling, but she finally had the good grace to look ashamed.

"I told her this was your son and that if she didn't leave, I wouldn't tell you about him. I said you'd already lost enough and asked if she wanted you to lose your son as well," Natalia said in a whisper.

"You told her to leave knowing she was in danger?"

"I thought she'd be safe enough at the hotel," Natalia replied. "I thought you and your parents and I could finally talk, make things right, the way they were supposed to be, and one of your friends would find her."

"But she's not safe. She's missing," he growled.

He and his team hadn't been followed, but that didn't mean Natalia and his parents hadn't been, and Natalia's lies had pushed Mackenzie right into the arms of the men he was trying to save her from.

* * * * *

October 6th
2:39 A.M.

Her head was pounding so painfully she'd gladly chop it right off.

Mackenzie groaned and blinked open her eyes, only to scrunch them closed again when pain ripped right through her skull.

Unfortunately, she remembered exactly why her head currently felt like there was a colony of fire ants running around in there.

Storm.

That man was the answer to every single thing that had ever gone wrong in her life.

Almost.

Luca's ex, Natalia, was partially responsible for her current predicament. If Natalia had never shown her the photo of Luca's son, she never would have run out of the bathroom and straight into Storm's men.

Not that it really mattered who was to blame. The bottom line was, once again, Storm got what he wanted.

Her.

Why did things always have to work out Storm's way?

Tears well behind her closed lids, and panic slithered inside her like a snake. She wanted to rant and cry and scream about the injustice of it all—and very well might have—but heard someone moving about close by. Not wanting anyone to know she was conscious, she did her best to regulate her breathing, even though her lungs felt like they no longer accepted air and she had to pant through each too small breath.

There was something cold and hard around her wrists and ankles—handcuffs, no doubt. That would be harder to get out of than rope or zip ties because she couldn't untie or break them.

She was lying on something soft, no doubt a bed, and could smell something smoky, but not like a fire, more like cigarette smoke. There was the sound of laughter and chattering nearby along with the unmistakable grunts and moans of people having sex.

She wasn't cold; there was no breeze, no musty smells. It seemed like they were in a house somewhere, but how far away were they from Luca's ranch?

When she'd left the bathroom at the hotel, Storm's men had shown her a gun and told her they'd shoot innocent people if she didn't go with them. So she had. But once they were outside, she'd made a run for it, confident they wouldn't shoot her, and they hadn't. Instead, they'd caught and hit her, knocking her unconscious, so she had no idea how long they'd been traveling or even what time it was now.

"I know you're awake, Mackenzie," Storm announced, and she felt a presence move closer to the bed.

So much for playing possum.

Still, he couldn't know for sure that she really was awake, and she wasn't ready to face him yet. Luca would realize she was missing sooner or later and go all out to find her. She knew that. She even believed it was possible that he *would* find her. But knowing what would happen to her in the meantime made it difficult not to panic.

"Come on, Mackenzie. Ezra didn't give you a high enough dose of sedatives for you to still be unconscious over twelve hours later, and it's only a small bump on your head. If you have a concussion, it'll only be a minor one."

What a great big brother she had. His men had drugged her and hit her hard enough to give her a concussion, but it was only a minor one, so why should she complain?

"Wake up, Mackenzie. Now."

She recognized that voice; it was his out-of-patience voice, but she was terrified and in pain and woozy and not quite in control of herself yet.

"Fine," Storm snapped. One of his hands circled her wrist, and he grabbed her pinkie finger and yanked, snapping the tiny bones in one smooth, far too easy movement.

Mackenzie gasped as pain shot up her arm, and her eyes flew open. It wasn't the first time her brother had broken one of her bones, and it wasn't the worst pain he'd ever caused her, so she managed to hold in a scream, but now he knew for certain she was awake.

As predicted, they were in a bedroom. The door was closed, but she could still hear sounds coming from on the other side. The walls were logs, the furniture rustic, and there was a large fireplace on one side of the room. She had to assume they were in a cabin and wondered if maybe they were still in Montana.

Could she be that lucky?

Storm stood beside the bed and watched her with a smug smile, the one she remembered so very clearly from her childhood. If he'd come back to the US, knowing he was a wanted terrorist, then he had to be here for a reason. Just for her, or something else as well? Was he ready to put his plan into motion?

A deep weariness, born of a lifetime of suffering at her brother's hands, had her swaying on the edge of despair. It wouldn't take her much to push her over. "What do you want with me, Storm?"

"You and I are going to produce a child that will usher in a new era," her brother declared.

Bile burned her throat, and she turned her head to the side and vomited.

He wanted to have sex with her?

Get her pregnant?

With a child he thought would create a new world?

She had always known her brother was insane, a result of a sad combination of the trauma of living with his father's brain injuries during his early years and his own head injury in the tornado that took his father's life. If their mother had gotten him appropriate help, maybe all of this could have been avoided.

Storm tutted disapprovingly and moved a step away from the bed. "You always were so dramatic."

"Me?" she asked incredulously.

"I never knew why Mother always picked you over me."

"What?"

How could he *possibly* think that? Was he really so delusional that he thought that he was the victim in this scenario?

"You were the one who tortured me from the time I was born, and Mom let it happen. Do you know how many times I begged her to keep me safe? To protect me from you? But did she ever do it? No, she didn't. She let you hit me, break my bones, torment me daily. *You* were her favorite because she felt sorry for you because of what happened with your dad."

"She kicked me out of my home! I was sixteen," Storm said, his gray eyes flashing with hatred. The clear disconnect with reality with highlighted by the tattoos he'd had done surrounding both of his eyes.

Did he really need her to remind him of the reason why their mom had finally protected her? She wouldn't think she'd have to, given that he wanted a repeat. Only this time, he wanted to get her pregnant. Once she'd given him the child he wanted, he wouldn't have a use for her anymore. He'd kill her.

Fear still swarmed inside her, but along with it was a red-hot fury directed squarely at her brother.

She hated him.

Hated him.

Prison was too good for him. He deserved to die.

Preferably a long, slow, painful death.

Tears trailed hot streaks down her cheeks as her entire body trembled with rage. Mackenzie yanked against the cuffs, frantic to get free, to tear her brother to pieces with her bare hands.

"I hate you!" she screeched. "I wish you'd died along with your father." It wasn't the first time she'd had that thought, but it was the first time she'd voiced it out loud. "You're an abomination. A sick, twisted monster who takes pleasure from other people's pain. From *my* pain. You're no hero. You're no martyr. You're no savior of the world, bringing in whatever insane utopia is inside your head. The world would be a better place without you in it, and I hope you burn in Hell."

Fire seemed to light in his eyes, and he lunged at the bed, backhanding her so hard her head snapped to the side. "You're the one who shouldn't exist," he growled as he started to hit her. "You and your father stole my mother from me. She was all I had, and she chose you over me."

Tears pricked Mackenzie's eyes, and even if she could have brought herself to form words in that moment, she'd never get the chance to speak them. Storm was still on his tirade.

"She threw me away like I was too broken, like I was nothing, just a piece of useless garbage to be discarded. I hate you, I hate your father, and I hate her for abandoning me. But it made me grow stronger, turned me into a man who is going to change the world for the better."

At this, his chest puffed out a bit, as if he actually believed this nonsense he was spewing.

"Your father thought his money could buy what he wanted," Storm raged on. "Send me to military school against my will, keep me from my mother. But I'm going to make it so no one has any money. I'm going to bankrupt the government, I'm going to destroy the military, and then the son you're going to give me is going to work alongside me to bring in a world where everyone is equal. No more rich people buying what they want."

His tirade of words and fists ended when he struck the side of her head, once again sending her into unconsciousness, where she was completely vulnerable and at her merciless brother's mercy.

CHAPTER TWENTY-ONE

October 6th
5:21 A.M.

Would they get a tornado today?

Storm watched the sky hopefully. In Mississippi, the main tornado season started in November, but that didn't mean there weren't some during other months of the year. And given that they were in October, just a month away from November, there was a very real possibility there could be one today.

As he sat on the porch swing, clouds began to gather. The blue sky of early this morning had gone and throughout the day clouds had slowly begun to fill the sky. A light covering at first, barely more than a mist of white, then growing darker and grayer, until now the sky was an angry dark gray.

A tornado could definitely touch down today.

It would be the perfect timing.

He had always felt like he was born more from the tornado that had taken his father's life and forever changed him than from his mother's body.

Despite what Mackenzie believed, she had always been the favorite child. What more proof was there than the fact that he had been kicked out of his own home and sent off to military school? He hadn't wanted to go there, hadn't wanted anything to do with the institution that had destroyed his father. One that his stepfather had used to turn himself into some sort of hero.

Those years in military school had been awful. He'd been picked on by the other students and mocked by the teachers. They had all known he was never going to join the military—there was no way he would have passed the psych tests—and yet still he had been forced to continue the charade. His mother wouldn't even take his phone calls anymore and all because he had violated some arbitrary code that said he couldn't take what he wanted from a woman just because she didn't meet their age criteria.

Even back then, he had known he and Mackenzie would create something special.

Tornados had given him rebirth, told him what his future was, and shown him that he belonged to the storms. They gave him power and strength, guided his path, and showed him how things could be. When Mother Nature was the only one ruling the earth, then her children would finally find peace.

Money, cars, houses, vacations, cell phones, brand-name clothes, jewelry—none of those things were important. Materialism had ruined civilization; the more you had, the more you wanted until you were consumed with greed.

In his vision of the future, there would be no material possessions to blind people. They would live off the land as their ancestors had done, growing their own food, raising their own animals, and living in small huts that allowed them to be sheltered from the weather but also one with the landscape.

Perfection.

Utopia.

And it was only fitting that while he would bring about the revolution, a child born of the storms would usher in that perfect utopia.

When the next tornado touched down, it would be time to take his sister and create that special child. If not today, then tomorrow or the next day or even next month. It didn't matter. He had waited thirty-six years to get to this point. He could wait a little longer. Wasn't like his sister would be going anywhere.

"Storm."

Irritated by the distraction, he turned to find Ezra standing in the doorway. His second-in-command had a scowl on his face, and he wondered if there was ever a time when Ezra wasn't in a bad mood.

Everyone seemed to spend more time than not in a state of anxiety. The pressures of constantly having to upgrade to a bigger house, a new phone, the latest car, or new seasons wardrobe placed a heavy weight on people's backs. If you weren't earning enough to keep up with all the things you were supposed to have, then you were looked down upon.

No one truly wanted to help those in need; they didn't care, too preoccupied with their own lives and the things they thought brought it meaning.

Soon that pressure would be gone.

People would be happier, they'd smile more, spend their days in the fresh air and sunshine, no longer hide inside when it rained but go out and allow the water to freshen their spirits and their souls.

"Storm," Ezra repeated.

"What?" he snapped, shoving up off the porch swing, the moment of peace as he watched for a coming storm ruined now.

Although he had never spent his days worrying over possessions, he wasn't immune to the stress and anxiety of those around him. He, too, would benefit from the peace and tranquility of the coming age. Perhaps the angry voices in his head would finally release him.

"What are we doing with your sister?"

"She is not your concern."

He might have promised her to his men once he was finished with her, but until he planted his seed inside her, he didn't want anyone else violating her. She had to be clean, pure, when that child was placed in her womb.

"Some of the men are getting ... antsy."

Was that some sort of code word?

Ezra should know Storm wasn't always aware of what people meant when they didn't just outright speak their minds.

"Do you mean they're wanting sex?" he asked.

"Sex, violence, they're ready to do something. You promised them they would get their chance to get their revenge, and they're getting tired of waiting."

Timing was everything.

Why didn't people understand that?

Patience was a virtue, and yet it wasn't something many were well acquainted with. In a world where everything was at your fingertips, where you could get whatever you wanted without having to leave the comfort of your own living room, people were losing the art of patience.

But Storm did believe patience was a virtue, and it was one people would learn when the world they had known was stripped away from them. When they had to plant crops and wait for them to grow, cut down the wood needed to build their shelters, and heat their homes with the crackle of an open fire that needed constant tending, they would start to learn that the necessities of life were worth waiting on.

"The time is coming and shall soon arrive," he said as he brushed past Ezra and headed back inside the cabin.

This piece of land was where another group of survivalists lived. He had several communities across the country and had spent his time moving between them before Dove Oswald and her fiancé crashed the party.

Coming back into the country was a risk, but a calculated one. The time was drawing near, and he could hardly ask his people to take those risks while he hid in the safety of a compound on the other side of the world.

He would be here to lead his people in the revolution.

He would be here to watch the world crash and burn and then be reborn.

As he surveyed the living room, the dozen men dressed in simple cotton shirts and pants sitting around in furniture they had crafted themselves, in a cabin built entirely by hand, the food on the table grown in the gardens, water from the wells they'd dug, he couldn't help but feel a surge of pride.

These people were as much his children as the boy who would be conceived in a storm. He had found them and shown them the truth of the world they lived in and the future that would come within their lifetimes. He had taught them the beauties of the land and the simplicity of living off it, and he had taught them how to fight for the future they all wanted.

They were anxious for that future to become a reality; he understood that and could hardly fault them for being a little impatient given how amazing that future would be.

Perhaps he owed them a little treat.

While he couldn't allow them to touch Mackenzie, maybe he could allow them to have some fun. As much as hard work would be a part of the future—after all, there was no way to live off the land without hard work—fun was equally as important. What was the point of living if you weren't enjoying your life?

Walking through into the bedroom, he looked at his sister shackled to the bed, bruises on her face, a streak of blood from the cut on her cheekbone, and defiance in the eyes that stared back at him.

Despite his hatred of his sister, he had to admit that he liked the fact that she had strength. She was a survivor, and she was going to create something beautiful with him. Even if she wouldn't be there to witness the new world, she would die knowing that she had played an important role in creating the perfect future.

"Come, the beginning is upon us," he said as he went to unlock the handcuffs.

A storm was on the horizon, and he was its creator.

CHAPTER TWENTY-TWO

October 6th
6:08 A.M.

He couldn't take his eyes off the clock hanging on the wall of the hotel room.

Each second that ticked past made the vice around his heart tighten just a little bit more.

Mackenzie had been gone for more than eighteen hours, and they were still no closer to finding her.

Bear was going to lose his mind.

Walking into a storm of bullets was fine, putting his life on the line to rescue a victim or take down a high value target was fine, but letting his heart be the one on the line had him dangerously close to losing it.

He couldn't help but wonder if, had he kept the lines of communication open between them when they left Uganda, things might be different. Mackenzie had done what Natalia demanded because she was trying to do the right thing for him, because she believed if he had a choice between her and his son, he'd choose his child.

If the boy, whose name he had learned was Lucas, had really been his son, he would have still chosen both of them because Mackenzie was … more than just a girlfriend.

She was someone special.

But she was also someone who believed he would never put her first because no one else ever had, because he'd shown her he might cave under emotional pressure when he'd refused to even say goodbye to her after Africa.

That was a mistake he would never repeat.

If he got her back alive—and he had to believe he would—then he was going to spend the rest of his life proving to her that she was his number one.

Love at first sight. He hadn't believed it existed, hadn't even thought real love existed, but he couldn't deny that from the moment he'd laid eyes on Mackenzie, he'd known she was his.

His.

There was no other way to describe how he felt about her, and yet he had failed her over and over again. Fought against what his heart and soul already knew because he couldn't face the truth. But it hadn't been Mackenzie who had hurt him; it was him who had hurt her, and it had to stop.

Now.

Bear stood. "I want to see the men from the ranch," he announced.

Tank and his team had flown over to Montana to take care of interrogating the men who had been sent to his property to grab Mackenzie, and while he trusted Bravo team as implicitly as he trusted his own, he knew he could get answers out of those men.

His team exchanged looks. "Are you sure?" Mouse asked.

One of them having a woman that was more than a one-night stand or a short-term girlfriend was new to all of them. Mouse was the only one who had ever been in love, and he'd lost his wife far too soon. It was something they were all going to have to get used to, though, because he wasn't letting Mackenzie go. He'd fight for her, work to earn her trust, and find happiness and peace.

He finally realized that when it was the right person, the risk was worth it, and Mackenzie was the right person for him.

"I'm sure."

There was no more questioning. The guys all stood, gathered their gear, and headed out of the hotel room. In the hall, they came face to face with his parents, who he had learned had known about Lucas all along, only they believed the boy was actually their grandson.

Maybe it should make him feel better that the reason they had sided with Natalia over him was because they believed the child was their grandson and they were doing the right thing, but it didn't. They'd tried to keep a child they believed to be his son from him, and that, he wasn't sure he could forgive.

If they'd just come to him, he could have told them that there was no way Natalia's child was his, but they hadn't done that.

Lack of communication had destroyed his relationship with his parents, but he was determined it wasn't going to destroy what he was building with Mackenzie.

"Luca?" His mother reached out a hesitant hand toward him, flinching when he took a step back.

Reality was finally sinking in for both his parents. Gone were the cocky, rude, condescending couple who had treated Mackenzie like she was nothing. In their place were a hesitant older man and woman who were forced to face what they were going to lose.

They'd thought they had a chance to mold Lucas into what they always believed their son should have been. Now they knew the boy wasn't their grandson and had lost their son forever.

"Not now," he said dismissively. It would take him a long time to sort out his feelings when it came to his parents, and right now, his time was much better spent finding Mackenzie.

"You really care about her," his mother called out as he and his team continued toward the elevators.

"If you'd actually cared enough to pay attention when we were at the ranch, then you'd know that I do," he growled without looking back at them.

"I'm sorry. You're right," his mother said softly. "We messed up with you from the beginning, trying to make you into something you weren't instead of respecting the man you are. A good man. Loyal, protective, strong, compassionate. You put your life on the line for people you don't even know. When you wouldn't come home after you lost your leg, we realized it was too late for the three of us, but your father and I thought maybe we could do better with your son."

Tears blurred his vision as his mom continued.

"Now we've lost Lucas as well," she said. "I hope you find your girl. She's lucky to have you." That was without a doubt the nicest thing his mother had ever said to him in his life and as close to an "I love you" as she was capable of giving. Perhaps it wasn't too late to mend fences with his parents, but not right now. First, he had to go find his girl and bring her home, where she belonged.

No one spoke as they took the elevator down to the garage and loaded into the SUVs. Nobody spoke on the drive out to an old, partially dilapidated cabin hidden between the trees on a remote part of the ranch.

Tension hung heavily in the air, a silent acknowledgment from his team that they understood he was about to do whatever it took to get answers.

There was nothing he wasn't prepared to do to get Mackenzie back.

Nothing.

He would sell his soul to the Devil himself if that was what it took.

Mackenzie had been through so much. She deserved to finally find peace, and while he wasn't sure he did, he would grab hold of the peace she gave him and refuse to let go.

As they pulled up outside the old cabin, Tank and the rest of Bravo team were standing waiting for them.

"We haven't been able to get them to talk," Tank warned as Bear and Alpha team climbed out of their vehicles.

Bear wasn't surprised to hear that. Storm found men and women who were former military, including some former special forces operators, to work for him. He had no idea how the man managed to turn men and women who had served and been willing to make the ultimate sacrifice for their country, but it seemed it was something he was good at. Storm would only have sent his best after his sister because she was important to him, so likely these men had been tier-one operators. The best of the best and unlikely to break.

But he didn't have a choice.

Mackenzie's life depended on him breaking them and getting a location.

"I'll get them to talk," he said with a confidence born of sheer determination.

"You sure about this?" Tank asked.

While they had all, on occasion, had to torture information out of a suspect, it wasn't something any of them enjoyed doing, and today Bear was willing to take it to another level. Nothing was off the table.

Rolling up his sleeves, he gave a single nod. "I'm sure."

He left the others outside. This was his line to cross, not theirs, and while he knew his team would support him in any way he asked, he couldn't ask them to do this with him. This was his fight, his heart, his *life* on the line. As he entered the dimly lit cabin and saw the two men tied to chairs, their faces already bruised and bloody, he knew he wouldn't walk away this morning the same man. This would change him, but it was a sacrifice he was more than willing to make for Mackenzie.

Getting her back was all that mattered.

* * * * *

October 6th
5:57 P.M.

These people were all lunatics.

That was the only conclusion Mackenzie could possibly come

to after spending the last couple of hours watching them.

They'd all sat and listened with rapt attention while Storm droned on and on about this new world that he believed he was creating. Apparently, that started with setting a number of explosions intended to cripple the government and the military and culminated in her and Storm producing a child who was going to build a new world.

Lunatics.

Was there any other way to describe people who believed in destroying their country, killing thousands of innocent people, and then moving civilization back a couple of thousand years?

It seemed that as well as living off the land and plotting to blow people up, another important part of these people's lives was sex. Lots of it. And it seemed they had no problem with having sex in front of others.

After Storm had brought her out of the bedroom, he'd set her in a chair at the kitchen table and bound her wrists and ankles; then the room had filled with a couple dozen men and women. They'd listened to Storm's monologue with rapt attention, then broken out their homemade alcohol and proceeded to get drunk and start making out.

This wasn't something she wanted to watch, and she'd scrunched her eyes closed, wishing she could do the same with her ears. The grunts and groans, the moans and screams, the begging and pleading ... it was all too much, and being forced to listen to it was making her feel sick.

Still, there was one benefit. After hours of drinking and having sex, everyone was now drunk and woozy. Her hands had been cuffed behind her back, her ankles attached to the legs of the chair with handcuffs, but the chair was wooden, and she thought there was a possibility she might actually be able to break its legs and get free. Or even just upending the chair likely meant the other end of the cuffs would slide right off the chair legs

All she had to do was hope everyone passed out soon.

In their drunken stupors, she was praying they wouldn't notice her getting free and fleeing.

It wasn't the best of plans, but it was better than nothing, and it certainly beat just lying on that bed helplessly, waiting for Storm to do to her whatever he wanted. It also gave her something to focus on so she didn't fall apart.

Any time thoughts of Luca snuck into her mind, she felt her composure cracking.

Every time it did, she quickly shored up her walls, shoved away all thoughts of Luca and her hopes and dreams of what the future could have been, and replaced them with pure determination.

She could do this.

She *had* to do this.

If she could protect herself and Luca in Uganda, literally shedding blood in the process, then she could find a way to save herself now too.

The moaning seemed to have died down a bit, so Mackenzie chanced a peek and found that while everyone was still naked and all kind of heaped together in the center of the room, most of them looked drowsy. A few had even passed out.

Cautiously, she moved one of her feet, trying to brace it on the floor so she could move herself. The floorboards meant there would be a crash when she knocked the chair over, drawing people's attention her way, but it was a risk she would have to take.

All she had to do was use her body motion, rock from side to side, and make the chair fall over. She'd probably hurt herself in the process, but after the beating Storm had given her earlier and the head injury from when she was abducted, it wasn't like she wasn't already in pain.

A rumble of thunder in the distance set off warning bells in her head. The sound felt like an ominous foreshadowing of what was to come.

It took a few tries to get up enough momentum, but then she

was falling.

The landing wasn't as bad as she had been expecting, although her head did painfully thump into the solid wooden floorboards. But with her hands cuffed at her back and her legs secured to the chair legs, they were somewhat protected.

As she'd hoped, the cuffs securing her ankles to the chair slid right off, and seconds later, she was free.

Choking back a somewhat hysterical laugh that tried to bubble free, Mackenzie stumbled to her feet. There were still the cuffs around her wrists, securing them behind her back, but she was off the chair, and nobody seemed to notice.

Hope swelled inside her.

She was really going to pull this off.

"Going somewhere?"

The voice had her whipping around to see that a man had been sitting in a chair further back in the kitchen, watching her with apparent amusement.

Mackenzie immediately recognized him as Ezra, her brother's second-in-command. He was the man who had beaten her in her bedroom the night she'd first been abducted, and he was the one who had beaten her in Uganda before she'd been thrown into that hole. The man was evil and enjoyed inflicting pain.

"I'd hate for you to disappear before I got a chance to spend a little one-on-one time with you," Ezra snarled. He grabbed her arm and dragged her back into the bedroom.

There was no one to help her. The others were all either passed out drunk or still engaged in an orgy. Even her brother had his head tilted back, eyes closed, pants shoved down, a woman's head buried in his lap.

None of them would help her anyway.

They were all sick and twisted.

Evil.

At the very least, they were brainwashed.

Regardless, they all supported this plan, so they'd just stand by and watch her be hurt, perhaps even join in themselves.

"You know the man whose throat you slit in Uganda?" He backed her up against the wall and ran a finger down her cheek, following the path of the cut that very man had given her. When he reached spot where the knife had dug deeper into her flesh, he pressed his thumb into the healing wound, making her hiss in pain. "He was my brother."

Of course he was.

Because that was absolutely her luck.

His hand moved lower, grabbing one of her breasts, and when she tried to buck him off, he tangled his other hand in her hair and twisted her head back until her scalp burned and she was staring at the ceiling.

"You know your brother is insane. He has these grand plans for you, wants to make a baby with you." His tone said he clearly thought that was sick but that he would happily stand by and let it happen to achieve his own goals. Which was every bit as sick. "He's just a pawn, you know, one more powerful men are using as a shield, but he doesn't know it. He buys into this utopia idea as though it could actually happen. But rebirth out of storms?" The man scoffed. "Come on, that's completely insane."

Keeping his hand tangled in her hair, he reached around her to unlock the cuffs and free her hands. Mackenzie knew her moment to fight for her life was upon her. Fail now, and she didn't think she'd get another chance.

Before she could make a move, a crash of thunder sounded almost right above them, and a second later, the door to the bedroom was thrown open.

"What are you doing, Ezra?" Storm raged as a heavy sheet of rain descended on the cabin.

Mackenzie reached for Ezra's gun.

Her shot hit Ezra in the head.

Blood and brain matter splattered her.

She shifted aim to her brother.

Could she kill her own flesh and blood?

After years of being tormented, she absolutely could.

She fired again.

Clutching the gun in her hand—no way was she letting go of the only weapon she had—Mackenzie ran to the window and used the butt of the gun to break the glass.

Once she'd scrambled through, she started running through the storm raging around her. She didn't know where she was or where she was going, but it didn't matter. She would keep running until she found safety.

"You can run, but you can't hide from me, Mackenzie," Storm's voice screamed behind her, and when she looked back, she saw him standing behind the broken window. "It's destiny."

CHAPTER TWENTY-THREE

October 6th
6:26 P.M.

"I got movement," Brick announced.

Bear had gotten the men to talk.

He hadn't doubted that he could. Those men were good, highly trained, and fighting for a cause they believed in, but that didn't mean they couldn't crack.

And crack they had.

He wasn't proud of the things he'd done to get them to talk, but neither did he regret it. Mackenzie represented everything good in the world, everything he sacrificed and fought for, and she was his. There wasn't anything he wouldn't do for her, and today he had proved that.

They'd taken Prey's jet to Mississippi, then hired vehicles and driven out to the property. While Bear would have preferred to go straight in, guns blazing, and get his girl, he had to acknowledge it wasn't the smartest plan and one that might wind up getting Mackenzie hurt or even killed in the crossfire.

They knew Storm's men would fight back. Those that weren't former military would have trained in weapons and hand-to-hand combat, same as the men on the compound in New York State, where Dove and Isaac had been taken. They'd throw everything they had at Bear and his team, and like the compound in New York, this one was likely well-armed.

So, they'd been smart, played things safe, and used drones to get a feel for the property. They'd identified the main cabin, surrounded by smaller buildings that appeared to be little more than one room shacks. Heat signatures indicated there were close to three dozen people in the cabin, with an additional dozen in the smaller shacks and surrounding areas.

Fifty people to his six. It might seem like the odds were in Storm's favor, but Bear knew they weren't.

Nobody beat his team. They were the best of the best, and this is what they did. They took down threats to the country, protected the innocent, and saved lives, and tonight, the life they would be saving was the one that meant the most to him.

They had been intending to wait to breach the property until well after dark, in the early hours of the morning when most of them would be asleep, but movement meant things changed.

"What is it?" he asked Brick. Since he was still injured from the bullet wound in Uganda, Brick was acting as their eyes tonight. He was manning the drones that had given them an aerial view of the survivalist property where Storm had taken his sister.

"Got one heat signature leaving the cabin."

"I need more than that."

"Hold on," Brick mumbled, and Bear assumed he was switching the camera view to try to see who was leaving the cabin. A moment later, a curse came through the comms. "Bear, its Mackenzie."

"What?" he snapped.

How could it be Mackenzie? Had she somehow managed to get free? And if she had, what had she had to do to make that happen? His heart ached for her if she'd had to take another life. He knew how much she was struggling after killing in Uganda, and he didn't want her to have to go through that again. But damn, if the idea that she had saved herself didn't make his heart swell with pride.

Brick swore again. "She's not alone. Someone left right after her. It looks like Storm."

"Which direction are they heading?" he asked, already shifting from his position hidden in the trees around the edge of the property.

"Down toward the river," Brick replied.

"Keep eyes on the cabin," he ordered Brick. "Let us know if anyone else comes out."

"Let's go get your girl," Surf said with a grin as they all moved from where they'd been hiding.

The cabin was only one klick from where they were, and thankfully, Mackenzie and Storm were already moving in their direction. The river was just off to their left. If they hurried, they would be there before Mackenzie and her brother, effectively cutting them off.

"Arrow and I will go to the river. Surf, come in behind them. Domino from the left; Mouse, the right. I want them surrounded. This ends here and now. I don't want Storm Gallagher leaving this property unless it's in handcuffs or a body bag."

"Preferably a body bag," Domino muttered, and Bear couldn't agree more.

As they split up, he prayed he was making the right move. He was banking on the fact that Mackenzie was scared and had no idea where she was. She'd pick a direction and run in it until she found a place to hide or help or safety.

When they were near the river, he and Arrow hid themselves and waited. It wasn't long before he heard someone crashing through the forest, and a moment later, Mackenzie came into view.

She was limping, clearly in pain, and even with his NVGs on, he could see the fear in her face.

As much as he wanted to go to her and drag her into his arms, they had to wait for Storm first. They didn't want him alerting his men that the compound had been breached until they had him in custody.

"There's nowhere to run, sister," Storm called out, appearing through the trees a moment after Mackenzie had.

She backed away from him until she was standing at the edge

of the drop down to the river. Then she lifted her arms, and he saw that she was armed. He had no idea how she'd managed to get herself a weapon and escape, but he was so grateful she had.

However, he wasn't letting her kill her brother.

He'd been her tormentor and was planning to do unspeakable things, but the weight of killing her own brother would be too much. He couldn't let her bear that burden.

"I won't let you kill thousands of innocent people, Storm," Mackenzie said, her voice strong above the raging storm. The irony that they were fighting Storm in the midst of a storm wasn't lost on him as he stepped out of his hiding place.

"It's over, Storm," he called out.

Brother and sister's attention both whipped his way, and Mackenzie swung her weapon in his direction.

"Easy now, sweetheart," he soothed, keeping his own weapon trained on Storm, who had been slowly advancing on his sister.

"Luca?" she asked, her voice trembling with emotion. "You found me."

"Never a chance that wasn't happening," he assured her. "It's over now, Storm. We can do this the easy way or the hard way, but my men and I will be taking you into custody tonight, and then we'll be rounding up the rest of your men."

A crash of thunder boomed right overhead. Lightning bolts lit the night. Storm looked from him to his sister and then tipped his head back and roared.

"Together we live, or together we die," he howled as he lunged at Mackenzie.

Three weapons fired simultaneously. Bear had no clue if it was his shot, Arrow's, or Mackenzie's that ended Storm's life, but when the man's body crashed into Mackenzie, sending them both falling backward over the cliff, he didn't care.

Mackenzie's scream as she fell struck him like a sword.

Even before it cut off as her body hit the river below, he was moving. It was only about a fifteen-foot drop, and as he dived off the edge, he hoped the water was deep enough he wasn't about to break his neck.

The water was cold but thankfully not freezing and indeed deep enough that he didn't hit his head on the bottom. He came up and spotted Mackenzie's head bobbing in the water a little further downstream.

Smooth strokes through the water brought him to her, and then he was pulling her into his arms and crushing his mouth to hers.

"Don't ever do that to me again," he said against her lips when he finally stopped kissing her.

"What?" she asked, and there was a thread of teasing beneath the pain, exhaustion, and fear. "Leave without telling you? Get kidnapped? Shoot someone? Fall into a river?"

Bear huffed a laugh, and it eased the pressure in his chest. "All of it, siren, all of it."

"You always said I'd end up dashing you against the rocks, and I'd say that almost happened," she said as she gestured to the rocks just off to the side.

As he pulled her close and started swimming them toward the shore, he shook his head. "I got it all wrong, honey. You aren't going to dash me into pieces. You're helping me put the pieces of myself back together."

* * * * *

October 6th
6:50 P.M.

Luca's strong arm kept her anchored to his side as he swam them both toward the shore.

It was over.

She was alive.

Storm was dead.

For the first time in her life, she was safe. Never again would she have to worry about what her brother was going to do to her next. And here, swinging her up into his arms to carry her the rest of the way out of the river, cradling her so very gently, was a man who could give her the future she'd thought she might never have. A home that was a safe haven from the world, a partner who would put her first, children of her own.

No.

Mackenzie shoved Luca's shoulders. "What are you doing here? You can't be here! She said that if I got in the way, she'd keep you from your son. You have to go. Now. Go back to your family."

Instead of letting her push him away, Luca tightened his hold on her. "Shh, siren. Stop worrying. I knew about the kid, and he's not mine. Natalia was just being Natalia and trying to manipulate to get her way. Only this time, it backfired."

What?

She must be more tired than she thought, because none of that made sense.

"She said he was yours."

"She lied. She knew he wasn't. The last time I was with her was six months before I lost my leg. If she'd been pregnant at the hospital, I would have known. She was cheating on me and passed her son off as mine to my parents so she could take advantage of their money."

"How could she do that to you?"

Mackenzie was outraged. Natalia had played with so many lives and almost gotten her killed. Without the other woman's interference, she would have already been back at the table with Luca and his team before Storm's men found her.

But more importantly, Natalia had hurt Luca again. She hated the other woman for that.

"Shh," Luca soothed as he set her down on the riverbank. "None of that matters right now. All I care about is that you're here and you're safe. Arrow is going to check you out now, okay?"

Feeling a little numb from too much information coming at her too quickly, Mackenzie nodded and allowed Arrow to take her vitals and poke and prod at her various wounds, including her broken finger, while she did her best to answer his questions.

Luca stayed beside her the entire time, holding her hand and talking to someone else. She didn't bother trying to figure out what he was saying, but she watched as Surf and Domino dragged her brother's lifeless body from the river.

So close.

Storm had come so close to getting what he wanted. If not for the team of special forces guys who had made her one of their own, her brother would have won.

"Kenzie, I'm going to take off your wet clothes, okay?" Luca was kneeling in front of her now, speaking patiently like he might have already spoken the words.

Her head was so fuzzy, and all she wanted was to just close her eyes and rest, preferably wrapped up in Luca's arms. "My clothes?" she echoed, trying her best to focus.

"You're shaking. Hypothermic," Luca explained.

"Oh. Okay."

With her assent, he quickly stripped off her soaked clothes, pulled on sweatpants and a sweatshirt that smelled just like him, then wrapped her in a foil blanket before the rain could drench her again.

"What about the others?" she asked as Luca gathered her back into his arms and started walking with her.

"Eagle called in the troops. Local cops are here along with Homeland and most of the alphabet agencies. They'll take everyone into custody."

Mackenzie shook her head. "No, I mean the men who were using Storm. What's going to happen to them?"

Luca froze, and she could feel his eyes on her even though

hers were closed, her head resting on his shoulder, sleep tugging at the corners of her mind. "What are you talking about?"

"Ezra said that Storm was just being used. Because he's crazy. Someone was pulling his strings, manipulating him, using him as a shield," she finished on a yawn.

"Did you get all of that?" Luca asked, and since she was pretty sure he wasn't talking to her this time, she allowed sleep to tug her under.

When she woke, she was warm, dry, and sitting on a stretcher in the back of an ambulance. An IV ran into the back of one hand, there was a blood pressure cuff around her arm and a pulse ox cable on one of her fingers, and the pinkie Storm had broken was taped to the neighboring finger. Aside from a medic, who smiled at her with kind eyes, she was alone.

Luca.

Where was he?

Panic spiked, causing the EMT to fuss over her.

But it wasn't until Luca stepped back into her line of sight and she realized he was only just outside the ambulance on his cell that she relaxed back against the thin mattress.

"I gotta go. Kenzie is awake," Luca said to whoever he was talking to on the phone, then he shoved it into his pocket and climbed in to join her. Perching on the edge of the stretcher, he reached out to caress her cheek. "How are you doing?"

"I'm okay," she said, glancing at the medic for confirmation. While she ached all over, she was mostly just tired.

"Probable concussion, suspected fracture of her cheekbone, possible cracked ribs, broken finger, dehydrated, and mildly hypothermic," the EMT rattled off, the corners of his eyes crinkled as he grinned. "But I think your girl will live."

"Yeah she will," Luca agreed as he reached for her good hand and laced their fingers together.

"Did I tell you what Ezra said?" she asked. Everything was still a little fuzzy, and she wasn't quite sure what was real and what she might have imagined.

"You did." There was a darkness to his gaze for a moment before he shoved it away.

No doubt he was worried that while Storm might be dead, his plans were still alive and in the hands of a more powerful man who had the resources to use Storm for his own purposes.

At least the part of Storm's plan about the two of them making a baby was over. While she might have been important to her brother, she doubted anyone else cared enough about her to seek her out.

"And Storm is really dead?"

"He is."

Knowing she was finally free of brother's sick, twisted grasp would take some getting used to. She was probably going to need him to tell her that a few more times before it sunk in.

"And you don't have a child with Natalia?"

"No. I don't know who the father of her son is, and I don't care. I just want her out of my life once and for all, and since my parents are kicking her off the ranch, maybe that will finally happen."

"Do you think maybe you can fix your relationship with them?"

"Maybe. But right now, the only thing I'm interested in is you. How about we get you to the hospital so you can get some proper rest?"

"Oh, no, I don't need the hospital. I just want to go home, only I'm not sure where home is right now."

Her house had been partially destroyed in the explosion, and even though she'd have the place fixed, she wasn't sure she wanted to live there. Luca's home was in New York, or maybe he was going to go back to the ranch. She wasn't sure, but home felt like wherever he was, only it wasn't like he had invited her to live with him.

Luca reached out a hand and smoothed a finger across her

forehead. "Stop looking so worried. We don't have to solve all the world's problems tonight, or all of our own. Eagle is giving Alpha team the next month off, Brick needs to heal from his injuries, and I've pushed my leg harder than I should have after I was shot. He thinks I need a proper vacation, so he's offering to send the both of us to a small island in the Caribbean for a month."

An island in the Caribbean? For a month? The thought made her smile, and Luca returned the expression, something soft in his gaze.

"I was thinking it's the perfect way for us to get to know each other without being shot at and blown up. We can finally do the dating thing right. I can bring you flowers and take you out for romantic dinners, and we can go for walks along the beach. What do you say?"

"And will there be lovemaking included?" she asked, ignoring the cough and chuckle of the medic.

"Wouldn't be a romantic beach getaway without it," Luca replied.

"Then I think it's a perfect idea."

"I was hoping you'd say that." His large hands framed her face, his touch gentle and careful to avoid the worst of her bruising, and then his lips feathered across hers in the softest, sweetest kiss she'd ever had.

The kiss felt like a promise that she would never be alone again, that she would never feel like second best, that she would know what it felt like to be cherished and protected.

That she would always be loved.

Giving Luca a chance, trusting someone else with her heart and giving them the opportunity to crush it beyond repair, had been a huge risk, only Luca hadn't done that. Instead, he'd soothed old hurts and shown her what it was like to be someone's top priority when he'd faced his own trust issues and pain.

Mackenzie knew he would spend his life making her his number one, and she would spend hers making sure he knew he was loved and accepted for who he was.

She was his number one, and he was hers.

CHAPTER TWENTY-FOUR

October 31st
8:11 A.M.

"Mmm," Mackenzie moaned when his lips closed around one of her pert little nipples. As he swirled the tip of his tongue across it, making it pebble, her chest lifted off the mattress, silently begging for more. "I could get used to waking up like this."

Bear laughed, loving the way another moan fell from Mackenzie's lips as the laugh vibrated across her sensitive flesh. "Pretty sure I've woken you up this way every morning for the last three and a half weeks. I would have thought you'd be tired of it by now."

Blinking open sleepy eyes, she gave him that sexy smile he loved so much, part sex appeal, part teasing, and full of love and affection.

They'd checked off exchanging "I love yous" on week two of their romantic island getaway. Words he'd never said to another human being before, not even to his parents, words he had always thought would be terrifying to say, had turned out to be easiest words he'd ever spoken.

They were so natural when it came to Mackenzie.

"You wake me up like this every morning because for some reason, you still feel the need to get up with the sun and work out even while we're in paradise and you've kept me up half the night making love to me," she said as her fingers reached out to curl into his short hair. "And just so you know, I won't *ever* get tired of being woken up by your hands or mouth on my body."

"Good to know." He smirked as he returned his mouth to her

breast and suckled it.

Some habits were hard to break, like getting up with the sun to work out, and he knew that while he felt like a new man when he was with Mackenzie, it didn't mean everything was always going to be this perfect between them.

Although they weren't married, this felt like a honeymoon, full of romantic strolls along the beach, candlelight dinners, and yeah, plenty of sex. When they went back to real life, there would be plenty of hurdles to overcome. They both had trust issues that would sooner or later rear their ugly heads, but he also knew they had what it took to make this relationship work, and that was all that really mattered.

Releasing her nipple, Bear trailed a line of kisses down her stomach until he was settled between her legs. Despite Mackenzie having no idea what she liked when it came to sex before he'd met her, she'd quickly discovered that she loved having his mouth on her. It was a sure-fire way to have her coming hard and fast in a matter of minutes.

Now, as he stroked his tongue along her center before spreading her legs wider and sliding it inside her, he could feel the beginnings of her orgasm starting to build. He added a finger, then a second, stroking deep as his mouth latched on to her little bundle of nerves.

When he curled his fingers to hit that spot inside her and then sucked hard on her little bud, she flew apart for him. As always, he didn't let up, stroking, sucking, and lapping at her until she had ridden the high for as long as he could make it last.

While his girl floated back down to earth, he shifted and plunged inside her in one thrust. She moaned as he filled her, her internal muscles still quivering from the intense orgasm he'd just given her. He loved coming at the same time she did. Feeling her clench around him set off an orgasm like none he'd ever experienced before, so Bear reached between them and began to touch them where their bodies joined.

Overly sensitive from stimulation, she pushed at his hands, and he clamped one of his around her wrists, stretching her arms up over her head. "Uh uh, siren. You know the rules. When I have you in bed, I get to do whatever I want with you, and that means making you come again."

"It's too much, too strong," she murmured as her hips began to move, meeting him thrust for thrust.

"No, siren, you can take it. You can take every ounce of pleasure I give you. Hands stay there, or I tie them there."

They hadn't actually gone there yet because he wanted Mackenzie to know how much he loved her, how special she was, before they did. Plus, she was still healing from her injuries from the night her brother died.

When they were back home, he had every intention of tying her up and spending the entire night making her come over and over again until she knew exactly who her sweet body belonged to, until she knew without a shadow of a doubt that he would worship every inch of her every day for the rest of their lives.

Bear took her nipple in his mouth again as his fingers continued to work her sensitive bud.

"Oh ... oh," she gasped as her breathing grew ragged. "I'm going to come."

"Now, baby," he ordered, tweaking her bud, and she did.

As soon as her internal muscles clamped around him, he found his own release. It rushed through him like a tidal wave, tossing him about until he didn't know which way was up and it felt like he was drowning in a sea of pleasure.

The tide of pleasure slowly receded, and he looked down to see his sweet woman watching him with heavy lidded eyes.

"I don't know how you do that. I swear, one day, you're going to kill me with sex. I didn't even know this kind of sex existed. I thought it was just made up for movies and books."

Bear laughed as he eased out of her. "Come on, let's get you up and into the shower so I can clean you up."

"So you can do that all over again, you mean," she teased as he took her hand and pulled her off the bed. "I know how you work."

"Are you complaining about all the sex?" he asked, guiding her through the bedroom and into the bathroom.

"No way. I would never complain about that."

"Smart girl." He swatted as her bare backside, making her yelp, but the heat in her eyes told him she'd like the gentle spank. This woman surprised him at every turn.

He'd kept her naked and in their bungalow right on the beach most of the last few weeks—his sexy girl in a bikini being ogled by other men wasn't something he wanted to endure—but when they did venture out, she'd been up for everything he'd suggested. They'd gone paddle boarding and snorkeling, and she'd even been up for cage diving with sharks.

She was fearless, something he wasn't even sure she'd known before her ordeal, and he loved that they had an entire lifetime to explore the wonders of the world together.

"Uh oh." Mackenzie yanked her hand from his and ran the rest of the way into the bathroom, dropping to her knees in front of the toilet a second before she threw up.

"Again, babe?" he asked as he turned on the tap and wet a washcloth, carrying it to her and kneeling beside her as she sank back onto her knees.

"That's three days in a row now," she mumbled, leaning into his touch as he blotted at her forehead. The first morning she'd been sick, they'd assumed she'd just eaten something that disagreed with her, but when it had happened again yesterday, he'd started to wonder.

"I picked up something on my run this morning." Leaving her where she was, he flushed the toilet, then went into the bedroom and grabbed the bag from the pharmacy.

"What is it?"

"This." He pulled out the home pregnancy test and held it up.

"You were late, and now you're getting sick in the morning. We thought it might have bene because of your injuries and the stress of what happened to you, but what if it's not?"

When she'd told him she was late a week ago and he'd broached this topic, she'd said it was more likely stress because they'd only had sex the one time before coming here and what were the chances of her getting pregnant in that one time?

"You really think I might be pregnant?"

"Only one way to find out." Bear took her hand and pulled her to her feet. "Why don't you take the test, then we can call back home and wish Cleo Oswald a happy fifteenth birthday while we wait for the results?"

The daughter of the oldest Oswald sister had been rescued two years ago on her thirteenth birthday after a decade in the hand of a sick monster. The girl was truly an inspiration, and no way was he going to miss wishing her happy birthday, even if they were on vacation.

"Oh, I don't want to intrude. Why don't you wish her happy birthday while I take the test?" Mackenzie said as she picked up the box and opened it, pulling out the stick.

"It's not intruding, Kenzie. Prey is like a family. The Oswalds make you part of that family when you start working for them. It's not just a job, not just a place to work. They're the people who kept me from falling apart when I felt like I'd lost everything. They were there for me, were the family I needed, and now you're part of that family, and I already know the Oswald sisters are planning something for when we get back. They're all dying to meet you."

"Really?" She looked shocked by the idea.

"Really. And if you think my team all but adopted you, wait till you see how overbearing the Oswalds can be. That family is all up in each other's business all the time, but they love big and protect their own with a ferocity you won't believe till you see it. Maybe we should wait till after we get the results. If you are pregnant, then I want them to be the first to know." Bear paused, wondering if he was overstepping. "Unless you want your parents to know first?"

Mackenzie shook her head emphatically. "No. I love my mom and dad, I really do, but they never put me first. Prey looked out for me when they thought I was in trouble, and if they hadn't, Storm would have gotten to me sooner, and you wouldn't have found me. If I am pregnant, I'd love for them to be the first to know."

Their eyes locked as she went to the toilet and peed on the stick; then she set the stick on the counter while she washed her hands. When she looked up at him nervously, he wrapped his arms around her and pulled her against his chest.

"Do you want me to be pregnant?" she asked hesitantly.

There was no hesitation in his answer. "Hell yeah. I'd love it if you were carrying my baby inside you."

He felt her smile. "I never really thought about having kids. I mean, I wanted to, but I wasn't sure I'd ever meet a man I trusted enough to want to make a baby with him. Then you jumped into that hole in Uganda, and everything changed."

"For the better."

"Definitely for the better."

"If you're not pregnant, do you want to start trying?" he asked.

"If we're pregnant, I'll be thrilled, but if I'm not, I'd rather wait till we're married to start trying. Not that I'm hinting or anything," she said pulling back to stare up at him.

"Didn't think you were, babe," he assured her as he thought of the other purchase he'd made this morning. Whether she was pregnant or not, he was proposing to her tomorrow morning on a sunrise hot air balloon ride above the island. "It's time."

With a shaking hand, Mackenzie reached out and picked up the stick, holding it so both of them could see it.

Two lines.

"We're having a baby," he said as he picked her up and swirled her around the bathroom. "Looks like Mouse isn't going to be the only daddy on the team anymore."

A kid.

Him.

He was going to be a dad.

Never in his life had he thought he'd be holding the woman he loved and a positive pregnancy test in his arms. Never had he thought he could be this happy. And it was all because he'd taken the risk and gone to Virginia to give being with Mackenzie a chance.

They still had lots to learn about one another, and they knew her brother had been manipulated, which meant there were still dangerous men out there that had to be stopped, but in this moment, Bear felt like his life was as close to perfect as he could get.

"Kiss me," he said.

"Your wish is my command," she teased as she wrapped her legs around his hips and her arms around his neck.

"Yeah it is." He laughed and then captured her lips in a scorching kiss that was only going to end one way, with them back in bed making love.

CHAPTER TWENTY-FIVE

When someone banged on Bear's apartment door, he looked up from the laundry he was folding.

Folding laundry was certainly a whole lot more fun now that it involved Mackenzie's bras and panties.

Though he grinned as he opened the door, that smile faded when he came face-to-face with Mouse, who's entire demeanor matched the worried scowl on his face.

"Hey, man. What's up?" Bear asked, stepping back to let his friend enter.

"Can I come in?"

"What do you think I'm standing back and holding the door open for?" Bear said with an eye roll. If Mouse was acting like this, then whatever was going on was bad.

Had to be something to do with Lolly and the custody case. Mouse's selfish former in-laws tried every couple of years to get their hands on their only child's daughter with no care of how it affected the little girl.

Maybe it was because Bear was going to be a dad in a few months, but this time, it hit harder. Mouse was an amazing father and didn't deserve any of this.

"Take a seat, and I'll grab some drinks?" Bear said as he ushered his best friend, a man who had been there for him without question throughout the decades, over to the couch.

"I'm ... not thirsty," Mouse replied. He took a seat and was barely sitting for more than three seconds before he was up, pacing, raking his hands through his hair.

Bear had never seen his friend this freaked out about a custody case. Well, not since the very first one when Lolly was a baby. Usually, he took it in stride, more upset about the impact on his daughter than anything else. Today, though, he looked like he was balancing precariously on a ledge.

"Prey got you a lawyer, right?" Bear asked.

Mouse gave a hard nod. "Yeah, same one as last time. They don't have a leg to stand on anyway."

"So ...?"

"So what?"

"What's going on? If you're not freaking about the custody case, then what?"

"My in-laws are using a different law firm this time around," he said slowly. "Some big-name law firm in LA."

"So then this *is* about the case?" Bear was thoroughly confused. He wanted to help; he just didn't know what Mouse needed from him.

"Not the case. The firm."

"You're worried about the firm ... but not what it means for your case?" This conversation wasn't getting any clearer. "Mouse, you're gonna have to give me more than that."

"Something is off there. I did some digging around, you know, because I always look into the lawyer representing my in-laws."

"Right. Seems smart since there are unscrupulous ones around who will do anything to win. But you said that's not what you're worried about."

Mouse nodded. "It's not. My daughter's life is on the line, so I can't afford not to do my due diligence, but this time, I found something I wasn't expecting. I don't know exactly what it is, Bear, but something has my gut screaming at me that this has something to do with ... well, us."

"Us?"

"Prey Security."

"Then we'll have to look into them more closely."

"Just like that?"

Bear frowned. "You really have to ask me that? We all know you trust your gut. Always. If you think something is up with this firm, then I take that seriously. I'm not going to let anything happen to Lolly, or to you, or anyone on our team for that matter."

"But all I have to go on right now are loose clues that keep leading to dead ends," Mouse warned.

"But that's what we do, right? We analyze evidence and take out bad guys." Bear gave his friend an encouraging smile. "And that's what we're going to do here. Just like Prey always does."

Jane Blythe is a *USA Today* bestselling author of romantic suspense and military romance full of sexy heroes and strong heroines! When she's not weaving hard to unravel mysteries she loves to read, bake, go to the beach, build snowmen, and watch Disney movies. She has two adorable Dalmatians, is obsessed with Christmas, owns 200+ teddy bears, and loves to travel!

To connect and keep up to date please visit any of the following

Amazon – http://www.amazon.com/author/janeblythe
BookBub – https://www.bookbub.com/authors/jane-blythe
Email – mailto:janeblytheauthor@gmail.com
Facebook – http://www.facebook.com/janeblytheauthor
Goodreads – http://www.goodreads.com/author/show/6574160.Jane_Blythe
Instagram – http://www.instagram.com/jane_blythe_author
Reader Group – http://www.facebook.com/groups/janeskillersweethearts
Twitter – http://www.twitter.com/jblytheauthor
Website – http://www.janeblythe.com.au

Faith is being sure of what we hope for and certain of what we do not see.

Hebrews 11:1

9 780645 643206